TROLLED

LEGACY OF MAGIC
BOOK 3

LINDSAY BUROKER

1

HAMMER RANG OUT AGAINST SWORD AS MY FIFTEEN-YEAR-OLD opponent feinted high and low, trying to find a way through my defenses. Despite the distraction of a dragon sharing the backyard, she didn't get through.

The dragon was in human form and ensconced in a steam room attached to a hot tub and sauna, so it wasn't as if he was paying attention, but it was hard to ignore his aura. Or that he'd informed me that he forbade anyone to harm the offspring of his mate. My joke that Child Protective Services already forbade that had either gone over his head, or he hadn't deemed it worthy of a response. Dragons were even haughtier than elves.

"I don't know what to do against a *hammer*," Amber told her mom and our observer as she backed off to wipe sweat out of her eyes. "It's not like a sword, and she does that weird spinning move that deflects *my* sword more than usual. I almost cut my own braid off."

"Braids are dangerous," Val said, though she had one of her own. "You could cut your hair shorter, like Matti." She waved to my tousled black hair.

It wasn't *that* short, but I did keep it trimmed so it didn't get in my eyes when I fought. Something I was doing a lot of lately since whoever had put the reward out for my magical hammer hadn't removed it yet.

Amber curled her upper lip at my hair—or maybe my entire look. My yoga pants and baggy T-shirt would have drawn snickers at the *dojang*, but I'd assumed we wouldn't be grappling this morning, and I'd wanted to grab a coffee afterward without drawing strange looks.

"*Your* hair is longer than mine," Amber told Val in lieu of insulting me.

This was our first meeting, and she must have decided she didn't know me well enough yet to deliver the surly snark she doled out to her mother. Either that, or Amber found my hammer intimidating. It couldn't have been my five-foot-one stature, not when she was as tall as her mother's six feet.

"Yes, but not wisely so. Colonel Willard calls this my vanity braid." Val flicked the long blonde rope of hair over her shoulder, then looked at me. "She texted to say she's on the way over. I think she has information for you about your father."

I lowered my hammer and stepped back. "*Quality* information about how she's pulled strings with the MPs and can get me in to see him for the first time in thirty years?"

"She just said information."

"Hm."

A deep rumbling sigh emanated from the steam room. Had Lord Zavryd been in his dragon form, some might have deemed it a roar.

"What is he *doing* in there?" Amber eyed the door.

"Just relaxing and enjoying the heat." Val waved toward the gray sky. The clouds had been spritzing us all morning, and a chill mist lingered, promising fall would come soon. "He's not that into the Seattle climate."

"Who is?" Amber asked.

"I don't mind it," Val said.

"Yeah, but you're weird."

"Yes, I am. Are you going to stick around after training? Freysha is supposed to come for a visit."

That was her elven half-sister, wasn't it? And a princess? I'd heard about but not met Freysha. Sarrlevi had suggested I might like her, since she was studying engineering and wasn't stuck up, like the *other* female elves I'd met.

"She's weirder than you are," Amber said.

"She's from another *planet*. Weirdness is to be expected." A knock sounded at the fence gate, and Val called, "Come in, Willard."

"Given all the people who'd like you dead," came Willard's Southern drawl as she opened the gate, "don't you think you should identify visitors before calling them back?"

"We're all armed, the magical topiaries don't let strangers into the yard, and there's a dragon in the steam room. Fort Knox has fewer impediments to inimical intruders."

Amber, who must have found such comments *weird*, rolled her eyes.

After closing the gate, Willard headed down the flagstone path toward our patio sparring zone. "I suppose you are well-defended."

The door to the steam room opened, the great gust of steam that rolled out not quite enough to hide Zavryd's naked body as he stepped out.

"Ew, Val!" Amber whirled away as she flung her arm over her eyes.

"One moment, Willard." Val held up a finger, then jogged toward a towel hanging from a peg by the steam-room door. She grabbed it to wrap around Zavryd, though he was heading toward the hot tub, the bubbles whirring to life before he touched a button. "What happened to your swim trunks?" Val asked him as she tried valiantly to cover his nudity.

Willard smirked as she watched, her gaze more appreciative than horrified.

Zavryd was handsome when he was in his human form, though I couldn't imagine that lusting after a dragon was wise. As I knew from recent experience, lusting after *elves* wasn't even wise. Alas, the thought put memories of the assassin Varlesh Sarrlevi in my mind. I hadn't seen him *fully* naked, but I'd seen him in nothing but bandages and a loincloth, an image that had imprinted itself on my memory.

"They are on the bench in the hot box," Zavryd said, slinging himself still naked into the hot tub.

"Sauna," Val corrected.

"Yes. They stick to my body when I sweat. It is most unappealing."

"I'm sure, but I need you to use a towel when you wander around the yard naked."

"You did not mind my nudity last night." Zavryd lowered his lids halfway as he eyed Val and flicked a finger in invitation for her to join him.

"Last night, my boss, colleague, and underage *daughter* weren't in the backyard."

Unconcerned, Zavryd let his head loll back. "Perhaps you should spar at the park instead of adjacent to a dragon-relaxation zone."

"They look at you funny when you try to hit people with swords and hammers in the park." Val was still holding up the towel, but it did little good with Zavryd in the hot tub now. She sighed and draped it near him. "Use that when you get out, please."

Rubbing her face, Val returned to us, her cheeks as red as if she'd been in the steam room with him. "I just got Thad to agree to let Amber come here again for sparring sessions," she muttered to Willard.

"I'm surprised he went for that." Willard's eyes crinkled as she waved toward the naked dragon lord lounging in the hot tub. "You'd damage your daughter less if you ran a porn studio back here."

"That can't be true." Val looked at Amber, who'd lowered her arm but still pointedly had her back to the hot tub. Fortunately, the bubbles now hid Zavryd's lower half. "Are you damaged?"

"Like a bug splatted on your windshield."

"Do you want my therapist's number?"

"I'd rather have fifty dollars. Retail therapy is soothing."

"Some find it healthy to talk to an expert."

"Some find it healthy to buy purses and makeup palettes."

When I met Willard's gaze, she nodded for me to join her in a private nook of the yard.

Anticipation made me bounce over ahead of her, in part because I hadn't seen my father since I was four, and in part because I'd run out of leads when it came to finding my mother. The dwarves who had once known her well and who lived in the area had disappeared. I'd never found more than Hennehok's empty cabin, and Artie, the owner of the ax-throwing business in Port Townsend, had vanished since I'd visited. Even though my father couldn't have possibly seen my mother since the night she'd supposedly died, thirty years earlier, he had to know more than I did about what had happened that night. Hopefully, he knew who had her today.

"I've been doing the research into Malosi Puletasi that I promised I would," Willard said.

I nodded hopefully, my eyes locked on her.

"I haven't been able to get confirmation that he's on Fort Lewis, which is what you believe, right?"

Disappointment crept in, dashing my hope, but if Willard had told Val she had information, she had to know something.

"It's where my grandparents said he was imprisoned, yes, and when I tried to see him after I turned eighteen, they told me he couldn't have visitors. They didn't say he wasn't there."

"I did learn that there's a separate maximum-security section of what's purportedly only a medium-security prison there. The person I talked to said some *hinky* stuff goes on around the building and that MPs hate being assigned there. I took that to mean the prison might be reinforced with magic."

"Magic that the military doesn't admit exists?" I asked.

"Precisely. The person I talked to also said some people have been held in there for decades, not only because they've committed crimes but for matters of national security."

I mouthed *national security*, wondering how my father could have been involved in anything like that. What kinds of matters of national security were in the Seattle area, anyway? We were a long way from DC and the Pentagon.

Willard arched her eyebrows. "How much do you know about your father's past?"

"Just that he was in the Army and married and divorced before he met my mother. When he got out, he drove commercial trucks. I assumed transport operator was his MOS when he was in."

"Not even close. He was a linguist who worked in Intelligence and had a top-secret clearance. He helped encryption specialists crack Soviet codes toward the end of the Cold War."

I stared at her, certain my grandparents had never said anything about that.

"How did he meet your mother?" Willard asked.

"I'm... not sure." I closed my eyes, trying to dredge up pertinent memories from the past, but I'd only been four when the soldiers had raided our apartment, arresting my father and shooting my mother before the building burned down around her. Everything before then was fuzzy.

"Do his parents know? They live in Marysville, right?"

"I'll pretend it's not creepy that you know that." I doubted I'd told her, though I supposed I had mentioned it to Val.

"You know we've kept tabs on you for a while. You and your *vigilante* justice." Willard looked pointedly at my hammer.

"I can't believe Val is scarring her teenage daughter with her mate's nudity, and you're looking at me like *I'm* the one with questionable morals."

"That kid was trapped in the fae realm and dragged through an orgy. I doubt a glimpse of dragon *cojones* is going to faze her."

I blinked, not having heard that story. "The kid may need a *hundred* dollars for purses."

"Yes," came a cry from across the yard as Amber pointed at me. "Did you hear that, Val? Your friend agrees that you should give me money."

Willard shook her head. "I always forget that they have enhanced hearing and that there's no such thing as privacy around this house."

"Is there any way you can get me into that maximum-security prison for a visit?" I asked, not caring if Val's entire family and even her vampire roommate overheard this, though I was glad when Val shooed her daughter toward the kitchen. This was a serious conversation.

"I can't get you in. I'm sorry." Willard glanced at Val as she walked over but continued on. "Not only did my superiors deny that your father is there or even exists, but I was simultaneously told to drop the matter."

"That implies he *is* there, doesn't it?" I asked. "Otherwise, they wouldn't care if you dropped it."

"Probably, but the Army is trying hard to get the world, including your family, to forget your father exists. After more than twenty years invested in the military, I can't do anything to jeopardize my career."

"So sneaking in to find him myself is my only option?"

"I can't be a part of that."

I looked at Val, who opened her mouth.

Willard said, "And neither can you."

"Right." Val shrugged apologetically at me.

"That elf is *not* permitted on our property," Zavryd announced from the hot tub. He was scowling through the fence toward the front of the house rather than at us.

"Elf?" I stretched out with my senses, trying to detect magical beings in the area. With a dragon nearby, not to mention all the magical protection, weapons, and trinkets in and around Val's house, it was hard to sense anything else, but I smiled when I picked out a familiar aura in the intersection out front. "Sarrlevi."

Willard eyed me. "Thorvald, is it right that she smiles so brightly when she says the name of a heinous assassin?"

"He gives her cheese," Val said.

I hadn't realized I'd been smiling—hell, that was almost a grin that I wiped off my face—and forced my lips into a neutral expression.

"And that excites her?" Willard asked.

"Apparently."

"He's not heinous. He's..." What? Misunderstood? He was hardly that. A decent guy? Even that was questionable. Handsome and a good kisser? That might be true, but I wouldn't admit to them that I knew that. "The product of a lot of dragon nudity in his youth," I said to end the conversation, not because I believed it true.

"Hell. I'd better go hug my daughter." Val headed toward the kitchen.

I have a warning for you, Sarrlevi spoke into my mind.

A WARNING? I RESPONDED TO SARRLEVI AS I THANKED WILLARD FOR her information and headed toward the gate. *I was hoping you brought more cheese.*

Was the last delivery not sufficient?

I have a goblin roommate who can eat her weight in snacks every day and reach things I hide on shelves twice her height.

I suppose that must be expected since she can climb to the roof of your domicile to shoot trespassers.

Yes. I'm fortunate she didn't like the pickled root vegetables.

Did you like them?

I noticed he wasn't answering my original question, but the banter was more appealing than being told I'd have to watch out for yet someone else angling for my back, so I didn't mind.

Yeah, I admitted, still wondering why he'd sent the gift. I'd done my best to keep Zavryd's sister Zondia from whisking Sarrlevi off to the dragon world for their loathsome *punishment and rehabilitation,* convincing her that I needed his help to find my mother, so maybe it had been his way of thanking me. But he'd also kissed me and then backed away and said it wasn't *appropriate,* so I didn't know what to think. When we'd first met, I'd inadvertently made it clear that I was attracted to him, and he'd been quick to point out that he wasn't interested in me. All I could assume was that the kiss had also been some kind of thank-you. Assuming assassins could feel gratitude.

After wrestling with the gate latch—why did tall people always install those for *their* towering convenience?—I trotted across the yard toward the intersection. Even if Sarrlevi drove me nuts at times, he was exactly the kind of person who could help me get into a maximum-security prison partially guarded by magic. And, unlike Val, he had no affiliation with the US military to worry about. He probably didn't care about the laws on Earth at all.

Mongrel friend of my mate's, Zavryd spoke into my mind, nearly causing me to trip over the large mushrooms comprising a fairy ring in the front yard, *you need not leave the premises and speak with that criminal.*

Uh, thanks, but he helped us fight those helicopters, remember? He's not a criminal.

He did little in that battle.

Except causing one of the helicopters to crash and vanquishing a bunch of enemies. Enemies who booby-trapped a forest with magical rockets that launched at dragons.

That was heinous and inexcusable.

Exactly. Your sister scoured my mind. She should know that Sarrlevi, unlike those people, is not a threat to dragons. I wished some of Willard's soldiers had found survivors from that battle to question. Since the helicopters had been made, or at least enchanted by my mother, those flying them would have been the perfect people to lead me to her. But they'd all either died in the fighting or disappeared.

The assassin is unappealing to dragons, Zavryd said, not disagreeing further that Sarrlevi had helped, not acknowledging it at all.

Because he challenged you to a duel, and you couldn't beat him?

I could *have beaten him,* Zavryd replied, his tone stiff, *had I changed into my natural and superior dragon form. This form has many limitations.*

It's hard being human.

Sarrlevi stepped out of the intersection but didn't go past the sidewalk, not presuming to approach the magical defenses of the property. Wise, since the crimson eyes of the nearest dragon-shaped topiaries flared, and smoke wafted from their foliage nostrils. Other traps and alarms buzzed against my senses, all poised to go off if an enemy—or innocent parcel-delivery driver—approached. Not for the first time, I envisioned Val's packages being chucked at the front porch from the street.

"Your expression is dyspeptic," Sarrlevi observed as I joined him on the sidewalk, the hilts of his twin longswords poking up behind his shoulders. Usually, he favored browns and greens—typical *Lord of the Rings* attire—but today, he wore dark trousers with a sapphire blue shirt that complemented his eyes. The copious wounds he'd received the last time I'd been with him had healed, leaving his handsome face striking and swoon-worthy. "I assume you're not thinking of cheese or root vegetables," he added.

"I was talking to a dragon."

"Ah. That *can* cause indigestion."

"Yes, I believe that's a known side effect, along with trembling, cringing, and spontaneously bursting into flame."

"*You* did not tremble or cringe when you faced his sister." Sarrlevi smiled at me, and the suggestion that he was pleased—or even *proud*?—warmed my insides. Unfortunately, it also made me think of our kiss, which I'd relived more than once in my dreams. The memory caused my cheeks to flush pink.

His smile widened, growing more knowing than proud, and I was sure he could read my thoughts.

I scowled and shoved the memory from my mind. "What warning do you have for me?"

His smile faded, his eyes turning grave. "Your mother's sister, Princess Barothla, is now aware of your existence."

His expression assured me that was *not* a good thing.

"She may have learned about you from Slehvyra, but many dwarves came with your grandfather when they visited you—" irritation flashed in his eyes, "—and when the dragons destroyed my home. Any of them could have said something to her. Perhaps your grandfather even mentioned you."

"She didn't hire you to kill me, did she?" I didn't seriously think that had happened, and couldn't imagine why my existence would matter to the aunt I'd never met, but I wondered where he'd been in the last few days that he'd heard about what the dwarf princess knew. The dragons might have destroyed his home, but the dwarves had been perfectly willing to stand by and let it happen. It had sounded like they'd even expected—and anticipated—it.

"She did not." Sarrlevi hesitated. "Since you are not trained in magic, she may believe she could defeat you without assistance."

"Defeat me? Why would she need to defeat me?"

"She did not sound pleased by your existence."

"Sound? Did you talk to her?" I frowned at him.

He'd said he wasn't welcome on the dwarven home world anymore, and from what my grandfather, King Ironhelm, had said, he knew Sarrlevi had once been hired to assassinate my mother... and hated him for it.

"I have been attempting to gather more information that could help me find your mother," Sarrlevi said, dodging the question.

"By talking to the sister who hated her enough to have her killed?"

"By listening to conversations."

"While stalking people and skulking in the shadows?"

His expression cooled, and I reminded myself that just because he brought me cheese and bantered with me didn't mean he wouldn't get pissed if I insulted him—and his profession.

"Often, information is not freely given," Sarrlevi said. "One cannot always acquire it openly."

"Did you learn anything? Besides that she knows I'm alive and doesn't like me for some reason? Even though I've obviously never done anything to her." I sighed, wishing the topiaries were less bristly so I could lean on one. Either the morning of sword practice had caught up with me, or I was tired of being targeted by people I didn't know.

"That is all I learned from her. She may not come after you. You are not in line to inherit the dwarven throne ahead of her."

"Or at all. The king made that clear. As if I'd be interested in ruling over strange bearded randos on another world."

"Randos," Sarrlevi mouthed, though I knew he'd heard me use the term before.

"I live here." I pointed at the sidewalk.

More smoke curled out of the topiaries' nostrils.

"Well, not *here*," I amended, "but you've been to my house."

"And organized your mess, yes." His face lightened, as if it had *pleased* him to clean my room. Or maybe amused him?

"Nobody asked you to do that, dude." It still mortified me to imagine him putting away my laundry, underwear and all, and the flush crept back to my cheeks. "It's not my fault *entropy* makes it hard for you to crash at a friend's house."

That had been the word he'd used to describe the state of my bedroom, as if a few scattered phone chargers, socks, and books constituted a whirling vortex of chaos.

"And yet you are grateful that I did so and also brought you this warning." Sarrlevi raised his eyebrows. "It is possible she will never seek you out, but I wanted you to be aware."

"I do appreciate that. Thank you. Can she make portals?" I

hoped not. If she had to catch a ride from a mage or a dragon, she might be less likely to come to Earth.

"Certainly. Like your mother, she is a powerful magic user."

Of course she was.

"An enchanter?" I asked.

"She has studied in many areas, but she is most renowned as an alchemist."

"A dwarf alchemist? Is that a typical field of study for them?" I didn't remember such being mentioned often in Dungeons & Dragons manuals, but it was possible those weren't the ultimate source on actual dwarves.

"It is not looked down upon, but it is not held in as high esteem as enchanting and smithing and training for war."

"So, if you were a young dwarf and became an alchemist, your parents wouldn't be as disappointed in you as if you became a hooker, but it's no doctor or lawyer?"

Sarrlevi gave me his trademark bland gaze, one I assumed meant he either didn't track my odd Earth vernacular or he did but didn't deem a response worth making. It was probably usually the latter since he didn't miss much. For a guy who twirled swords for a living, he was no dummy.

"Can I ask you a favor?" Maybe I should have brought *him* a gift before making requests, but it wasn't as if I'd expected him this morning.

Sarrlevi opened his mouth but paused and looked past my shoulder. A pair of moms with babies in strollers were walking briskly toward us. The topiaries had stopped glowing and smoking, but the women kept glancing at them and looked like they wanted to get past the sketchy house quickly.

I almost clasped Sarrlevi's hand to draw him onto the grassy strip, but if he found kissing inappropriate, he might have decided touching of other kinds was too, so I simply waved for him to step out of the way with me. Assuming discussions of sneaking into military prisons would prompt odd looks, I waited for the women to pass. But one saw Sarrlevi and slowed down and whispered to the other.

"Who is that guy? He's *gorgeous*."

Even though dwarves might not be known to have as keen of hearing as elves, I had no troubling catching that.

"His ears are pointy," her friend whispered back.

"So? It's exotic. I should have worn my good bra."

"You're a single mom pushing your kid in a stroller. He's *not* going to be interested."

"Single moms have game. Just because *you're* married and can't ask him out doesn't mean I can't."

"If he came out of *that* house, you don't want to ask him out. Trust me. Only kooks live there."

"Watch Susie for me." The single mom waved at her stroller, flipped her hair back, and walked toward Sarrlevi with impressive self-confidence.

If she noticed me, she must have assumed we weren't a couple. That was insulting, though, judging from the way she never looked away from Sarrlevi, she hadn't registered my presence. Or she thought I was an ambulatory mailbox.

"Hi." She beamed a smile at him. "You're probably busy with… things." She glanced at the house, then at me, but only briefly. "But can I see your hand?"

Sarrlevi looked at me. I *knew* he wasn't mystified by women hitting on him and assumed it was only the request for his hand that puzzled him.

"He's not interested," I told her, wanting to get back to planning a visit to Fort Lewis.

"I'm sure *you* wouldn't know." She sniffed dismissively at me and pulled out a pen. "Your hand?" she prompted Sarrlevi with another sultry smile and pantomimed writing her number in the air. "The kid is asleep by eight."

Sarrlevi didn't have a phone, but he must have gotten the gist, for he kept his hand at his side. "I do not seek to mate with the females of this world."

"*This world?*" she mouthed.

Her friend rolled her eyes and pushed both strollers ahead. "I *told* you anybody from that house is weird. Come *on.*"

The pen wielder let her friend grab her arm and tug her away, but the glances she sent back toward Sarrlevi were more disappointed than confused.

"Not up to elven standards, huh?" I asked, though I shouldn't have. I didn't want to hear his confirmation on that since I knew he lumped me in with *females of this world.*

"I am on a mission." Sarrlevi faced me. "What favor do you seek?"

"You know I've been trying to get into the military prison to see my father. Willard said she can't help. Neither can Val. I do have a camouflaging charm now and believe I could get in on my own, but there could be magic further securing the place. I... might need help." I grimaced, hating to admit that and hating to ask for favors. Especially from him. It galled me that I kept needing to do so.

"You don't think you can simply bash the magical prison security with your hammer?" He raised his eyebrows.

At first, I thought he was teasing me, and maybe he was a little, but I *had* taken out the gnomish enchantment on that brick wall, not to mention the entire brick wall, with a cry of *Hyrek!* and a swing from the hammer.

"Not stealthily. I need time to *talk* to my father once I get in." Unless I intended to break him out completely. I couldn't help but grow wistful at the thought. After thirty years, I barely remembered him, and, after Willard's revelations, I realized how little I knew about him at all. Not only did I want to talk to him to ask if he knew who had my mother, but I wanted a chance to get to know him and let him know me.

"Yes," Sarrlevi said, "he may be disinclined to speak with you if there are bricks piled atop him."

I squinted at him. "You *are* teasing me."

"I am." Eyes gleaming with amusement, Sarrlevi rested a hand on my shoulder. "I will help you with your quest to reach him."

"Because you've decided I'm a delightful and valuable person or because my quest to reach him could help you with *your* quest to find my mother?"

"Indeed." He touched my cheek before lowering his hand, but I had no time to debate what *that* gesture meant before he tilted his head toward the gate beside the house. "Will *they* be coming?"

When I looked, I was in time to spot Val and Amber, their height allowing them to see over the fence. Amber ducked and fled as soon as we made eye contact. Val arched her eyebrows and walked more slowly away.

"This *is* a weird house," I said, though Val had probably only been concerned for my safety. "And, no, they're not coming."

"Good." Sarrlevi inclined his head toward me and took a step back. "I will come for you at midnight."

"Wait," I blurted, relieved he'd agreed to help but disappointed that he was leaving so soon, especially if it was because we'd had *spies*. "Do you want to come to my house for dinner first?"

He tilted his head. In puzzlement? Confusion? ...Horror?

"Not like a date," I hurried to say, realizing he would consider that *inappropriate*. "Just as a thank-you. For helping me. I'll feed you. And myself. So we're properly nourished before sneaking into a maximum-security compound. Nourishment is important." Damn, I was babbling. That cheek touch had flustered me. As much as I did not want it to be so, *he* still flustered me.

Sarrlevi hesitated.

"Do you *eat* what other people prepare? Or are assassins paranoid that everyone is out to get them? I mean, I've seen dragons destroy your home, so maybe everyone *is* out to get you. But I'm not. You know that by now, right? If you want, I could lick everything before you eat it." As soon as the words came out, I realized how gross that sounded. *Taste* was what I should have said. I'd taste things before he tried them.

His mouth opened, but he didn't respond right away. I'd probably flustered *him*. "How much cheese would I have to bring to ensure you *don't* lick my food before serving it to me?"

"Uh, a wheel would suffice. Two if you want to be generous so I can share with my roommate."

"Will she not eat it regardless of whether *I'm* generous?"

"Yes."

"I'll bring two." Sarrlevi bowed once more before heading into the street, forming a portal, and leaping through it.

As he disappeared, I caught myself grinning, even though I had a new problem to worry about and most certainly did *not* have a date later.

3

WITH MY MOTORCYCLE HELMET AND LEATHER RIDING JACKET MOSTLY deflecting the rain, I took the Marysville exit off I-5 and headed toward my grandparents' house. Midnight was a long way off, and I figured I'd better learn as much about my father as I could before then.

I also had a dinner to plan and shop for. Unless I wanted to get takeout. But what takeout would an elf like? Not pizza, surely. Despite having purchased food for Sarrlevi before, I couldn't remember ever seeing him eat, unless a dubious-looking protein bar he'd once pulled out of his pack counted.

When I'd had my spur-of-the-moment urge to invite him for dinner, I hadn't considered this new conundrum. I would have to buy or make numerous options, so he could choose. *Make*, most likely, since I wouldn't be flush with cash until the project house closed. That was what I got for taking on a roommate who didn't help pay the bills.

Not wanting to waste time, I hadn't swung by my place to trade the Harley for my truck and make sure my industrious goblin roommate wasn't disassembling any more of my kitchen appliances this weekend. The night before, she'd mentioned finishing all of her homework. That was never a good sign since it meant she had more time for *projects*.

My phone rang as I turned into the residential neighborhood by Jennings Memorial Park, and Val's name popped up. I pulled over under a tree to answer. Between the people hunting me for my hammer and Sarrlevi's warning that the dwarven aunt I'd never met might be a threat, I couldn't risk calls from friends, relatives, or colleagues dropping to voice mail.

"Hey," I answered.

"Hey, Matti. I wanted to apologize for spying on you earlier."

"Are you worried Sarrlevi is out to get me, or did Willard order you to listen in on any plans I might make related to prison visits?"

"She warned me *not* to learn anything about your plans, as it would be better for both our careers if we had no knowledge of that. As to the rest, Amber dragged me over."

"*She's* the one worried Sarrlevi is out to get me?"

"No, she's the one who said I had to see the *straight fire* guy out front. I was pretty sure she meant Sarrlevi, but I was hoping an age-appropriate teenage boy might be skating past. Preferably one who gets good grades and respects girls. I understand she and the last boy parted ways."

"Sarrlevi's grades might have been okay. Three hundred years ago." I paused, thinking of the story Sarrlevi had told me of his past, of his father abusing his mother and killing his sister. Grimly, I added, "And he does respect girls."

"Good to know." Val's tone turned dry. "Amber said she can give you some fashion advice if you want to get more than a touch on the cheek."

"I do not, thank you." I scowled at my phone. How long had those two been spying on us?

"She also said you'd be a way better catch than that thirsty stan who hit on him."

"That thirsty what?"

"You're younger than me. I thought you might be able to decode the slang."

"I'm not *that* young. This isn't really what you called about, is it?"

"I did call to apologize. But also because, after you left, Willard mentioned that someone broke into her office again. Nobody stole anything, but I know you've still got hammer hunters after you, so I thought I'd let you know. People have broken into her office before to look up her records on *me*."

"It sounds like she needs a better security system."

"Believe it or not, she's got a good one, mundane and magical. If anyone gets in, that means they're powerful. *My* stalker was Zondia."

I didn't think the lilac dragon cared much about me, and she'd already scoured my mind. Sarrlevi's warning about Princess Barothla came to mind. But it couldn't have been my aunt. How would someone from another world know to look for information on me at Willard's office? How would she even know who Willard was? I shook my head. It had probably been someone from the same organization behind the theft of Willard's artifacts. Maybe they wanted to steal them again.

"All right." I tugged my collar up as the rain came down harder, the tree branches overhead only modestly effective at keeping water off me. "Thanks for the warning."

"No problem."

After hanging up, I headed deeper into the neighborhood where I'd grown up, riding slowly and looking around while stretching out with my senses. When all I'd had on my mind was learning more about my father, I hadn't thought anything about coming up here, but what if someone was watching me? And I led them to my grandparents' house?

They were almost eighty-five, which was far too old to deal

with hostile magical beings that would happily hurt them to get to me. Or my hammer.

I glanced at the weapon in my saddlebag, wistful for the days when nobody powerful or dangerous had been aware of or cared about me. In addition to the reward-seekers, I had to worry about dwarves. Even though my mother's father, the king, had been nice and supportive, he'd implied that his advisors thought my mother's hammer should be back with their people, not in the hands of a mongrel. If I could find her, the dwarves had implied they would let me keep it, but if I didn't... who knew?

Instead of pulling into my grandparents' driveway, I left my Harley at the park. Maybe I was being overly cautious, but I grabbed my hammer, headed down one of the trails, and ducked behind a tree. I rubbed the camouflage charm Artie had given me, the hammer-shaped trinket my mother had made, and let out a sigh of relief once I was invisible to the outside world.

Hopefully hidden from assassins, princesses, and anyone else who might spy on me, I jogged to the unassuming ranch house that I'd grown up in. It was one of many on the cul-de-sac, and kids played basketball at the hoop set up at the end. The rain wasn't dampening the spirited game, and the normalcy made me relax an iota. Everything was fine. Nobody evil was in the neighborhood.

Since I'd texted my grandparents that I was coming over, I stepped inside without knocking. Only after I shut the door did I deactivate the charm and call out a greeting.

Not surprisingly, I found Grandma in the kitchen. She was baking cookies, the cheery scents of oatmeal, raisins, and cinnamon wafting through the house, but I knew better than to get too excited. Grandma made *amazing* Samoan food, but she'd never mastered American desserts, likely because she refused to use recipes. Apparently because they stifled her creativity. As kids, my sister and I had gotten a lot of cookies in our lunches with the density and heft of paperweights.

"Hey, Grandma." I greeted her with a hug. "How's it going?"

"Fine, dear. It's nice to see you." She squeezed me with her meaty arms, her height even with mine. Dad was taller, but even without dwarf blood, I never would have reached the top shelves of kitchen cabinets.

"You too. Is Grandpa around?" I suspected he would be more aware of what his son had done in the Army, if I could get him talking. They usually got terse and quiet when I asked questions about Dad. Maybe I should have brought some whiskey, a known lubricant for Grandpa.

"In the garage." She pointed me toward the door but also grabbed my wrist and put an oatmeal-raisin cookie in my mouth before letting me go. It was neither soft nor chewy. "I saw them make these on the cooking channel. Let me know what you think."

"It's great." I took a polite nibble, the cookie crumbling oddly in my mouth, then fled toward the garage.

Maybe it was good that Grandma's desserts weren't scintillating. If Sarrlevi ever saw me naked again, I didn't want to jiggle too much. Not that he would. There were no flying soap dispensers to assail me on Earth, and it wasn't as if I would strip down to try to entice him with my feminine wiles.

I was bemused that Val's daughter had apparently implied that I might be able to. She didn't know anything about my odd relationship with Sarrlevi, such as it was, or that he didn't *mate* with Earth women.

When I walked into the garage, the floor was covered in wood shavings, with Grandpa sanding the sailboat he'd built from scratch and had been working on since he'd retired. Since it hadn't yet been painted, I assumed it wasn't ready for the sea or lake or whatever he had in mind, but it looked close. Of course, it had looked close for at least five years.

"How's it going, Grandpa?" I leaned my hammer against the wall by the door.

He grunted and nodded toward me, as verbose as ever.

"Do you want the rest of this?" I held up the cookie.

With another grunt, he pointed at his work bench where a tray of them rested.

"Right." I set my half-nibbled offering with the others, something I wouldn't have done at someone else's house but that seemed perfectly normal at home. "You're not using a planer?" I waved at the boat.

"I did earlier. Down to the fine work now."

"Are you going to let me carve you a figurehead?"

"You agree yet that an *aquatic* one would be best?"

"There's nothing wrong with lions." Now that I'd met Zavryd and Zondia, I might be inclined to carve one of *their* heads on a boat, but if he objected to lions, he would definitely object to dragons.

We debated figureheads and the best tools for carving them before I worked up the courage to ask him about Dad.

"I ran into someone who works for the Army," I said as casually as I could. *Ran into. Was working for.* They meant almost the same thing. "A colonel."

Grandpa grunted.

"She said she knew a bit about Dad."

He eyed me. "*She?*"

"Yeah, the Army has female officers, you know," I said, though I wasn't sure that was his objection. "It's the modern era."

My sarcasm only earned me another grunt.

"She said he used to be in Intelligence. Is that right? I thought he drove trucks."

Grandpa frowned as he focused unnecessarily on sanding a spot that was already glass smooth. Would he answer?

He had to miss his son as much as I missed my father. Maybe

he never admitted it, but I'd seen his eyes get far-off and misty numerous times over the years when someone in the family had talked about Dad. When I'd first tried to get permission to visit him in prison, Grandma had said it was a lost cause, that Grandpa had attempted the same thing every year since the arrest, and it had never been allowed.

"That's right," he finally said. "I don't know what all he did. He always clammed up about it and said it was safer if we didn't know anything. I figured he was being melodramatic, but he *was* stationed at the Pentagon for a few years, so maybe it wasn't all hokum."

"Why'd he get a job as a truck driver when his enlistment was up? If he had that kind of experience..."

He gave me a long sideways look that I struggled to read. It seemed to suggest I should know already. "His enlistment never *was* up. That was part of the problem. That's why they treated him so badly when he got arrested, I assume. And because of whatever *she* was involved in."

"She? Mom?"

He frowned and went back to sanding.

"They didn't think she was a Russian or something dumb, did they?" My mind boggled at a dwarf from another world being mistaken for some Cold War enemy.

"They knew what she was."

"Was she... a prisoner?" I scowled at the thought. All along, I'd mistrusted the Army, so it didn't take much to get my hackles up.

"Don't know. They had her for some reason." Grandpa shrugged. "Brought the boy in to learn her language and talk to her. Guess they did more than talk since it broke up his first marriage." He glanced at me, and I shifted uneasily.

I'd always thought Penina's mother and my father had been divorced a long time before Dad had met my mother. Or at least a reasonable amount of time. Logically, I knew Penina was only a few years older than I, so it couldn't have been *that* long. The idea that Mom might have been the Other Woman, someone who'd prompted Dad's divorce, was one I hadn't considered. And I didn't want to consider it. It wasn't why I was here.

"She was a sweet girl," Grandpa relented with a sigh. "Not as rigid as Maryanne and not... well, drugs weren't *her* problem. I didn't approve, but I understood the temptation. And if she was a prisoner, well, maybe she fell for her captor. Something like that."

"I came more because I was wondering about his work, but does this mean he was *AWOL* when I was born? Like hiding out in Seattle in that apartment?"

"We didn't know *where* he was. Not at first. The Army came by and questioned us that first year he went missing."

I rubbed my face.

"He said he was protecting her. That they'd hurt her and wanted to force her to do things. I always figured that was some fanciful shit the boy made up as an excuse for leaving, but who knows. The Army did come by a bunch of times, looking for him. For *them*. More than you'd expect just to round up a wayward soldier."

"I can't believe he managed to stay hidden for years. Didn't he have to sign a lease? Get a background check for his job?"

Something twanged at my senses, and I frowned toward the garage door. Was there a magical being nearby? I'd never sensed anyone like that living in my grandparents' neighborhood.

Before I could home in on the aura and identify the owner, it disappeared. As if he or she had activated a camouflage charm. I touched my own, but I couldn't disappear from the garage while I was in the middle of a conversation with my grandfather.

"Those were different times. You could pay cash for everything and get paid in cash if you had the right employer. He was in Canada at first too. That's where you were born."

"Huh."

The brush with magic made me realize that, as an experienced enchanter, it probably would have been easy for Mom to use her power to hide her family in plain sight. I hadn't been by Val's coffee shop yet, but I'd heard it was virtually invisible to normal humans. They walked right by it without realizing anything interesting was there. Mom might even have crafted Dad a charm that made normal people see him differently.

The more pertinent question was... what, after years of successfully hiding, had allowed the Army to find my family that awful night?

"That's all I know," Grandpa said. "There's a metal box of his belongings in the cupboard over there if you want to look. Some things from his childhood and some from when he came home on leave." He shrugged. "Penina was never that interested. Didn't want to be associated with a father in prison. Guess that's understandable, even if I know it would have hurt him. Anyway, you might as well have it."

"Thanks." Though it sounded like stuff from before he'd met my mother, curiosity sent me toward the cabinet. I swept out with my senses again, worried about whoever I'd briefly detected, but if they'd hidden themselves, I would have to wait until they got close to sense them again. Hopefully, they *wouldn't* get close while I was in the house.

I made the mistake of opening Grandpa's metal bait box first and couldn't keep from gagging. I'd been willing to do more outdoor things with him as a kid than Penina had, but fishing hadn't ever been a favorite of mine.

"The *other* metal box," he said dryly.

"I'm sure Dad appreciates you storing his baseball cards next to the stinky tackle box that you never clean."

That only earned me another grunt. There probably *were* baseball cards in Dad's box. Hopefully, that wasn't all there was.

I found it and tugged it out. There wasn't a lock, just a clasp. A tremble went through my fingers, and I fumbled with it before managing to open it. For some reason, I was nervous, as if I were poking into someone's diary.

"If he'd kept a *diary*, figuring out what went on would have been a lot easier," I mumbled, then glanced back self-consciously.

But Grandpa was heading inside and didn't seem to hear. Maybe he'd decided I should have privacy for this. That immediately made me think there was more inside than baseball cards, and I almost fumbled the entire box before settling myself and resting it on the workbench.

There *were* boyhood treasures inside. They ranged from the aforementioned baseball cards to an Eagles ticket stub to a troll doll to what might have been a pet rock. A stack of Polaroids rested on the bottom, and I sorted through them, hoping for one of my mom, but of the ones with women in them, she wasn't among them. Judging by the clothes and haircuts, the photos had been taken in the seventies. That was before my time and also probably before my parents had met. There was Penina's mom. I'd never known her, but I'd seen pictures of her before. The only Army-related thing was a copy of what must have been his first orders for training at Fort Huachuca in Arizona.

"This was all before Mom." I was about to close the box, certain there weren't any clues to Dad's adult life, but folded notes at the bottom made me pause.

The paper was yellowed, and I unfolded one carefully. Then sucked in a breath as my heartbeat thundered in my ears. The ink hadn't faded so much that I couldn't recognize the language: Dwarven.

4

I COULDN'T READ MORE THAN A COUPLE OF THE DWARVEN WORDS, but I recognized the language, the hieroglyph-like runes my mother's people favored over an alphabet. A dozen of them were carved into my hammer, and hundreds if not thousands existed in their language.

My fingers shook as I found and opened four different messages. There weren't any translations. Meaning that by the time my mother had given them to my father, he'd already been fluent in her language?

I folded the papers and tucked them into a zipper pocket. I *had* to get them translated. Willard had mentioned people who could do such work for her, but the idea of some Army officer deciphering what might have been love letters from my mother to my father made my skin crawl.

Maybe Val's half-sister Freysha would do it. I'd heard she'd studied languages and done translations for Willard.

While I was debating if *her* reading my family's letters would be less weird, the being I'd sensed before returned to my awareness.

I swore. Whoever it was—whoever *she* was—wasn't doing anything to hide her aura now. It radiated power from the front yard. Worse, she had the aura of a dwarf. Unless my mother had decided to make her first appearance in thirty years, I could only imagine one other person this might be.

"Hiding my Harley was a waste of time," I muttered, closing Dad's box and tucking it back inside Grandpa's cabinet.

For a second, I thought about activating my camouflage charm, but she knew I was here, and if I disappeared, she would question my grandparents. Possibly with force.

Horrified by the idea, I grabbed my hammer, intending to charge out the front door and face her. On the way, I paused and grabbed a couple of the cookies. Maybe I could bribe her to leave me alone. If that didn't work, they made decent projectiles.

"I'll be back later," I called as I headed through the house and to the front door.

Hopefully, I could lead the dwarf away from the house, and she would never bother my grandparents.

"Do you want some cookies to take with you?" Grandma called from the kitchen.

"Already got some from the garage. Thanks."

"The garage." Grandma humphed as I let myself out. "They're probably covered in sawdust."

The dwarf female stood on the sidewalk out front, her beefy arms folded over her chest as she studied the house and—as soon as I stepped out and closed the door—me. Even if I hadn't already been certain who she was, Princess Barothla resembled my mother closely enough that I would have believed her a close relative. She had frizzy red hair clipped back from her broad face, a squat nose, and eyes that were gray instead of green like my mother's. They were also cool and wary instead of warm and friendly, as I remembered Mom's being.

Barothla wore plate armor and boots, and had a horned

helmet like the king's tied to a backpack. The short single-headed hammers belted at either hip looked more like weapons than tools, and I doubted her arm muscles had come from alchemy. A warrior as well as a crafter, then, and probably a dangerous one. Her aura certainly suggested that. It was as powerful as Sarrlevi's.

As an heir to the dwarven throne, she might also have body-guards around. I didn't sense any, but I also hadn't sensed *her* until she'd chosen to reveal herself.

"Maybe I should have brought a better bribe," I muttered, then forced a smile as I descended the steps. "Hi, I'm Matti. I guess you're Princess Barothla, huh? Do I bow or curtsey?"

She kept studying me and didn't reveal whether she could understand me or not.

"I'm surprised they let you out of your palace without body-guards," I added.

Her bushy red eyebrows rose, and she tapped a charm on a metal bracelet around one wrist. It glowed faintly before fading, and she nodded to me.

Assuming that was a translation charm, I repeated my questions. It occurred to me that *she* could read the notes in my pockets, but there was no way I would ask the dwarf who'd hired Sarrlevi to assassinate my mother to translate love letters she'd written to my father.

Palace? Barothla asked telepathically, maybe realizing I didn't have a translation charm and wouldn't understand the Dwarven tongue.

Since Val had only lent me hers, I'd given it back after returning from Sarrlevi's wild world. But, as usual, telepathy somehow bypassed language, and I understood Barothla even though the words were in Dwarven.

Does dwarf royalty not have a palace inside their caves and tunnels? I asked.

It is true. You are ignorant of your heritage and know nothing.

That's right. I decided not to be offended. Better to have her think that I was an idiot and not a threat than someone she had to worry about or speak carefully around. *I've lived on Earth my whole life, and my mother died when I was four.* I squinted as I watched her for a reaction. *I guess you know all about that.*

Barothla's face was hard to read. She had a haughty upward tilt to her chin that reminded me of the elf ex-princess, but she was half a foot shorter than I, so maybe it wasn't fair to judge her by that. There were plenty of other things I could judge her by.

We have recently learned she may not *be dead,* was all that Barothla said.

No kidding.

This time, she squinted at me. *Where is she?*

I have no idea.

The inside of my skull itched, and unease bordering on fear crept into me. Would she prove more gifted than Sarrlevi at reading my mind? I still wasn't that sure he struggled as much as he'd claimed. He had no trouble knowing when I was thinking about his hotness.

As the itching grew stronger, my fingers tightened around the haft of my hammer. I thought of physically convincing her to stay out of my head. But did I want to challenge her to a fight when she appeared capable? And had magic in addition to hammers to throw around? Besides, since I truly didn't know where my mother was, how much could she learn?

Her cool gaze held mine, and the itching grew more painful, like fingernails—or talons—raking my mind. It started to remind me of the dragon Zondia's mind scouring.

Growling, I strode toward her, rethinking my decision to avoid a fight, but the sensation halted abruptly. I also halted, not because I wasn't fantasizing about knocking her head off with my hammer, but because I sensed an invisible wall in front of her. A magical barrier that was *stronger* than a wall. It was possible I could smash through it with my hammer, but I wasn't positive.

I see, Barothla said after the itching faded from my mind.

If my approach concerned her, she didn't show it. She hadn't stepped back or lowered her hands toward her hammers.

That is unfortunate, she added. *I've come to look for her, find her, and apologize.*

"Apologize?" I blurted skeptically before remembering we'd switched to telepathy. *For hiring an assassin to murder your own sister? My* mother?

Yes.

Mentioning Sarrlevi brought his face into my thoughts and reminded me he would show up at my house in a couple of hours and that we had an incursion into a maximum-security prison on a military post to plan. Standing in the yard and talking to the dreadful dwarf who'd been responsible for my mother fleeing her world and being captured by the Army was a waste of time.

You invited Sarrlevi to dinner? Barothla asked, proving she was still sauntering through my mind. She threw back her head and laughed.

I gritted my teeth, contemplating trying my hammer on her barrier.

You know he's the one I hired all those years ago, right? I see that you do. Are you so overcome by his beauty that you are trying to court him?

Nobody's courting anyone.

His tastes don't run toward dwarves. Trust me. Barothla smirked at me. *I did ask.*

Everybody does. But I'm not interested in him. I'm just working with him to— I halted with the realization that she knew the answer to the question I'd never stopped wondering. *He's not still working for you, is he?*

He is not interested in working for me these days, and I would be a fool to attempt to harm my sister again. Once my father found out what I'd done, he officially removed me from the line of succession. He almost cast me out of the city altogether, but with our mother passed, he and I — I have been his only close family these past decades.

It concerned me that she hadn't straight-up said Sarrlevi wasn't still working for her. I didn't think the answer had conveyed that he *was*, but it was ambiguous.

Who's supposed to inherit the throne if both of his daughters are out of the picture? I asked.

Not a mongrel from another world, if that's what you're thinking.

If you've been in my head enough to know about my dinner plans, you ought to know I'm relieved that could never happen.

Barothla gazed at me, my skull itching again. I glared defiantly back at her but didn't attempt to keep her out of my head. I *wanted* her to know I meant what I said.

It's good that you're not completely stupid, she said. *I didn't think you could be since my sister wasn't—isn't. We need not be enemies, you know.*

You don't think so, huh? I rubbed the haft of my hammer with my thumb.

Barothla snorted, her expression unconcerned. *To answer your question, I don't know if my father has an heir selected currently, but he informed me that if I want to remain in his good graces and stand to inherit anything from him, I had better find my sister and bring her home. Since you seem to have the same goal, we could work together.*

You also don't inherit anything if she returns, do you? Why would you care about getting her?

As the second-born, I would stand to inherit lands and one of the golden smithies. Further, if Rodarska never has children—real dwarven *children—my offspring, should I marry and have some, would be in line to inherit after her. It is only the throne that I myself would not inherit if my older sister returned.*

I mulled that over. If Barothla had already had adult children, I might have thought this was some plan to appease her father while continuing to scheme to get rid of her sister and rule through her kids one day. But those kids sounded hypothetical.

Though our people might object to Rodarska as a ruler when they learn of you and that she dallied with a male of an inferior species. Barothla raised her eyebrows.

Are you sure we shouldn't be enemies?

Barothla surprised me by laughing again. I tried to decide if it was the maniacal Machiavellian laugh of someone plotting to gain power. When she was done, she waved toward my hammer. *Do you know how to fully use Rodarska's weapon? Are you aware that she crafted it?*

I've heard that.

There are power words. Did she teach you?

I know a few of them. Admittedly, because *Val* had shared them, not because my mother had. Mom presumably hadn't thought teaching a toddler how to use a magical hammer to smash things was a good idea. Since my hobby had been applying crayons to the apartment walls at the time, that had been wise.

I could show you more, Barothla offered. *If I can't guess them all, I can find the rest. One of the reasons I sought you out is to warn you that some of our people believe such a powerful weapon shouldn't remain on another world in a mongrel's hands.*

I'm aware of that.

Ah. She spread a hand. *If you prove yourself capable and act honorably in battle, they may agree to let you keep it. You should fully know its capabilities though. If you don't wish instruction from me, I can simply help you find my sister so she can teach you.*

Even though Barothla was clearly trying to manipulate me, I couldn't help but feel longing. I'd wished for that often, to have my mother back in my life so she could teach me more about the hammer and my dwarven heritage. And just so I could get to know her.

If she's a prisoner somewhere, I have the means to be helpful in breaking her free. Barothla patted one of the hammers on her hips. *Whoever has restrained her all this time must be dangerous and powerful themselves if she wasn't able to escape on her own.*

That was what I feared. *I thought you were an alchemist, not a warrior.*

I am both. Her eyes narrowed. *Who told you about me? Sarrlevi?*

Someone mentioned your career, I said vaguely, though Sarrlevi had told me that morning. *Is it a secret?*

Barothla lowered her hand from her hammer. *It is not. Do you wish my help?*

No.

You would be foolish not to make use of me and my abilities.

I'm often that.

She gazed coolly at me for a long moment. *I will continue to seek her on this world, regardless of whether you assist me.*

Because you can't inherit a smithy if you don't? I asked, skeptical of her motives.

A golden smithy, lands, and, as I said, a place in the succession for my children.

If she didn't have kids already, was it strange that she was planning on having them? How much younger than my mother was she? Since dwarves were long-lived, I couldn't guess. I didn't even know how old my mother was. Maybe dwarven fertile years lasted for centuries.

These are not unimportant things, Barothla added. *I also would prefer to be back in my father's favor. You have no reason to believe me, but I regret my actions in the past—hiring Sarrlevi.*

Why did you do it? Just because she was in line to inherit the throne instead of you?

Please. I am not such an ambitious and callous person. The thought that I could inherit if she was gone was certainly part of my consideration, but it was not everything. You see, she was our parents' favorite.

And our people's favorite. Dwarves love enchanters, and she was the best to come along in many generations. She got praise from our parents, from our people, from our tutors, from everyone. Barothla's mouth twisted. *And then there was me, someone who had little interest in or aptitude for enchanting but had a knack for alchemy. I mastered hundreds of helpful existing formulas and also made new and useful creations. But* alchemy *is not one of the favored careers for dwarves, not something they respect. They would prefer to trade armor and weapons and tools to elves for formulas, not make their own, and they thought I was addled for studying the craft.*

Barothla looked toward the park, her eyes growing distant.

I couldn't tell if it was all an act. The bitterness was believable, but why was she sharing all this with me? I was a stranger to her and vice versa. And if she was as capable and powerful as she said —and as I believed—she ought to be able to hunt down my mother on her own.

Or maybe not. Sarrlevi hadn't been able to find Mom, and he was an expert at tracking people down. Neither of them knew Earth, which was probably one of the stranger and more confusing *wild worlds* to magical beings from other places.

Even if the praise she received and that I didn't hadn't bothered me, Barothla continued, *it was clear she was our parents' favorite. You probably don't know what it's like to have a perfect older sister and constantly be held up beside her for measurement.*

"Uh." I glanced at my grandparents' house, memories of going through school in Penina's wake coming to mind. Her perfect grades, socially acceptable hobbies and friends, and the fact that *she'd* never gotten in trouble for fighting. Yeah, I knew what it was like to have an older sister who was hard to live up to.

It was difficult following in her footsteps, Barothla said. *The night I hired the assassin, I was drunk and angry over a squabble my sister and I had in the wake of more praise she'd received—praise and an* award *for a power generator she'd led a team to craft, an improvement over the* one lighting up our great city. I'd made drugs that could cure diseases that plagued our people, but she got an award. Barothla shook her head. I was furious that night. That doesn't make my actions excusable. For what it's worth, I'm relieved the assassin didn't succeed.

Good to know, I said neutrally.

And her absence these past decades has taught me that removing her from my life didn't fix all the problems I'd imagined it would.

The problems sounded like they existed solely in her mind.

I don't blame you if you don't believe me, but will you accept my assistance? Let me join you in seeking her. Her gaze was back on mine, intent now. If you come face to face with powerful enemies, you may need my help.

I almost pointed out that I had Sarrlevi for that, but I didn't trust her and didn't want to admit anything of my plans to her. The way she'd laughed when I thought of Sarrlevi as an ally—or as a dinner companion—also made me hesitant to bring him up again.

Let me join you, she repeated. I believe you'll need all the help you can get.

Surprisingly, I found myself nodding in agreement. It was possible I could use her help, that Sarrlevi wouldn't be enough. After all, if the fight on the logging land was an indicator, my mother had been building enchanted helicopters, weapons, and who knew what else for her captors. When I found their next base, I might have to get past powerful defenses to reach her. And then, if some magical artifact—such as one of the elf pilots had worn—had her brainwashed or enslaved to work loyally for her captors, would she attack me instead of fleeing with me? If she was as powerful as I'd come to believe, she might be able to kill me with a hand wave.

That thought sent a chill down my spine, and I took a step closer to Barothla, about to say I did need her help.

But a hint of triumph in her eyes and smugness curving her

lips rang alarm bells in my mind. Damn it, she'd used magical coercion on me when she'd spoken those words. It had been subtle, and I hadn't sensed it, but I was positive that only *magic* could have changed my mind so quickly.

I planted my feet. *I know what you're doing.*

Oh?

I won't let you manipulate me, and I don't need your help to find her. If you save her on your own and take her back home to your father, I'll be delighted, but— I squinted at her, *—my instincts tell me that's not what you're* really *after.*

Anger replaced her triumph, turning her gray eyes to storm clouds, but only for a second before she recovered and smoothed her features. *I suppose it is only through my actions that I can prove that what I say is true and that you can trust me.*

That's right.

Very well. She bowed toward me, then turned and walked away. Before she'd gone more than ten yards, she activated a camouflaging charm and disappeared from my sight and senses.

5

THOUGH GRAY CLOUDS AND DRIZZLE MADE THE SKY DARK, IT WAS still daylight when I arrived home, so I hoped to have plenty of time to prepare before my dinner guest showed up. After parking my Harley under my newly rebuilt carport, I headed to the door with a pair of canvas grocery bags that held prepared salads from the deli and ingredients for one of my favorite dishes: scalloped potatoes and ham smothered with cheese.

It wouldn't win any awards on the Food Network, but it had been one of my staples during the lean years after I'd first started my business. The secret ingredient was the balsamic vinegar that gave it zing.

Whether my elitist elf guest would like scalloped potatoes, I didn't know, but I planned to tell him it was considered fine-dining fare on Earth. It wasn't as if he would know. Besides, I had some green offerings for him, in case his tastes ran more toward vegetables. Three different kinds of salads, though the spinach-flavored green pasta salad might not count as a vegetable. The other two definitely were. Personally, I couldn't imagine anyone wanting Kaleo Twist or Chard Rock instead of cheesy potatoes, but elves were odd. To round things out, two baguettes stuck out of my bags, and I planned to make my favorite garlic-butter spread. For dessert, we would have cookies and brownies.

The lights were on in the living room, and I spotted movement inside as I carried my load to the door. Unexpectedly, Zadie's electric vehicle and Abbas's truck were out front. Given how distracting the afternoon had been, it was possible I'd missed a phone message coming in.

I hoped they didn't plan to stay for dinner. I had enough food, since I'd wanted to make sure to have plenty of whatever Sarrlevi ended up liking, but... I wanted to plan the night's mission with him, not host a dinner party. I hadn't been that worried about Tinja being around, but I didn't want to discuss breaking into a prison while my business partner and real-estate agent were present. True, Zadie and Abbas were friends, not only my agent and partner, but... the less they knew about my plans for illegal activities, the better. Too many people around me these days had the ability to read minds. I didn't need Barothla showing up to question them while Sarrlevi and I were sneaking in.

"Hey, guys." I lifted a bag in greeting as I passed through the living room to the kitchen.

Abbas and Zadie knelt on the floor next to a laptop, and Zadie sprang up when she saw me.

"*There* you are," she blurted.

"Here I am," I agreed, setting the grocery bags on the counter. "Tinja," I said into the dining room, where she was sitting on papers covering the small portion of the table not occupied by toolboxes and half-started contraptions. "Can you clear that stuff off? I've got a guest coming for dinner."

"Clear it off?" Tinja looked blankly at me.

"I know it's usually our joint project space, but the technical function of that room and that table is for dining."

"I can't reach the table when I sit in these chairs."

"Yeah, but other people can, and not everyone wants to perch on the edge of a sofa with projects piled up behind them while they eat."

Tinja scratched her head with a pencil, further mussing her perpetually mussed white hair. "Huh."

"I've got two kinds of desserts and will share if you clean everything off. Just for tonight. And, ah, you could eat in your room if you don't want to join us. It's kind of a..."

"A date?" Zadie guessed, her eyebrows rising. "Is it that Tyler? Aren't you meeting him for coffee tomorrow morning?"

Hell, *was* that tomorrow? I glanced at the date on my phone, having forgotten tomorrow was Sunday. "I guess I am."

If I didn't get arrested tonight.

"But that's not who's coming," I added.

"I'm not invited?" One of Tinja's pointed ears drooped.

"You are if you want to come, but I wasn't sure you'd want to spend time with my guest. He's... aloof."

"Who is it?" Zadie asked.

"Sarrlevi. You've met him." They'd *all* met him, but I wasn't sure I'd ever formally introduced everyone. The last time Zadie and Tinja had seen Sarrlevi, he'd been bleeding all over the floor as I led him back to my room.

"You invited *him*?" Zadie looked at the bags. "To *dinner*? Every time I've met him, he's been in the process of lopping off someone's ear. Or *head*."

"Last time, he was injured and leaning on me," I pointed out, though I couldn't deny their first meeting, which had also been my first meeting of Sarrlevi, *had* involved him beheading werewolves.

"While he bled all over the place. Matti, that guy has a bad vibe."

"Because he's an assassin. If he came across as a kindergarten teacher, nobody would hire him."

Zadie mouthed, "*Assassin*," and looked at Abbas.

He'd been scrutinizing whatever was on the laptop and only shrugged at the conversation. We had an unspoken agreement to stick to discussions about work, with occasional forays into macroeconomics and how they would affect the Seattle housing market. In the years I'd known him, he'd never brought up my love life. All I knew about *his* love life was that he liked sweet, shy women—a couple of his girlfriends had come by the work-site in the past—and was saving himself for marriage. I was fairly sure that was something that came from his mother's Muslim religion and not his father's troll religion. Though I hadn't spent a lot of time with trolls, the males had leered at me often enough that I doubted premarital abstinence was a big thing for them.

"Zadie brought us an interesting house to look at," Abbas said, as if her incredulous look had been about that. "It's where Bothell, Maltby, and Woodinville all mash together. Not far from the free-way. A real fixer that we could improve, and here's the interesting part. It's on five acres and already approved and platted for more houses. This could be an incredible investment. You've been talking about building some houses from scratch, and I would dig the challenge too."

"I thought we agreed not to put in an offer for anything new until the Bridle Trails house closed." I started unpacking groceries, relieved to talk about work rather than my dinner plans.

Zadie had followed me into the kitchen, and I willed her to refocus, but her face was still twisted in distress as she watched me remove items from the bags. "You can make an offer contingent on the sale of the other house," she said. "It's a buyer's market now. Contingency offers are back in vogue."

"Good to know. I suppose we could look at it tomorrow."

"After your date with the normal guy? The *human* guy?" Zadie asked.

"Yeah."

She pointed to the salads. "I know you didn't get those for yourself."

"I want my guest to be able to eat his fill of things he likes so he'll..." I caught myself before saying *have plenty of stamina tonight,* certain Zadie would misinterpret the heck out of that. "Get enough food. I think he might be a vegetarian. Or partially one."

"A partial vegetarian is just a normal person, Matti. And is this a *date*?" Zadie waved to the potatoes I was pulling out. "I've never seen you make food for someone. You don't even feed me, and I sell your houses for you."

"It's not a date."

She scratched her jaw dubiously. "I didn't think you were the type to be involved with two guys at once."

"It's not, and I'm not." Not that there was anything wrong with dating two men at once. Besides, aside from meeting at my sister's house, Tyler and I had only talked on the phone a couple of times. We were having our first get-together in the morning. That didn't count as dating, not yet. We hadn't even kissed. And Sarrlevi... Well, whatever that kiss had been, he'd made it clear it had been a mistake. "Look, I didn't even get a bottle of wine to go with dinner. I would have gotten wine if it were a date."

Also, since we were going to break into a prison later, being sober tonight seemed wise.

"Oh, that looks good." Zadie grabbed one of the baguettes and smelled it. "If it's not a date, Abbas and I can stay, right?"

"And I can stay," Tinja added brightly from atop the dining-room table.

So far, she'd only pushed papers around, and I added clearing it off to my mental to-do list.

"You *want* to stay?" I asked her.

Though Tinja never voiced complaints about people lopping off heads in her presence, she'd expressed fear before at those who could do such things. Understandably so.

"I do not believe he will threaten me," Tinja said. "We've gone into battle together. He's seen the Goblinator in action! If enemies come again, I'm prepared to spring onto the rooftop to defend our home once more. I've replenished my supply of ammunition."

"You have?" I looked around the kitchen, hoping she hadn't disassembled anymore of my small appliances for parts. "Where's the blender?"

Tinja gave me a wicked grin. "I could not help myself. The blades were *so* enticing. Perfect for incorporating into my ammunition. They could slice the tusks off an orc!"

"Their purpose is making smoothies." Shaking my head, I fished in drawers until I found a vegetable peeler so I could start on the potatoes. It wasn't my *favorite* peeler with the ergonomic handle, since that had gone mysteriously missing, but a rusty, dented, all-metal one that had been in a drawer when I'd bought the house.

"You can stay if you help," I told Zadie, handing her a paring knife and pointing to the bag of potatoes. "I need to get these in the oven soon so they'll be ready for dinner."

"When is your... not-a-date coming?" she asked.

"I'm not sure. He doesn't wear a watch or have a phone, so I didn't give him a time. We just have to be done and ready to go at midnight."

"What's happening at midnight?"

I hesitated and started slicing potatoes. "Laser show at the Seattle Center."

"Your assassin is a fan of loud music? Doesn't that hurt his ears?"

"He likes Metallica."

Zadie blinked.

"Metallica is great," Abbas said. "I like Grunge more, but you know."

"I do know," I said. "I've spent many a day rocking out to your music choices while installing drywall."

Shaking her head, Zadie picked up the peeler to help.

As a pile of sliced and peeled potatoes grew, I left her to finish the task while I prepared the sauce and cut up ham. I remembered the notes in my jacket pocket and vowed to call Val later to see if her half-sister had arrived. If any of the Chard Rock was left over, I would offer it to Freysha as a bribe. Though with the number of people inviting themselves to my dinner, I doubted there would be leftovers. I hoped Sarrlevi wouldn't feel waylaid when he arrived and encountered more of a party than the private planning meal I'd envisioned.

Once the scalloped potatoes were in the oven, buried under not one or two but *three* kinds of cheese, I took a break to clean off the dining-room table and call Val.

"Hey, Matti," she answered. "You're not in trouble, are you?"

"No, I can handle clearing off a table." I tugged at half-rolled blueprints for Tinja's forthcoming tiny-home-plans business only to find them stuck to the surface. "Probably."

"Ah, you're having dinner? I thought you might be... on a mission."

"The mission I wouldn't be able to tell you about, even if I were on it, since Willard forbade you from getting involved?"

"That's the one."

"If I *were* going to undertake such a mission, I would wait until the middle of the night."

"That's wise," Val said.

"I called because I was wondering if your multilingual elven half-sister has arrived yet."

"She has. Do you want to meet her?"

"Yes, ideally while she's translating some old letters for me."

"Letters in Elven?"

"Letters in Dwarven. I found them in a box of my dad's things and think my mom might have written them before I was born."

"So they're full of topical news then."

"They may have something useful in them. Mom has been missing for a long time. Is your sister available for hire?" Though I hoped the notes would be easy for a linguist to translate, I didn't want to presume she would do a favor for someone she'd never met for free.

"She doesn't have a lot of interest in Earth currency, but if you bring her a plant, I'm sure she'll be delighted and take on the task."

"Great. I'll bring over the letters tomorrow morning." I remembered the coffee date. "After noon."

"After noon tomorrow morning, got it."

I snorted. "Maybe around one or two. Does that work?"

"Sure." Val hesitated. "If you were to go on a mission that you can't tell me anything about tonight, I would hope you would be careful and take backup. If you end up in a military prison yourself, Willard might not be able to get you out."

"I'm a civilian. Wouldn't I be sent to a regular prison?"

"Willard would have even less pull to get you out of one of those," Val said dryly.

"I'll keep that in mind."

6

THE HOUSE SMELLED OF CHEESY GOODNESS, AND I'D GOTTEN THE sticky papers—and the pine pitch responsible for the sticky papers—off the table and laid out my one set of matching plates. They weren't fine china, but they weren't chipped, and they were all the same color. To add further posh, I'd found glasses that hadn't come with a McDonald's happy meal and didn't have cartoon characters on them. Mostly. The two Moose Drool pint glasses from my trip to Missoula did have illustrated moose dripping saliva painted on them. I found them whimsical, but, on second thought, I put them away and grabbed the *Shrek* glasses I'd managed to keep in good condition for more than a decade.

Maybe Sarrlevi would be amused by the Hollywood version of an ogre. Or he would be horrified at the hodgepodge of dining implements. As I recalled, *he'd* had silver trays and glasses that had probably been blown by elven artisans. They doubtless hadn't been acquired from garage sales and Goodwill, as much of my stuff had.

"At least my table is pretty cool," I murmured, admiring it for the first time in months—it was usually covered in projects. After buying the house, I'd found a slab of reclaimed wood and made it myself. Though I didn't know how to enchant anything, it always struck my senses as slightly magical. Something within the wood itself rather than anything I'd done to it, I was sure.

"You're going to give an assassin a *Shrek* glass?" Zadie asked as she walked in with the salads, the contents transferred from the store containers to bowls.

"Is that not appropriate?" I asked. "I used to have *Zorro* glasses, but they broke."

She arched her eyebrows.

"Don't judge me. I've seen your *Star Trek* juice-glass collection."

"Those are collectibles. I don't serve water to assassins in them." After setting down the salads, Zadie patted me on the shoulder. "Here's a tip: if you're going to throw dinner parties, invest in some nicer stuff."

"I wasn't planning to throw a dinner party. You invited yourself."

"Only because I'm concerned about you being alone in the house with that guy."

While I was wrestling between pointing out that Tinja would be around and that Sarrlevi wasn't going to do anything nefarious to me, Zadie continued. "Besides, you do okay with the business, right? You don't invest *everything* back into it, do you?"

"No, but I have a roommate with a bottomless stomach, and I'm saving up to buy a cottage on the lake."

"Your roommate doesn't buy her own groceries?"

"She doesn't even pay rent. Last tax season, I was debating if I could claim a goblin as a dependent."

Zadie blinked. "I didn't know you were running a charity, though I suppose I shouldn't be surprised since you so often accept the *sentimental* offer on your houses instead of the highest one."

I was about to mention that Tinja helped in other ways, but I sensed a portal opening out front. Nerves ricocheted through my gut. Whether I was nervous because Sarrlevi was coming to dinner, or he was coming to what he didn't know was a dinner *party*, I didn't know, but I thanked Zadie for her help and hurried out front to greet him.

It was raining harder, puddles forming on the walkway up to the house, and I halted on the covered stoop to wait for him. He could use magic to keep from getting wet. I couldn't.

Our eyes met as Sarrlevi strode toward me, dressed all in black like Death on a mission instead of in his more typical *Lord of the Rings* browns and greens. It startled me, for it made him look much more like an assassin. I reminded myself we were going on a stealthy nighttime excursion, so the choice made sense. Besides, he carried two large wheels of cheese tucked under his arm, and I smiled, certain people with assassinations on the mind didn't tote around such items.

As he approached, I considered asking him about the events surrounding Barothla hiring him so I could find out how much of the story she'd told had been the truth. *Had* she been drunk and angry and made a mistake? Since then, had she shown any sign that she'd regretted it? Sarrlevi hadn't said he'd spoken to her in the past forty years, but he'd found out somehow that she'd learned of me and might visit.

But when he reached the stoop, joining me under the covered area, I hesitated to bring up Barothla. They'd known each other a lot longer than he'd known me. How *well* they knew each other, I didn't know, but that comment about her trying to woo him made me wonder if she had reached out to him more than once. Was there any chance they'd been in communication recently and that anything I asked would make its way back to her? I thought I could trust him more than that, but... I wasn't the one who'd hired him. What did he owe me?

"Your cheese." Sarrlevi inclined his head but didn't bow as he offered the wheels to me. On the small stoop, it would have meant clunking me in the head.

"Thank you."

"I have rope and a few other items that may be helpful with an incursion." He waved over his shoulder, toward his twin longswords and the magical backpack that could hold far more than it should have.

I hoped Zadie wouldn't freak out when he walked in armed. Had she truly invited herself to dinner to watch out for me? I was touched that she cared but wished everyone could grasp how helpful Sarrlevi had been to me over the past weeks. Even if I couldn't trust him fully when it came to my quest and telling the truth, I did trust that he wouldn't hurt me in any way. He might *tease* me, but I teased him too.

"You have company." He looked toward the window.

Three noses were pressed to the glass, and I rolled my eyes. "Friends, yes. But they won't be coming with us tonight."

"You do not believe your formidable roommate and the *Goblinator* would be useful?" he asked dryly.

"If we were going into battle, she might be, especially now that she's incorporated my blender blades into her weapon, but we can't hurt anyone tonight."

Sarrlevi arched his eyebrows.

"I mean it. Nobody. We need to get in and out without being seen, or I'm going to end up in jail myself." I waited, expecting him to object or state that he would defend himself if attacked.

"I am practiced at stealth," was what he said.

"I've noticed."

He smiled slightly. "Though *dwarves* aren't known for their light feet."

"Since you're here to help me tonight, I'm going to allow you to tease me without glowering at you or being snarky."

"Oh? There will be no snark at all?"

"You can't tell me you like it."

Not when he got all huffy and glared when I did it.

"Mongrels of modest talents should be respectful to assassins, but I prefer spirited people who stand up for themselves to ambulatory lumps of defeat."

"My talents are *amazing*, not *modest*," I said, locking onto the first half of the sentence before realizing it was something of a compliment—inasmuch as he gave them. Maybe he wasn't the only one who got huffy and glared.

"I refer to your lack of training in the magical arts, not your... plumbing abilities." His eyes gleamed as they reflected the porch light.

"You're such a bastard."

"Yes." Sarrlevi tilted his head toward the door. "I smell cheese baking. Is the meal almost ready?"

"Yes, but hang on." I gripped his arm, though he hadn't reached for the knob. "My friends don't know anything about this, but you should know that Barothla showed up today." I watched him, wondering if he would be surprised.

"Ah?" He didn't look or sound surprised, but the humor faded from his face.

"She said we didn't have to be enemies, that she regretted hiring you in the past, and that she wanted to help me find my mother." I raised my eyebrows. "She also tried to use magical coercion to get me to agree to work with her."

Sarrlevi's face had grown closed, and he didn't comment. I wished I could read *his* mind.

"My instincts told me she was full of shit and that I should do my best to avoid her. What do you think?"

There, a question. He had to answer. If he wanted scalloped potatoes, he did.

Sarrlevi gazed toward the yard and the rain pattering into the puddles in the street.

"You should heed your instincts," he finally said.

"And not trust her any more than I should trust assassins?" I asked, still wishing I *could* trust him fully.

"Correct." Sarrlevi managed another faint smile, but his eyes seemed troubled. He lifted a hand and rested it on the side of my head as he gazed into my eyes. He looked... apologetic.

There was a warning for me in his gaze, I was sure, but my libido kicked in at his touch, and I started thinking about how much I wanted him to use his magic on me again, as he'd done after the battle and while we'd kissed. I wished I had magic that I could use on *him*, to make his insides quiver with pleasure and anticipation. Maybe then he would forget that elves and half-dwarves were not *appropriate*.

A *thud-thump* came from the living room, and Sarrlevi lowered his hand.

I shook away my silly fantasies and opened the door to lead him inside, where Tinja was picking herself up from the floor as Abbas and Zadie lunged away from the window, though I'd known they were all there. I might have *forgotten* it when Sarrlevi had been touching my face, but it wasn't as if I would have kissed him out there.

"Must be hard to spy effectively when you're three feet tall, and the window is three and a half feet off the ground," I said.

"You have no idea," Tinja said.

Zadie and Abbas looked like they might say something, but when Sarrlevi walked in behind me, armored and armed and his face back to grim, they only glanced at each other and backed toward the fireplace. As if my dinner guest would spring at them with his swords.

Abbas hadn't encountered Sarrlevi often, but I hoped he knew Sarrlevi had attacked the *brysarrusi* that night in the park and possibly saved his life. He'd also gone to Zadie's apartment and driven away orcs that had been threatening her. Of course, he'd afterward questioned her for information as he read her mind... but we hadn't been as staunch of allies then. I hoped he wouldn't feel compelled to read my friends' thoughts now.

"Have a seat at the table." I waved Sarrlevi toward the dining room. "The cheese has been melting deliciously over baked potatoes and ham. I'll bring it out shortly. Do you eat meat? If not, the ham cubes are easy to eat around. And there's bread and lots of salad."

"You made a main course comprised of root vegetables?" A hint of his humor returned, a reminder that he'd been amused that I preferred vegetables that grew underground to the chewy green stalks he'd tried to foist on me at his place. He'd been tickled, apparently finding it appropriate for someone with dwarven blood.

"Potatoes grow underground, yes, but Zadie assures me they're a starch and not a vegetable." I waved toward her for confirmation, but she only nodded, her usual snark evaporating with Sarrlevi present. She was eyeing not only his swords but the numerous daggers visible in sheaths around his body.

He might be capable of stealth, but he always traveled prepared for battle. I hoped we could get into the prison without hurting anyone.

Zadie, Abbas, and Tinja followed Sarrlevi into the dining room. At a distance. Watching him uncertainly, they gave him a wide berth as they maneuvered toward seats. They positioned themselves at the far end of the table from where Sarrlevi stood.

"Your servants will dine with us?" he asked me.

"My what?"

"Servants." Sarrlevi extended his arm toward my friends.

"*Servants!*" Zadie found her tongue, as Abbas shook his head.

Tinja nibbled on a slice of baguette and appeared indifferent to the word.

"They're friends," I said. "We don't have servants in Seattle. I mean, some people might, but that's not a thing in my, uh, economic stratum." Nor could I imagine wanting a butler or maid. Well—I eyed the stacks of tools and project materials I'd moved out of the way—maybe a maid wouldn't be so bad. "I don't even have a robot vacuum."

Of course, that was more because Tinja would gleefully disassemble it as soon as it came out of the box, not because I couldn't afford one.

"That one sells the homes you repair." Sarrlevi pointed at Zadie. "That one assists you in their repair." His finger shifted to Abbas, then Tinja. "I do not know her function."

"Repurposing my small appliances to maul home invaders, but she's not a *servant*. None of them are. Abbas is my equal partner in our business, and Zadie's business is to sell houses for many people. It may be a service business, but that's not the same as being a servant."

"Damn straight." Zadie tore off a piece of baguette and chomped angrily on it.

Had Sarrlevi not been an intimidating figure with weapons on display, I knew she would have given him a far more vitriolic response.

"We're all equals here," I said.

Sarrlevi's eyebrows twitched. He probably didn't think any of us were *his* equals.

"So they will dine with us." His tone was flat. Had he wanted a private dinner? That *had* been my plan when I'd invited him, but it wasn't as if we'd intended to have a date with soft music and candlelight.

"Yes." I pulled out a chair for him. "But if you feel it's more fitting with your superior station in life, you can sit at the head of the table."

That earned me a look as flat as his tone. *Superiority is not my concern. I had assumed we would discuss the infiltration while consuming this meal. And that your... colleagues would not partake.*

Friends. Is that not a word in your vocabulary? Reminded of the solitude of his house—his former house—and the fact that his people wouldn't let him visit his dying mother, much less hang out on his home world, I regretted the snark. Assassins probably *didn't* have friends. *And they won't partake in the mission. You're right. Fortunately, thanks to your ability to use telepathy, you can whisper sweet nothings in my mind without them hearing.*

Sweet what?

It's an expression. It— never mind.

Sarrlevi's gaze shifted from me to the table, and he rested a hand on it. *You crafted this?*

Yeah. It surprised me that he could tell.

What does the enchantment do?

Uh, I don't know.

He lifted his brows.

I don't know how to enchant anything. I always thought the magic came from the wood.

No. It feels like an enchantment for longevity and durability, but I'm not an expert on such magic.

Huh. I guess my subconscious mind knew a goblin would one day be crafting projects on it.

Sarrlevi's eyes narrowed. *You need an instructor.*

So I'll know what my furnishings do?

So you will better know how to use your magic and be able to protect yourself.

I would love that. If I find my mother, maybe she'll teach me. Once again, an ache of longing filled me.

That would be ideal, but it might be possible to find an interim teacher.

On Earth?

Sarrlevi hesitated. I doubted there were many enchanters around Seattle.

I don't know, he said. *Possibly.*

Zadie cleared her throat. "You okay, Matti?"

"Yes. Sorry." I grew aware of the others watching as Sarrlevi and I gazed at each other. Our telepathic sweet-nothings whispering had to appear odd from the outside. "I'll get the food."

Not yet sitting, Sarrlevi moved his hand from the table to one of the *Shrek* glasses, which he picked up to examine. That made me glad I hadn't left the Moose Drool drinkware out.

"I thought alcohol might be a bad idea," I said as I headed toward the kitchen, "but I have three kinds of sparkling water. Lemon, grapefruit, and—"

Sarrlevi clunked the glass down and drew a sword as he whirled toward the front door, the blade almost slicing into the ceiling.

"—blood orange," I finished, staring at him from the doorway.

"Is one of the dragons invited to your meal as well?"

"No. Uh, which dragon?" I thought I'd convinced Zondia to leave Sarrlevi alone so he could help me find my mother, but Zondia wasn't the dragon queen. Her decision might have been overruled.

"Thorvald's mate," Sarrlevi said with distaste.

"Oh." Why would Zavryd be coming here? Or was he? I couldn't yet sense him. "Is Val with him?"

My hand strayed toward my pocket, but I'd taken off the jacket with the letters in it. Since I'd mentioned I would bring them by her house the next day, I hadn't expected Val to come here.

"Yes. Also an elf that I'm less familiar with."

"Maybe they heard about the dinner party," Tinja said.

"And the copious amounts of flavored water that would be served," Zadie said. "Matti, do you really not have any wine?"

Sarrlevi frowned. "I *do* know that elf. It's the princess."

"Uh. Val's half-sister, right? Not your ex-princess, er, friend."

"Slehvyra is not a friend," he said, though his gaze remained toward the wall in the direction of the street.

"Just a bedmate, huh?" I asked, then winced at my big mouth. Given their complicated history, and the fact that she'd started the rumor that had prompted the dragons to destroy Sarrlevi's home, I shouldn't have made a joke.

Besides, I had problems of my own to worry about, like what I was supposed to do if an elf *princess* came to my home. Offer her scalloped potatoes? I looked around my modest abode and at the *Shrek* glasses. I'd been self-conscious enough about my things when only Sarrlevi had been coming. Sarrlevi who still had his sword drawn.

Will you put that away? I asked silently, hoping he was still monitoring my thoughts. *Nobody wants to watch you duel a dragon in my front yard.*

Are you certain? He eyed me. *Are matches of gladiatorial combat not popular with spectators on this world?*

Not in this century. We spectate over sports these days.

Are there not combat sports?

Yeah, but beheadings are against the rules.

Alas, there would be repercussions with the Dragon Justice Court if I succeeded in beheading a dragon.

Alas.

"Matti," Zadie whispered.

"Sorry." The dragon—Zavryd—was close enough now that I could detect him. His powerful aura made it harder for me to detect Val and Freysha, but I trusted Sarrlevi's keener senses. "I'll see if I can find some wine in my stash."

A princess might expect wine. Something fancier than grapefruit seltzer water anyway.

"I'll take a malbec or a cabernet."

"My *stash* isn't that comprehensive. Your options are going to be red or white."

"You have the sophisticated palette of a French sommelier, Matti." Zadie elbowed Abbas. "I can't believe that elf thought *we* were the servants."

"Are you going to be able to appreciate it properly if she pours it into a *Shrek* glass?" Abbas asked.

"No, but I don't think I'll want to take extra time to sniff and swish anything from her collection anyway."

"Tea for me, Matti," Abbas called as I headed into the kitchen, hurrying to fill drink orders and grab more place settings. It was possible Val was stopping in to grab the letters for her sister while on some other errand, but I would feel obligated to invite them to dinner.

"Anything bubbly," Tinja called. "While we're all here, is anyone interested in seeing the blueprints for the projects I'm working on? Lord Elf, I heard you lost your domicile recently. Are you aware of tiny homes? They're mobile, so you could roll one to another part of a world if a dragon approached. Their merits are many."

I groaned and hurried out with drinks, hoping Sarrlevi was too busy monitoring Zavryd's approach to be bothered by Tinja's spiel. It surprised me that it was taking so long for Val's trio to reach us, as I'd assumed they would be flying.

But I sensed their leisurely approach and decided they had to be in her Jeep, with Zavryd in his human form. If I'd known he would show up for dinner in any form, I would have purchased entire hams, not a few slices to cube up in my potatoes.

Why is that vile dragon-hating elf assassin here? Zavryd's voice boomed in my mind—in all of our minds—as Val's Jeep pulled up in front of the house.

Sarrlevi, his sword still in hand, clenched his jaw.

Why did I have a feeling this dinner wouldn't go well?

7

As the doors to Val's Jeep opened outside, Sarrlevi strode toward the front door with his swords in hand.

Abandoning my hostess job, I ran past, almost bumping his hip to get in front of him. Before he reached the doorway, I whirled with my hands up, envisioning Zavryd and Sarrlevi dueling and drawing blood in my yard while a beautiful and sophisticated elf princess watched in horror. While *I* watched in horror.

"I'll handle the introductions. Thanks, Sarrlevi. Maybe you can leave your weapons there." I pointed at the coat hooks mounted by the door and my hammer leaning next to the umbrella rack. "I forgot to mention it, but it's an Earth custom that we don't bring swords to the dinner table. Or prong guests."

"What if I prong him *before* he reaches the table?" Sarrlevi asked.

"You fought together up on the mountain. Aren't you over wanting to prong him?"

"He called me *vile*."

"I call you things all the time, and you don't draw your swords."

"Because I *need* you. Nobody needs dragons." Sarrlevi looked past me toward the door and used his magic to open it, revealing Val walking up with a young female elf. Zavryd, clad in his usual black robe, remained by the Jeep, his arms crossed over his chest as he glowered after them.

Had he refused to come in? Or had Val requested that he stay outside? Either would help the situation.

"Hey, Val," I said brightly, turning my back to Sarrlevi and leaning casually against the door frame. I had no doubt that he could get past me if he wished but hoped he wouldn't knock me aside with a gust of magic. "I wasn't expecting you."

"I know. I'm sorry." Val lifted an apologetic hand toward me as she glanced back at Zavryd. "But Freysha is interested in meeting your roommate, and I... have arranged some assistance for you on the mission you're not going on tonight and wouldn't be able to tell me about even if you were."

"Uh, how did you know I'm... not going tonight?"

"Just a hunch."

I will not assist if that elf is involved, Zavryd said. *My sister said he attacked her with magical weapons.*

At first I thought he meant during the battle against the helicopters, but Sarrlevi had *helped* Zondia there. Zavryd had to be referring to when Zondia and the black dragon had come to Sarrlevi's world.

Those so-called attacks came from the magical defenses around my home that she and another dragon were destroying, Sarrlevi said, the iciness of his tone conveyed even through telepathy. *They were not harmed, but had they been, they would have brought it upon themselves.*

I am not positive it was a rumor *that he seeks to assassinate the dwarven king,* Zavryd said. *I know he fantasizes about slaying me.*

"No, he doesn't," I called toward the Jeep. "He's too busy fanta-sizing about the delicious dinner I've made. Uhm, you're all invited of course, Val. Wait, did you say your sister came to see my *roommate*? Not..." I waved toward the jacket on the hook with the letters in the pocket, then looked curiously at the elf who had to be Princess Freysha.

Though blonde, slender, and tall like Val, she had a youthful and innocent face. Had she been human, I would have assumed she was a teenager. If she carried weapons, I couldn't see them, nor did she have the mien of a warrior. She didn't have the mien of a *princess* either. She wore a leather apron over simple tan and brown clothing, with tools jutting from the large and copious pockets. She clinked faintly as she and Val came to a stop in front of me.

"Freysha agreed to translate your letters," Val said, "but she's studying engineering and is a fan of goblin ingenuity when it comes to building and projects. She hasn't met a goblin architect before and is intrigued."

"I *am* intriguing," Tinja spoke from behind Sarrlevi, though she hadn't presumed to move past him. Not surprising since he still held his swords and radiated displeasure in addition to his powerful aura. "I would enjoy speaking to an elf interested in engi-neering, especially engineering that involves tools and alloys, not magically manipulated plants."

"I do both," Freysha said, her voice gentle and lilting.

Val did introductions, though she didn't know Zadie and Abbas well—they'd abandoned the table to peer out the front window at the new arrivals. Zadie must have decided my *sommelier* duties were inadequate, for she'd found my wine stash and filled a glass for herself.

After the introductions, Tinja slipped past Sarrlevi. "Do you want to see my room, Princess Freysha?" she asked brightly. "I have blueprints all over it, not only for houses and tiny houses but for multistory buildings too. We're doing a big commercial project as an assignment right now."

"I would like to see your work, yes." Freysha smiled briefly, but her gaze had shifted to Sarrlevi and his storm cloud of a face. Despite Tinja's encouraging wave, Freysha didn't come closer.

Had Freysha encountered the assassin before? Or maybe she knew that he'd once targeted Val.

"Maybe you can bring your blueprints outside," I whispered to Tinja as I dug the letters out of my pocket. "Here are the dwarven messages, Freysha. Er, Your Highness. Is that what we call you?"

"Freysha is fine."

"She originally came to Earth incognito," Val said, "and was living under a bridge with Gondo."

"Mm, it was more *adjacent* to Gondo than with him," Freysha said.

"I'm just saying you're not one for airs," Val said.

"I *do* like air, but more the fresh forest air outside of your city. The bridge under the busy vehicle thoroughfare was not ideal."

Val lifted a finger but dropped it. "Never mind. You've got a room and a conservatory here now."

"Yes." Freysha smiled.

After I handed the letters to Freysha, Val tilted her head and drew me aside. No, she drew me toward Zavryd, whose storm-cloud face mirrored Sarrlevi's. I eyed him as warily as Freysha was eyeing Sarrlevi.

"As you know, Willard has forbidden me from assisting you with your task," Val told me.

"Yes."

"But she can't forbid Zav from anything. He's not affiliated with the Army—or anything on Earth."

"A dragon does as a dragon wishes." Zavryd lifted his chin. "Nobody who values his or her life forbids him from partaking in any activity."

"Your mom forbids you from doing things," Val pointed out.

"Nobody but a more respected and powerful dragon forbids a dragon from partaking in any activity."

"Right. Matti, Zav has agreed to fly you to your destination. He's not going to get involved or do anything that could potentially harm a soldier—and I hope you don't plan to do that either—but I thought it might be helpful to get a ride down there." Val raised her eyebrows. "And a ride away in case you're being chased."

"I hope that won't be the case, but a delivery and getaway dragon would make things easier." I didn't think Sarrlevi could make a portal to a place he hadn't been—or seen in someone's mind—so I'd planned to drive us down. We would have had to park well away from the post, and then the installation itself covered more than a hundred square miles.

"Dragons can make *all* things easier," Zavryd said.

"I'm not sure I'd agree with that," Val murmured. "But dragon flight is handy if you don't get airsick."

I didn't *usually*, but his flying over that logging operation had threatened the contents of my stomach numerous times. Further, I had a healthy and natural aversion to heights—and falling from them. Even so, I wouldn't object to a ride past barbed-wire fences and security checkpoints on a dragon's back. But... would he take Sarrlevi too? And what would it cost me?

"Would he expect something in exchange?" I asked. "I'm afraid I haven't gotten barbecue takeout lately."

"This favor has been pre-negotiated," Val said, "and Zav will receive his payment upon its completion."

"My mate has placed many racks of ribs in the smoker." Zavryd smiled contentedly, thoughts of meat apparently overriding his ongoing disgruntlement that Sarrlevi was on the premises. "With the agreed-upon sugarless spice rub applied liberally."

"Sounds tasty," I offered. "We're not leaving for some time, so the activity on the post will be light. Will you... join us for dinner?"

I couldn't imagine such a meal going smoothly, but it didn't seem right to ask Zavryd to wait outside in the rain until we were ready to go on the mission.

Zavryd's eyelids drooped as he regarded me. "You are serving meat?"

"There are some cubes of ham in the scalloped potatoes, but it's more of an elf-centric meal. I didn't know you would be coming, Lord Zavryd."

"Cubes? Like the meat cubes that my mate makes?" Zavryd used his hands to sketch meat-loaf-sized shapes in the air.

"No." I held up a thumb and forefinger. "They're secondary to the potatoes in the dish. And possibly the cheese."

"Potatoes and cheese," he said as if I'd suggested he eat dog food.

"Go ahead in, Zav." Val pulled out her phone as she pointed him toward the door. "I'll have some additional supplies delivered."

"Substantial cubes," he said.

"Of course. Don't get in a fight with Sarrlevi on the way past, please."

Zavryd grunted. I couldn't tell if it conveyed agreement or if he was envisioning changing back into a dragon so he could spew forth fire on his elven nemesis.

I rubbed my face, wondering what craziness had prompted me to invite *anyone* for dinner.

"Is he going to balk later when I point out Sarrlevi is also going to need a ride?" I asked quietly as Val pulled up a delivery service.

"Yes. I assumed that was why he was here, and that you don't usually invite him for dinner dates—" Val's eyebrows rose again, "—but I'm not sure Zav has made the connection yet."

"What should I do to convince him that he wants a vile elf on his back?"

Val showed me the order she'd tapped into her phone. "I'm hoping ten pounds of bone-in ham will do the trick."

"Ah."

~

Earlier, when he'd been fondling my table and examining the glasses, Sarrlevi had seemed open to sitting with my other guests, but now that Val, Zavryd, and Freysha had come in and we were eating, he stood with his back to the wall, holding his barely-touched plate. The fork in his free hand was poised more like a dagger than an eating implement. Not surprising, since he was eyeing Zavryd, who stood with *his* back to a wall on the other side of the table. He also held a plate of food while glaring.

Wisely, my other guests had left the seats between them empty. Tinja and Freysha sat at one end of the table, while Val, Zadie, and Abbas had taken chairs at the other. My seat was next to Freysha, whom I would have enjoyed speaking with, but I was busy bringing in dishes and filling people's glasses with sparkling water. Additionally, Freysha seemed distracted, for she kept glancing nervously at Sarrlevi, only nodding occasionally as Tinja chattered to her about how interesting combining elven magic and goblin engineering would be.

Zadie, Abbas, and Tinja didn't appear that relaxed with Sarrlevi against the wall either. To my eyes, it wasn't right that they —that *anyone*—would be more concerned about an elf, even an elf assassin, than a dragon. Zavryd's aura was far more noticeable than anyone else's in the room, and his scowl made it clear he wasn't happy to be here. I hoped Val's ham delivery would arrive soon and put him in a better mood.

After setting down the garlic-butter spread for the baguettes, the last item that needed to come out of the kitchen, I sat and debated if there was a way I could make my guests realize that

Sarrlevi was a worthy dinner companion—and person—and wouldn't do anything to them, as long as they didn't do anything to him.

"Sarrlevi has assisted me a number of times of late with mercenaries and other thugs who've decided my hammer is wondrous and should be stolen. He's a good ally." I beamed a smile at him, which was hard when he gave me a why-are-you-speaking-of-me look across the table.

"A *dragon* is a good ally," Zavryd said. "I would incinerate anyone who wished to steal my mate's magical weapon."

"Incineration is illegal here on Earth," I pointed out.

"Dragons obey only the laws that *they* create," Sarrlevi said coolly, stabbing some greens with his fork.

"I'm certain Lord Zavryd is a wonderful ally as well," I hurried to say over whatever indignant response the dragon would have made.

"Lord Zavryd'nokquetal is my name," he told me coolly.

"Like many humans—" Val waved her fork, a ham cube on the tines, "—Matti may also struggle with that mouthful of a name."

"Does she *also* have a tongue impediment?" Zavryd asked her, though his voice lost its cool edge. He waved a finger, and her ham cube slid off her fork and levitated to him.

"It's common on Earth." Val didn't comment on the meat theft.

Sarrlevi slid his greens into his mouth. At least he wasn't so affronted by the dinner company that he wasn't eating.

"The beings of this world have *many* weaknesses." Zav chomped on his stolen cube, then eyed the mound of potatoes on his plate. He'd already fished all of the ham out and curled a lip at the rest. He didn't even seem to like the cheese, which was hard for me to believe.

"He calls us *beings* now," Val told me, "not *vermin*. He's come a long way."

"That's very gracious of him," I said, hoping to butter him up before he found out about his second rider for the night.

"Yes." Zavryd lifted his chin. His haughtiness made Sarrlevi's haughtiness seem modest in comparison.

"But dragons don't think elves are weak, right?" I asked Zavryd. "They're strong warriors and mages. Worthwhile allies." I smiled at Freysha as well as Sarrlevi.

She looked dubiously at me, and I had a feeling she didn't want me to bring attention to her.

"They are not weak," Zavryd said, his gaze back on Sarrlevi. "But only *some* are worthwhile allies. Some vex their own kind and should be taken for punishment and rehabilitation as soon as possible."

Hell, not that again.

Sarrlevi's eyes narrowed, and he pointed his fork at Zavryd. "You will take me nowhere, dragon."

"Actually." I raised a finger. "He has offered to take us on the mission we're not going on tonight."

"I have *what*?" Zavryd looked not at Sarrlevi but at Val. "You did not say *he* would go along and ride on *my back*."

Val dropped her face in her hand, peering at me between her fingers. "You were supposed to wait until after the extra ham got here to mention that."

"My mate, you cannot want me to assist one as nefarious as he." Zavryd pointed his fork across the table.

A trickle of magic wafted toward Sarrlevi, and I tensed, afraid Zavryd was attacking. The small mound of scalloped potatoes on Sarrlevi's plate quivered, and several ham cubes floated into the air.

"You steal my meat, dragon?" Sarrlevi stabbed two of them, managing to strike quickly enough to thrust the fork into them instead of knocking them across the room, then jammed them into his mouth. "You are the lawless one here, not I."

"I break no laws. Lesser beings know it is proper to please a dragon. And it pleases me to enjoy this salty meat offering."

"I am not a *lesser* being," Sarrlevi said. "Perhaps you'd like to join me on the lawn to discuss it with blades."

"No," Val said firmly. "No dueling during dinner. It's a human custom. You shouldn't have even brought weapons in here." She frowned at Sarrlevi, but she also frowned at Zavryd, even though he didn't carry any visible weapons. Of course, a dragon *was* a weapon...

"How do we escape," Zadie whispered to Abbas, "if they spring across the table for each other's throats?"

Wordlessly, Abbas pointed at the dining-room window.

"I will *not* take the assassin who once hunted my mate on my back," Zavryd told Sarrlevi before frowning at Val.

"He's going to help Matti," Val said. "It's not a long flight. You'll barely notice him there. He'll be quiet, and I bet he won't even insult you." She raised her eyebrows toward Sarrlevi.

But he was looking at me. *We do not need that dragon to give us a ride. If any magical beings are in that prison, they will sense him from a great distance.*

I doubt any of the human prison guards will be mages. It'll be easier for us to get in and find the prison on dragon back. I don't have a map, so we'll have to search.

The doorbell rang. Sarrlevi tensed, as if he expected a threat.

Val stood. "Thank goodness." She waved her phone. "That's the delivery person."

"What's being delivered?" Tinja asked curiously.

"More ham." Val lifted a finger, eased past Sarrlevi, and strode for the front door.

"A dragon must have sufficient meat in his belly if he is to fly with *a rider.*" Zavryd pointedly made that singular and looked at me.

"Can't you accept that he's a useful ally?" I asked. "Like I told you, he took down one of the helicopters in our battle on the mountain. And he attacked another one that was after your sister."

"An assassin cannot be trusted. He targeted my mate, and he would have slain her if he were strong enough to do so. He is only here on this world because he now targets someone else." Zavryd squinted at Sarrlevi. "I cannot read his mind, but I know he cannot be trusted. You should know this too, mongrel."

Sarrlevi's jaw clenched as he watched us.

"That you invite him into your abode and *feed* him is extremely unwise," Zavryd continued. "Is my mate not advising you on the ways of the Cosmic Realms?"

"She doesn't need your mate's advice," Sarrlevi snapped.

"In the matter of elf assassins estranged from their people, she does," Zavryd said.

Sarrlevi set his plate on the table—he looked like he was tempted to *slam* it down—and strode out of the room. His aura disappeared as he camouflaged himself, and I had no idea if he went out the back door or the front.

Are you still going to help me tonight? I asked, hoping he was monitoring my thoughts, but only Zavryd frowned at me, as if he'd heard the words.

As soon as Sarrlevi was gone, Zadie smiled and stood. "Who wants wine? I think I'll get some more. Abbas, did you and Matti get a chance to look at the sub-dividable property yet? I really think that will be perfect for you two. Tinja, how's the tiny-house architecture going? Have you finished your first plans yet?"

"Oh, I've completed three sets of blueprints," Tinja said with excitement. "After dinner, I will show our new elf friend." She clasped Freysha's arm.

I thought a princess might disapprove of such familiarity, but Freysha smiled, more relaxed now that Sarrlevi was gone.

Everyone was more relaxed, and conversations blossomed. When Zadie returned with a fresh bottle of wine, numerous glasses lifted. Those who'd only been nibbling at their meals before, as they warily watched Sarrlevi and Zavryd, now dug in with gusto.

I slumped in my chair. Even though I was glad my friends and visitors were enjoying their meal, it saddened me that nobody would acknowledge how good of an ally Sarrlevi was. And also that his presence had been what inhibited everyone. He was the entire reason that I'd made this dinner.

Val came into the dining room holding a huge ham. It wasn't on a serving platter, probably because she was carrying it straight to Zavryd.

"My wondrous and thoughtful mate," he proclaimed, levitating it from her hands and onto his plate, where it stuck out over the edges.

Val stood beside him and patted him on the stomach. *I'll work on him after he's eaten,* she told me silently. *He'll take Sarrlevi. Assuming he's still coming.* She looked around and perhaps *sensed* around as well. *Is he?*

I hope so. I looked glumly toward the window, imagining Sarrlevi eating one of his unappealing ration bars alone in the yard instead of dining with us. With me.

8

MY NERVES THAT HAD BEEN FRAYED ALL THROUGH THE TENSE DINNER party shredded further as I headed to my bedroom to pack a few things for the trip. Despite Willard's insistence that I was a vigilante, I hadn't sneaked into many places in my life, certainly no government installations, so I didn't know exactly what I would need. Sarrlevi had mentioned having rope. I'd grabbed some protein bars, water, and tools, but if this mission took longer than the night, it was a foregone conclusion that I would be caught and thrown behind bars myself. These thoughts did nothing to settle my nerves.

In the dining room, glasses were still clinking as Tinja spoke with enthusiasm, trying to get people's opinions on her tiny-house-plan empire. The last I'd heard, she was asking what built-in storage solutions elves and dragons enjoyed.

As I finished packing, I sensed Sarrlevi coming down the hall. Good. I had worried he'd left permanently.

Glancing around my messy room, I debated between springing out and shutting the door, so he wouldn't see that the tidying he'd done weeks earlier had failed to stick, and rushing to put away my laundry in case he wanted to speak privately. Since I wouldn't mind a moment alone with him, to make sure he hadn't been deeply offended at dinner, I hurried to sweep my stack of laundry off the dresser and into drawers.

He waited in the doorway for an invitation, though he watched me tuck things away, his expression lightening for the first time that evening. Before he'd arrived, I'd made sure there wasn't any dirty laundry about, but I hadn't tidied as much as I'd wanted. Zadie, Abbas, and Tinja inviting themselves to dinner had thrown off my plans.

"You kept my storage addition." Sarrlevi nodded toward the two shelves mounted on the wall over the headboard. Made from woven vines he'd conjured out of the ether, they were by far the greenest things in my room.

"They're magically embedded in the wall," I pointed out, though I hadn't considered removing them. Green vines didn't fit in with my decorating style, but after recovering from the mortification that he'd cleaned my room, I'd been touched that he'd made the shelves.

"I've seen you demolish brick walls enchanted by gnomes. Two shelves would be a simple matter for you to remove."

"Probably not without demolishing the wall too, but they're useful." Had I not admitted that? Or thanked him? Probably not. For whatever reason, I was more inclined to snark with him. Or engage in flustered rambling. "I like them," I added, waving to my belongings stacked on them.

His gaze snagged on a photo I'd leaned up there, the Polaroid with my mother and her two dwarf friends. The lightness faded from his expression, and it grew more thoughtful. Or... pensive?

"Do you think her sister has any way to keep tabs on me?" I asked. "It's concerning that she not only figured out where my grandparents live but knew when I was there and showed up."

"You had the hammer with you?"

"Yeah. I take it everywhere with me these days. I even sleep with it."

His gaze drifted to the bed, eyebrows rising, and I blushed, anticipating a comment related to sex.

"The better to punish inadequate lovers?"

And there it was. "I don't *beat* guys for not satisfying my needs."

"No? How better to motivate them to improve?"

"I gather meat does the trick for dragons. I don't know yet what motivates elves. You didn't wolf down any of the dinner offerings."

Sarrlevi had eaten but lightly, keeping his eyes locked on Zavryd until he'd strode out and disappeared.

"I hadn't imagined you with a lot of dragon or elf lovers in need of motivation," he said.

"Right, because mongrels can't possibly be of interest to such vaunted beings." I almost pointed out that Val and her half-human blood had managed to snag Zavryd, but, for all I knew, her willingness to feed him multiple times a day had done more to woo him than her blood or beauty.

Sarrlevi turned his palm toward the ceiling. A dismissal of the statement? Or an acknowledgment? "There aren't many dragons or elves on this world for such purposes. As to Princess Barothla, I doubt she's been to this world often, if at all previously, but she may be able to track that hammer."

"From miles away? I didn't think the auras of even powerful magical items were noticeable from that far."

"Farther for those who are full-blooded dwarves, elves, and such, and she may have ways to enhance her abilities."

"Like with potions? Can alchemists make such things?"

"Perhaps." His earlier amusement had disappeared, and I wished I'd kept trading jokes with him about motivations. "It is not an area I'm well educated on, but many things can be accomplished with an alchemist's formulas."

"Well, I can't go anywhere without my hammer, not when there's still a reward out for it. I hope she doesn't show up and get in the way of things." I waved vaguely to the south to indicate the night's mission, though I didn't want to see her anywhere again. "If she really wants to find my mother and take her home alive, fine. I'll wish her success, but I'm skeptical that she does."

Sarrlevi didn't reply, but he'd already semi-agreed with my assessment when he'd said that I should go with my instincts and not trust her.

"Can I ask you a question about her and... when she hired you?" As I'd been thinking earlier, I was leery about talking too much to him about her, in case they still spoke, but he could likely confirm or deny some of the details of the story she'd told me.

At first, Sarrlevi didn't reply, his face growing more closed, and I worried he would clam up.

"Go ahead," he finally said. Tersely.

"Was she drunk and angry that night? Like she was doing something she might later regret?" I wondered how much he remembered after forty years. If he'd been hired to kill a lot of people since then, the details might have become a hazy blur.

Again, Sarrlevi was slow to answer, but I couldn't tell if it was because he was dredging up the memory or if this topic was fraught for him. Because he didn't know how I would react? Or because... *she* might react poorly if she found out he was sharing information?

"She was neither," he said. "In general, I don't accept assignments from inebriated people for exactly that reason. Because loose inhibitions could prompt them to make decisions they'd regret. Regretful people either renege on the deal later and refuse to pay, or they end up committing suicide or fleeing their residence after the fact. To avoid those outcomes, I arrange the initial meeting several days after the client contacts me."

"So... it was premeditated. And calculated."

"Yes."

"Okay. Thanks for letting me know."

I touched the camouflage charm on my key chain, wondering if I should start activating it all the time, even at home. Would Barothla be able to sense my hammer through the protective magic? Since my mother had made the charm, maybe it would be strong enough to cancel out the weapon's aura. The problem was that the camouflaging magic was only temporary and wore off after time. I was fairly certain that even sleeping with my hand wrapped around the charm wouldn't keep it engaged during the night.

"Are you ready to depart for the prison?" Sarrlevi asked.

I glanced at the time. "I guess. We don't want to get there too early."

Freysha and I are leaving, Val spoke into my mind from the living room. *Thank you for the meal. She enjoyed the kale and Swiss chard dishes.*

I'm glad there was something she liked. I'd watched with bemusement as Freysha had removed the ham cubes from her potatoes and deposited them on Zavryd's plate. Once his meat delivery had arrived, he'd dumped the potatoes and cheese from his plate onto hers, resulting in quite a mound. Sarrlevi had eaten a couple of cubes, so I didn't think all elves were completely vegetarian, but Freysha seemed to be.

Zav is ready whenever you're ready, Val said. *Freysha asked me to remind you that Sarrlevi shouldn't be trusted. He's assassinated people she and our father knew. She was concerned for your well-being when I admitted you were going on a mission with him and have been working with him here on Earth.*

I wondered how many telepathic conversations had been taking place during dinner. *Are you still concerned? He's helped me a lot over the past weeks.*

Val hesitated. *I'm not unconcerned. But he wouldn't have had to come to dinner at your house if all he wanted was to use you toward some evil end. Or even a non-evil end.*

So you think he likes me, huh? I smirked with self-deprecation.

Well. I doubt your roommate's tiny-house scheme was what drew him here.

That only draws elf princesses?

I believe so.

Mongrel female, Zavryd boomed into my mind. *You will come now if you wish a ride to the soldier lair.*

Sarrlevi arched his eyebrows and stepped into the hallway. Maybe Zavryd had boomed his words into *everyone's* mind.

"I guess that means he's ready to go." I grabbed my belongings and headed for the door.

"One wonders if *Thorvald* takes her weapon to bed," Sarrlevi muttered.

9

HARD RAIN FELL AS ZAVRYD FLEW SOUTH TOWARD FORT LEWIS, Sarrlevi and me riding on his back. The dragon's magic kept the water from reaching us. I doubted he cared that much about ensuring we stayed dry and that his solicitude was more a byproduct of our location astride him. Since I'd seen Zavryd go out of his way to avoid landing in puddles, I knew of his aversion to rain.

Will we break your father out of this prison or simply speak with him? Though he sat behind me, Sarrlevi had been communicating telepathically to keep our plans private.

I doubted Zavryd cared, his participation being only at Val's behest, but I replied in my mind. *Just talk to him. As much as I would love to break him out, since I don't believe he's been fairly incarcerated all this time... I would then be making the choice to become a criminal myself. A real criminal, not just someone who's gotten in trouble for knocking thieves into soda refrigerators. Aiding and abetting a felon is a big deal here.*

What if you could do it without being caught? Isn't the goal of this mission not to be discovered?

It's the goal, *yes. Goals involving breaking people out of prison are difficult to achieve. I wish I could take him with me though.* I stared bleakly at the headlights snaking along the freeway below. *Like I said, I think he was only defending his family that night, and I don't believe he deserves to be there. Also... I miss him. Both of them. I wish...*

I shook my head, not wanting to babble to Sarrlevi about how much I'd missed my parents when I'd been growing up and how I would love to have them in my life again. He'd only asked because he wanted to know the parameters of the mission.

But he rested a hand on my shoulder, as if he understood all that I hadn't said. I had to resist the temptation to lean back against him. During our flight, I'd already been doing my best not to think about how close behind me he was. He hadn't put an arm around me or pressed his thighs against mine or anything as intimate as sharing a horse would have involved—Zavryd's back was roomier than that—but he was close, and flying through the rainy night, with the city far below, created a feeling of privacy. Which was an illusion, since Zavryd spoke now and then when he asked for directions.

We'll talk to him and ask him who messed up everything for my family, I said. For *me,* I almost added, but that was selfish. The Army had screwed up my parents' lives more than mine. I'd still had my freedom and my sister and grandparents. What had they had these past thirty years? Loneliness? Forced servitude? Worse? *Though if the opportunity to leave a file behind comes up, I might be tempted.*

A file? Sarrlevi asked.

In cartoons, people are always sending cakes to prisoners with nail files in them so they can grind away the steel bars. I don't know if that ever actually worked or if it's all fictitious.

Your hammer would be a more effective tool.

You can't bake a hammer into a cake. Not one the size of mine anyway.

·

Sarrlevi snorted softly, patted my shoulder, and lowered his hand. Again, I fought the urge to lean back against him. We weren't on a date, and I shouldn't find an assassin's touch comforting.

As we flew past Tacoma and continued south along the freeway, Zavryd spoke. *Mongrel, what portion of the outpost contains the prison you seek?*

She has a name, *Zavryd'nokquetal,* Sarrlevi said, surprising me with his frosty tone and comment. He scooted closer and returned his hand to my shoulder. For some reason, I remembered the battle with the orc mercenaries and how he'd stood protectively beside me with his sword raised. *It would be appropriate for you to use it when you address her.*

Zavryd didn't answer right away, maybe surprised as well. *She has not given it to me. My mate calls her Matti, and her employer says Puletasi.*

"Matti would be great." I gave Zavryd's scales an encouraging pat, hoping he wouldn't mind the touch.

The use of a pet name is not overly familiar from the mate of another female?

"It's my first name, not a pet name. But you can call me Puletasi if that's better. Anything is an improvement over *mongrel.* Almost anything," I amended, thinking of more derogatory things I'd been called over the years.

Very well.

"There's supposed to be magic at the prison, so if you sense magic on the post, that should be the spot."

Very well, Zavryd repeated.

I looked back at Sarrlevi. "How come it's not okay for dragons to call me mongrel when you do it yourself?"

"I call you plumber too," he said.

"Don't remind me."

He smirked.

"So it's okay for *you* to tease me, but others can't?"

He did seem to use *mongrel* more to get my goat these days, but it wasn't as if he used my name either.

My question prompted his smirk to widen into a smile. *Correct.*

I almost asked if he even knew my name, but when he'd sent the gift of cheese and pickled vegetables via the delivery goblin, he'd addressed it to me by name, my *full* name.

He was not using it to tease you, Sarrlevi added. *Only friends tease each other.*

Is that what we are? Friends? I raised my eyebrows.

He hesitated. *We should not be.*

Despite the statement, he squeezed my shoulder. This time, instead of releasing me, he pulled me back and wrapped an arm around me.

Because it's not appropriate? I thought about scooting away, but my body wasn't interested in that, and I found myself giving in to my earlier urge and settling back against him.

Yes.

Because you're a full-blooded elf, and I'm a mongrel? Why did it have to feel so amazing to ride like that with him? To have the muscles of his arm and chest against me, to remember what he looked like without clothes, to imagine him in my bed that way...

Because I'm on a mission.

I blinked and looked up at the dark sky. Was that *really* the reason? Not because he considered me some lesser being? Some scruffy half-dwarf?

Do you not allow yourself distractions when you're on a mission? I asked.

I almost brought up the elf females, but they'd manipulated him into having sex with them. Other than his interlude with them, I hadn't seen Sarrlevi veer off to hit on any women. Nor had he accepted offers when he could have. The horny mom angling for a booty call might not have been that much of a catch, but the werewolf lady who had wanted him had been sexy and beautiful.

My memory replayed Val's comment that Sarrlevi wouldn't have come to dinner if the mission was all he cared about. Was it possible he *liked* me?

Rarely. Do you prefer Matti or Mataalii?

The question caught me off guard. Was he asking because he would deign to use whichever I preferred? Instead of calling me mongrel?

I'm used to Matti at this point. My parents were the last people who used my real name.

But which do you prefer? he asked dryly.

Whichever you like, I said, though I was tempted to see if he would use Mataalii. It would be kind of intimate since nobody else did. But did I want that from him? Probably a dumb question since I'd snuggled back into his arms and was having fantasies of him in my bed. *I'm easy,* I added, letting him decide.

That can't *be true.* Sarrlevi brushed a lock of my hair behind my ear, the gentle touch sending a thrill of pleasure through me. *Not when you sleep with a giant war hammer in your bed.*

You're not going to let that go, are you?

The imagery amuses me. He shared a telepathic picture of me snuggled under the covers with my arms around it.

Well, at least I wasn't the only one imagining the other person in bed.

So, you'd be disappointed if I admitted it was bed-adjacent, leaning against my nightstand? I turned my head to look at him.

Very. His eyes crinkled with humor. *Mataalii.*

Hearing my name, even telepathically, from him sent as much pleasure through me as his touch had. My emotions took over, trampling over the thoughts from my rational mind, and I kissed him.

I shouldn't have, since nothing had changed, and he was still on his mission, but, damn it, I wanted him to know that it meant something to me that he'd used my name. I was sure he knew—he knew way too much when it came to my feelings for him—but I couldn't stop myself.

He didn't draw back or push me away. As he had on the mountaintop, he returned the kiss, his arm tightening around me. His free hand brushed through my hair, magic flowing from his fingers.

This time, I wasn't injured, so it wasn't intended to heal. Instead, it had to be meant solely to evoke pleasure—*desire*—and make me crave his touch and wish we were already on the way home from our mission, not about to start it.

Zavryd banked and headed toward the lights of Fort Lewis, flying over a barbed-wire-topped chain-link fence.

Sarrlevi sighed and broke the kiss. I swallowed and looked away, afraid I would only snuggle closer and grip him tighter if I didn't. This was *my* mission, and I wouldn't screw it up with lust. No matter how amazing his touch was.

I sense magic infusing walls and doors of a building in a cluster set apart from the main compound, Zavryd reported, indifferent or oblivious to our kiss. *I am heading toward it.*

Thank you, I replied silently.

Mataalii? As we soared toward our destination, Sarrlevi's arm still around me, he tightened his grip again, as if he feared I would fall off. Or be subjected to some other danger? *Stay away from Barothla.*

With those words, my heart switched from beating rapidly due to arousal to hammering in my chest because of fear.

The night she hired me, she was cold and calculating and offered sex after I said yes. To celebrate her future acquisition of the throne.

Barothla's mention that she'd hit on Sarrlevi came to mind.

With utter certainty, I knew he was telling the truth even before he shared what I assumed was his memory of that night, Barothla in a skimpy gown, showing off her dwarven curves and offering him wine as she smiled and gestured to a bed.

Her decision was not made on a drunken whim, he added. *She was as sober as a sword. If she wants to work with you, it's so she can find your mother and make sure what she started forty years ago is completed.*

I guess I should have thrown cookies at her after all, I replied, too chilled to come up with anything more intelligent to say. It was what I'd suspected, but the image of my aunt lounging in bed and trying to seduce the assassin she'd just hired to kill her sister disturbed me on another level.

Do your best to avoid her.

Is she going to be angry with you for warning me?

Sarrlevi hesitated. *Likely.*

But you're as powerful as she is, right? You can take care of yourself around her?

I'll just have to be careful about what I eat and drink.

Right, because she was an alchemist and probably had a thousand recipes for poisons memorized.

Your mother was, Sarrlevi added. *According to Barothla, some of the first enchanted trinkets Rodarska made for herself and their father were protections against poisoning.*

So she knew her sister was gunning for her?

I assume so.

Did the king know she might be after him too?

I'm not sure he believes his daughter is a threat to him, but he continues to wear the trinket.

As we neared a set of squat buildings set apart and fenced off from the main post, I rested my hand on Sarrlevi's leg. *Thank you for telling me.*

Thank you for convincing Zondia'qareshi not to take me off for punishment and rehabilitation. Sarrlevi kissed the side of my neck.

I swallowed again, aching to be able to call him friend. And more.

10

AFTER DEPOSITING US IN A DARK AREA BEHIND A CEMENT BUILDING that radiated magic, Zavryd flew off, saying he could be reached telepathically when we were ready to leave.

I thought the message was for Sarrlevi, since he was the tele-pathic one, but Zavryd added, in what must have been a private message, to me: *I will also come to the sound of gunfire or explosives. It is my mate's desire that you not die tonight.*

I appreciate that.

She would be less aggrieved if the presumptuous elf did not return.

She would be, or you would be?

Mm. With that vague answer, Zavryd ended the conversation.

Maybe he hadn't appreciated Sarrlevi correcting him about calling me a mongrel.

Though I'd activated it during the flight, I rubbed my camou-flage charm again to make sure its magic wouldn't wear off. I trusted Sarrlevi had already enacted his stealth measures as well and only my proximity to him kept him in my sight.

Without the magic, we would have been visible to soldiers in a guard tower that rose above the fenced compound. Even though we'd landed in the back, the single road stretching away from the prison on the other side of the buildings, pavement devoid of brush and bathed in bright lights would have kept us from hiding.

Sarrlevi took the lead, veering toward a back door in the sole building that emanated magic. This close, even I could sense it. More than that, I sensed magical beings inside. An orc, a few shifters, and people like me, half-bloods. Vile prisoners that someone like Val had once captured? Or people the military wanted kept quiet but for some reason hadn't done away with?

One couldn't question or *use* the dead, I supposed.

Their presence and that thought made me question my earlier claim that I wouldn't free my father. A vision of me breaking down doors and gates left and right so that prisoners could escape sauntered through my mind.

I wished I could sense my father, but he was fully human, so I had no way to detect him.

Sarrlevi stopped in front of the sturdy metal door. Though he couldn't know the area any better than I did, I was content to let him lead. Between my nerves and the day's revelations, I struggled to stay a hundred percent focused.

The door had a lock in the latch as well as a deadbolt. A magical enchantment emanated from them, but the locks clicked open as soon as Sarrlevi pressed a hand against the door. He didn't, however, reach for the latch, instead leaving his hand in place as he sent more tendrils of his power into the metal.

After a long moment, I sensed some of the magic enchanting the door disappear. I almost asked him if he specialized in picking locks, mundane and magical, but decided it was a dumb question. Of *course* an assassin would have learned those things.

The thought cheered me with the certainty that I'd chosen the right person to help with this endeavor.

Sarrlevi pulled open the door a couple of inches, listening and peering in before committing. *How do you want to deal with guards?*

Avoid them, if possible.

He shook his head slightly. Did he already hear someone?

I don't suppose you have the magical equivalent of a phaser set to stun?

A what?

A way to knock people out without hurting them.

I can try to sneak up on them from behind, choke them, and deprive them of air for long enough that they pass out, but it doesn't last long and will cause harm.

I grimaced, not sure that was better than cracking someone on the head with my hammer. *Try it, please. But avoiding them is better. It's why we're camouflaged, right?*

Sarrlevi opened the door further, enough to slip in, and did so, waving for me to hurry after. We stopped right inside, and he pointed to the lit cement hallway ahead—and a burly guard in a tactical vest with an MP armband on his uniform. The man stood with his back to a wall, so taking him from behind wouldn't be easy. When we'd slipped in, he hadn't been facing the door, but he was doing a scan, alternately looking toward banks of cells, aisles, a front door, and in our direction.

When his gaze skimmed over us, I froze, not daring to breathe. But his face showed no indication that he saw us. We had to keep it that way, for a radio handset on his vest hung within easy reach, and I had no doubt he could call in more men in seconds.

A camera high on the wall pointed at our door, and I cursed silently. Did magical camouflage fool such technology? Even if it did, were we far enough away from the lens to ensure it wouldn't register us?

I touched Sarrlevi's shoulder and pointed at it. He'd been considering the guard and probably trying to detect other threats inside. The magical beings I'd sensed were in the cells, not on duty. I assumed the military only employed humans or half-bloods that appeared fully human, though I didn't sense anyone like that outside of the cells.

That is for security, yes? Sarrlevi asked. *For monitoring?*

Yes. Suspecting he had limited familiarity with such Earth devices, I envisioned a control room somewhere with a bank of screens displaying numerous camera feeds, and attempted to share the thought with him.

I am not certain if your technological seeing devices penetrate magical camouflage. Sarrlevi took several steps so that we weren't directly in front of the camera and stopped ten feet from the guard.

I'm not either.

We will hurry in case our presence has already been noticed. Before he finished the words, and as soon as the soldier's head rotated toward the cells, he sprang.

Sarrlevi twisted the man so that his back wasn't to the wall, wrapped an arm around his neck from behind, kicked the backs of his knees so they buckled, and clasped his free hand over the soldier's mouth. Sarrlevi moved so quickly, doing everything at once, that the man didn't get more than half a grunt of surprise out before he was pinned and silenced. *Mostly* silenced. As the soldier struggled and tried to yell, some noise did get out. Grip tightening, Sarrlevi bore him to the ground with his leverage and greater strength.

I ran past them with my hammer, afraid even the minimal noise would get us in trouble. It would take time for the soldier to pass out from lack of oxygen.

A bored orc in the closest cell looked curiously at what, from his point of view, must have looked like the guard by himself, dropping to his knees and flailing at the air.

The cell across from him held a shifter, not a wolf but a bear. He was sleeping on the ground in his bear form and didn't stir. I jogged farther, grimacing since all the cells held magical beings.

What if my mundane human father wasn't in the maximum-security area, after all?

I spotted more cameras high on the walls and hoped none were pointed toward the guard Sarrlevi was choking.

At the front of the building, where a closed front door led out toward the guard tower and road, another soldier walked into view. "Thompson?"

He peered toward me—and toward the other guard. His eyes widened, and his hand dropped to a firearm holstered at his hip.

I swore silently, certain he saw his buddy. Hammer raised, I sprinted toward him, intending to jab him in the solar plexus hard enough to steal his breath—and ability to yell. But the front door opened before I'd covered more than half the ground toward him.

Damn, the cameras must have seen something—the guard, if not me and Sarrlevi.

I ran faster, anticipating having to leap into the middle of a group of guards and start swinging. I had little choice. The last thing I wanted was for them to have the room to shoot.

The soldier in view had drawn his firearm, but he whirled toward the front door instead of me. It was still open, but the expected reinforcements hadn't charged in. Instead, several smoking canisters—smoke grenades?—soared into the building. They flew in several directions, clattering as they struck cell walls and the cement floor.

As smoke poured forth, the guard fired out the door. He spread out his shots, aiming high, then middle, then low. Because whoever had thrown the smoke grenades wasn't visible?

Confusion surged up in me, and I didn't know whether to run up and try to knock him out while he was distracted or use the smoke as further camouflage to look for my father.

Deciding on the latter, I turned toward a side aisle as the guard kept firing. But he reached for his radio, and I worried we would *all* be in trouble if he reported in.

Springing toward him, I kicked his hand away from his radio, then tore it off his vest. His focus shifted from whatever was outside to me, and he whipped the firearm toward my head. I smashed his wrist with the haft of my hammer, knocking his arm aside. His knuckles cracked against the wall, and he swore and dropped his firearm. With his other hand, he launched a jab at my face, but I blocked him again.

Smoke swirled between our skirmish and the doorway, and a wave of magical power came out of nowhere. It struck us both, and we flew apart. The soldier hit a cell wall as I soared back down the aisle. I might have landed on my ass, but someone caught me. Sarrlevi.

Who else is here? As soon as he steadied me, he ran past, clearly intending to deal with them.

Hell if I know.

The smoke swirled again—someone coming in? The soldier I'd battled, his form just visible through the haze, had hit the floor. Abruptly, he screamed. He *appeared* to be alone, but I knew better. Sarrlevi and I weren't the only ones here with camouflaging magic.

The soldier's cry broke off with a crunch, as if someone had stepped on his throat and crushed his trachea. I hoped not, and not only because *I* might get blamed for it.

Another wave of power flowed through the open door. Prisoners who'd risen to peer out from their cells fell to the floor. Even Sarrlevi had to pause and brace himself. I sensed him wrapping defensive magic not only around himself but using it to provide cover for me. Thanks to that, the second wave didn't strike me.

Search for your father, he said as he waded into the power, like someone walking in chest-deep water.

My senses told me the magic originated outside the still-open door, but smoke filled the prison now, and I couldn't see anyone. The haze extended outside too, maybe blanketing the entire courtyard. I thought I sensed a magical artifact out there—was that *dwarven* magic?—but wasn't certain if it was responsible for the continuing waves of power knocking people off their feet or if some mage out there was casting spells.

I ran down the side aisle so I could search the cells, but once I was out from behind Sarrlevi's defenses, the power struck me, hammering me against a wall. A shifter on his hands and knees in the back of a cell snarled in surprise when my weapon clanked against his gate. In the haze, I sensed and heard him more than saw him.

Footsteps pounded in the courtyard outside, and Sarrlevi sprang through the doorway. Clangs rang out. He'd found someone to engage in a sword fight.

Gunshots followed the metal clangs, and I hoped he wore his armor that protected him from bullets. If the intruders were firing, not the guards, those might be *magical* bullets with the power to burrow through mundane defenses.

Though I finally passed a couple of cells with full-blooded humans in them, the smoke made it difficult to see their faces. Then the lights went out. I cursed in frustration. Red emergency lighting came on, but it wasn't that helpful. The smoke was getting thicker, making it hard to see anything.

"Is Malosi Puletasi in here?" I risked calling.

With the gunfire outside, I doubted it would matter if I made noise.

"Let us go," a nearby shifter urged, grabbing the bars of his gate, then reaching through them for me.

I darted around the grip. "Malosi Puletasi?" Realizing my father wouldn't recognize my adult voice, I risked adding, "It's Matti—Mataalii."

Maybe it was foolish—those cameras might record audio as well as video—but I was desperate. The roar of trucks and screech of a siren grew audible over the continuing gunfire and sword clangs in the courtyard.

At least I'd moved far enough from the front door that the waves of magic weren't reaching me. I whispered, "*Eravekt,*" and my hammer glowed silver-blue. It helped with the dark but not the smoke.

"Mataalii?" an uncertain male voice spoke from a back corner.

Hope surged in my chest. Even after thirty years, I recognized that voice.

"Dad," I rasped and ran down another aisle, trying to find my way to him in the dim, smoky light.

There are numerous enemies out here, many with magic, Sarrlevi reported. *They are attacking the soldiers as well as me. The men in the tower are dead. Two soldiers in the courtyard are also dead.*

Who are they? I asked, realizing I would *have* to break my father out. There wouldn't be time for a leisurely chat through the cell bars. Further, he might be in danger from these intruders.

"Dad?" I called again, still trying to pinpoint him in the maze.

"Here. At the end."

Look out, Sarrlevi said, though he still was outside.

I spun and raised my hammer, afraid of a threat about to spring from behind.

But that wasn't why he'd warned me. An explosion ripped through the prison with a thunderous boom. Metal wrenched, and cement cracked as a shockwave knocked me against a cell gate. The floor quaked, and it took me a second to find my feet and regain my balance.

Before I could step away from the cell, two strong hands grabbed me from behind. Another shifter had reached through the bars, one hand gripping me around the neck.

"Release me," he snarled, tightening his hands painfully.

I tried to ram my elbow back into his gut but clipped one of the bars, and a jolt of pain burst from my joint. Damn it.

"I don't have a key, you idiot," I said, though his grip half cut off my air.

Cement clunked and thudded—part of a wall tumbling down? It worried me that it came from the same direction as my father's call had. I had to get to him, not waste my time on this shifter.

I rasped, "*Hyrek.*"

Turning my hammer in my grip, I rammed it backward between the bars. The angle made the strike awkward, but the head clipped my attacker's ribs, and the weapon's magic did the rest. Lightning sprang forth, the smoky air sizzling with electricity as branches arced and wrapped around the shifter.

Screaming, he released me. After springing away from the bars, I whirled, tempted to strike him again, but he stumbled back, his hands up as he begged for lenience.

He wasn't my enemy, just someone desperate, and my father was my priority. With my throat and elbow aching, I ran toward the end of the aisle.

Fresh air rushed in from that direction, swirling the smoke. An ominous sense of foreboding filled me even before I reached the end of the cell bank.

With my hammer still glowing and crackling in my hand, I gaped at a great hole that had been blown in the wall. Rubble littered the floor of... Had that been my father's cell?

If so, he was gone.

11

"Dad?" I called.

The barred gate of the empty cell was intact, but the back wall was open to the night. From the aisle, there was no way to reach it, so I couldn't rush out after him—and whoever had taken him.

"Dad?" I cried again, frustration making me swing the hammer at the gate, connecting with one of the bars.

Lightning branched up and down the metal, the hammer denting the bar. I swung again, this time with more precision. I needed to get through the gate, not beat it up. It would be faster to go out through the hole than run back to the front door, with prisoners eager for their freedom trying to grab me the whole way.

Gunshots continued to fire outside, and the sound of helicopter blades grew audible over the sirens. No sooner had I thought of the aircraft we'd battled in the mountains than I sensed magic. It came from the sky, from two helicopters similar to those we'd fought approaching.

Sarrlevi? I asked silently, though I was sure he was part of the battle out front, especially if the guards had been killed. *Don't let them get away with my father. Please!*

With the gate smashed enough for me to squeeze through, I pushed into the cell, then jumped through the hole and into the courtyard.

Gunshots pinging off walls and cracking the pavement kept me from running straight out. I also didn't know where *to* run.

Since I couldn't sense my father, I didn't know which way he'd been taken. I did, however, detect magical artifacts—weapons, I was sure—near the front door where Sarrlevi continued to battle. I could sense him, meaning his camouflage had worn off or been knocked out by the fighting. That wasn't good, especially if there were cameras out there.

As I headed in that direction, worry that we would be blamed for this entered my mind. So far, I hadn't seen any of the intruders, and I was reminded of the invisibility rings the trolls and men who'd attacked my house earlier in the month had worn. Hopefully, the smoke grenades spewing their contents into the air would muddle the view for the cameras.

The *thwump-thwump* of the helicopter blades came closer. I could sense but not see them through the smoke. One seemed to be coming in for a landing. To retrieve the people who had my father?

I sprinted in that direction and glimpsed Sarrlevi, who was somehow deflecting bullets as he battled a knot of magical beings —orcs and shifters, who were, for some reason, working together. As the helicopter descended toward the courtyard, Sarrlevi sprang over his opponents, clearing the heads of even the towering orcs, and landed and ran toward it.

People inside the aircraft threw several projectiles—grenades. They weren't *smoke* grenades but explosives. They struck the ground in front of Sarrlevi and one also landed near me, blowing a crater. Once more, the shockwave sent me stumbling. Chunks of pavement flew everywhere, several pelting me.

I caught my balance and again started toward the helicopter, but more explosions followed. More clods of dirt and pieces of pavement struck me hard enough to make me stagger. I had to pause, turning my back and trying to protect my head. A jagged piece of pavement the size of a dining-room chair slammed into me from behind and smashed me to the ground.

Swearing, I clawed my way out from under the chunk of rubble, but I sensed the helicopter rising, leaving the courtyard. The crew had come down to retrieve their people—and my father?—and were throwing the grenades to guard their escape.

As I reached my feet, stumbling from the pain that battered my body, someone limped out of the smoke toward me. Sarrlevi. I sensed him before I could see him fully.

I was not able to keep them from getting away. Sarrlevi wrapped an arm around me and guided me toward the rear of the compound, toward where Zavryd had dropped us off. *They brought too many men—humans, orcs, and shifters. They all wore magical bracelets and appeared to be under a compulsion to fight me.*

I don't understand. How could they have known we were coming and beaten us here? I glanced back into the smoke at the front of the compound and grimaced. With the intruders' escape, the gunfire had stopped, but lights flashed, and we could hear the shouts of soldiers demanding to know what had happened and calling for their colleagues. *And why would they have wanted my* father? *I could understand my mother having value to them, but...*

Wait until we've escaped to contemplate it.

A good idea. Especially since the sounds of trucks and sirens promised the compound was now surrounded, with us inside. Further, I heard more helicopters approaching. Not magical ones but aircraft belonging to the military, and the smoke wouldn't mask the courtyard for long.

Can you call to Zavryd? If the dragon was nearby, I couldn't sense him, and that gave me a fresh reason to feel uneasy as we reached the back wall. The *tall* back wall with barbed wire lining the top. He'd said he would come if he heard explosions, but what if he'd decided to abandon us instead? I didn't think Val would do that, but she wasn't here, and Zavryd didn't like Sarrlevi. I didn't think he *dis*liked me but also doubted he cared much about my continued existence.

I've done so.

Did he answer? I reached for my pack and a coil of rope buckled to it, but my feet grew light, startling me.

Activate your camouflage again, Sarrlevi said as his magic levitated us from the ground. As we rose toward the wall, we also rose above the smoke.

Sorry, I thought I had. I hurried to rub the hammer-shaped charm and willed it to hide us from sight.

Vigorous activity or having magic used in close proximity can cause the illusion to falter.

Sarrlevi guided us over the barbed wire. Before we started descending on the other side, I had a view of the chaos: trucks spewing soldiers into the courtyard, helicopters arriving, and the still-smoking hole in the side of the building. In addition, craters had been blown in the pavement in numerous places, and men had to skirt them as they searched the courtyard for intruders and fallen comrades.

"What the hell are those *things*?" someone shouted in disgust or horror, pointing at a large tusked figure.

"Orcs," someone else said.

We descended below the wall, and I didn't hear the rest.

I shouldn't say this, Sarrlevi, but I'm glad you killed some of the other intruders, so that whoever pieces this together from the camera footage doesn't see only us. I hoped the cameras didn't see us at all, but I didn't know if we would be that lucky. If what Sarrlevi said of camouflaging charms was true, we'd both likely been visible during parts of this. He'd been out front fighting for several minutes.

When I'm battling so many, it becomes pure self-defense. I had to take them down any way I could.

I get it. I didn't ask if he'd killed any soldiers. I hoped he hadn't and that the other guys had been responsible for that. *Our enemies got my father,* I added, my shoulders slumping.

I gathered.

We'd reached the ground, and he wrapped an arm around my shoulders for a squeeze before releasing me. It was a light squeeze, and I suspected we'd both been injured.

Zavryd says he's chasing a helicopter, Sarrlevi added.

Oh? I brightened. *Maybe he'll catch them and get my father back.*

The new information made me feel guilty for believing Zavryd might have abandoned us.

Limited to walking on foot until the dragon returned, we headed toward the distant border of the post. Helicopters flew overhead, search lights probing the area all around us, but Sarrlevi didn't react, even when a beam lit his face. The lack of gunfire and shouts implied our camouflage was keeping the crews from seeing us. That was one good thing, but as I glanced back at the prison, I couldn't help but believe we'd failed.

Maybe Zavryd would have some luck. Hearing my father's voice, however briefly, had been heartening, since it meant he was still alive, but if my decision to come see him had prompted our enemies to swoop in and snatch him... I would regret this sojourn.

Explosions sounded, not from the prison but off in the distance, to the north of the post.

Zavryd? I couldn't sense him and glanced at Sarrlevi.

Yes. I can sense him and *the dwarf-enchanted helicopter he's battling.* He gave me a long look.

I thought I detected dwarven magic again.

Yes. Your mother's dwarven magic.

I wonder how many of those helicopters they've made. Whoever *they* were.

All along, I'd blamed the military, since they'd been the ones to attack my mother and arrest my father thirty years earlier. At least, I'd assumed they had been, since Dad had ended up in an Army prison. But maybe Val and Willard had been right, and the men who'd been harrying us lately had been wearing uniforms but had no affiliation with the Army. I wasn't, however, ready to absolve the military from blame. I could easily believe one unit or one branch of service was acting without the knowledge of the others.

I sensed two helicopters during the battle. One went that way. Sarrlevi pointed in the direction of the explosion, where Zavryd was fighting. *The other went south.* He pointed in the opposite direction.

At least the odds are decent that he's fighting the one full of the people who took my father.

Sarrlevi looked at me, his face grim, but didn't respond.

I halted and gripped his arm. *Do you think Zavryd got the wrong one? Can you tell? My father is a normal human, so you wouldn't be able to sense him. Or... did you see which one he was taken in?*

The smoke had kept me from spotting the helicopters, much less the occupants, but who knew what elven eyes could see through.

I did not, but they had magical beings among the crews. It's possible they were here before we were and sensed the dragon arrive. If so, they might have intentionally split forces, sending one helicopter in his direction to lure him away while the other took their prisoner. Sarrlevi nodded for us to keep walking.

Though his words had dashed some of my hope, I continued on. It wasn't as if we could stay here. And what if something happened to Zavryd, and he wasn't able to fly us back home? At least Sarrlevi could levitate us over fences. Though I wondered how injured and weary he was after that battle. I felt guilty at how many enemies he'd faced when all I'd done was run through aisles and knock down a gate with my hammer.

Thank you for helping me tonight, I said. *I'm sorry you were hurt. Again.*

Sarrlevi gave me another sidelong look. *I have been injured more times in the three months since I've met you than in the three years prior. Maybe the thirty years prior. As an assassin, I usually face off against single opponents. Only fools leap openly into battle against multiple foes.*

I'm sorry, I said again, hoping he wouldn't decide he'd had enough and leave. I would miss him, and not only because he'd been helping me.

The memory of Sarrlevi sitting behind me on the dragon's back, with his arm wrapped around me, made me ache to have that experience again. Even if he had been warning me about my conniving aunt.

It is not your fault that I'm being a fool, he said.

Are you sure? Because this has all revolved around me, so it seems like it might be.

You are *at the nexus.*

And you can't stay away because of your quest. Hoping to lighten both of our moods, I added, *And my sexy mongrel allure.*

You don't think it was the proffer of cheesy potatoes that drew me?

They are *good,* I said, though he hadn't shared his opinion of the meal.

Another explosion came from up ahead, the flash visible through the trees, though we had to be miles away.

I have vanquished the mechanical foe, came Zavryd's telepathic call.

I sensed him at the edge of my range. *Good. Did anyone survive?*

Like my father? Or people we could question?

Sarrlevi looked at me. *When you wish to speak telepathically to someone far away, imagine their face in your mind, and project your thoughts toward them, as if through a tunnel.*

That probably meant he didn't think Zavryd was close enough to hear my thoughts without such a projection.

Though I was sure he could relay the message, I attempted to do as he instructed. Supposedly, I had enough of my mother's blood in me to learn some magic, and telepathy would be handy to master.

I will search the wreckage for survivors, Zavryd replied after my second attempt. He'd either heard me that time, or Sarrlevi had passed along the message. *Then I will come for you.*

Thank you.

Sarrlevi nodded at me.

Did I get it right?

Yes. You have good range too. Some human half-bloods, even after much instruction and practice, can only manage a whisper to those around them.

So I'm a special mongrel, huh?

I meant it as a joke and expected him to tease me, but he nodded again. *Your mother is very powerful.*

He'd mentioned that before, but, for the first time, it occurred to me that he might mean he knew that from personal experience.

Have you met her? I asked.

For some reason, I'd assumed he'd taken the assassination gig without ever having met my mother. Maybe because that had made it seem less deplorable. If Sarrlevi hadn't *known* she was a good person, or had only her sister's version of the truth, which had doubtless painted my mother in a poor light, then he couldn't have known how awful that assignment was.

Briefly in passing when Barothla first called me to the dwarven court. She did have a noticeable aura, but it's the significance of your mother's enchantments that speaks to her power. Sarrlevi waved toward my hammer. *Also, as I've recently been reminded, her sister is very powerful.*

The confirmation that he'd been around my aunt lately chilled me.

You were reminded when Barothla called you back to ask if you're going to finish her original assignment? I asked.

When she threatened me for not having completed it, he said and looked toward where the explosion had gone off.

The Army helicopters with their searchlights were no longer close, and my hammer's glow had worn off, so I couldn't see his face well, but it made me uneasy that he'd looked away. He kept warning me that assassins shouldn't be trusted, that *he* shouldn't be trusted, and what did I do? Snuggle up to him on a dragon's back and fantasize about him joining me in bed one day.

Somehow, I doubted *he* was the fool.

There are no survivors, Zavryd reported. *An elf and three humans were in the craft, but they are all deceased. I believe two of the humans died from the crash. The elf was dead due to a bullet shot into the back of the head. The final human died from a bullet in the side of the head.*

Meaning one guy shot the elf and then killed himself? I asked.

It appears so.

Who are these zealots?

Even a dragon cannot mind scour the dead.

Which had to be why they'd made sure they all died.

I hesitated before asking my next question. *Were any of the humans wearing prison clothing?* I formed an image of the green outfits the prisoners had been wearing and attempted to send it through the telepathy tunnel toward Zavryd. Then I held my breath while I waited for an answer, afraid my father had been one of the men who'd died.

No. They wore the camouflage uniforms of your military personnel.

I blew out a slow breath, though I didn't know how relieved to be. Dad wasn't dead. But he was on his way from being a captive in one prison to, most likely, being incarcerated in another. Possibly a worse one. At the least, it was a prison I had no idea how to find.

.

12

SARRLEVI AND I DIDN'T TALK ON THE WAY BACK, NOR DID HE TOUCH me. Maybe he sensed that I was... I didn't know.

I wasn't mad at him. That wasn't it. Not when he'd again fought on my behalf and was the only reason I hadn't been captured or killed. But I was freshly concerned about his allegiances and goals.

Even so, when Zavryd landed in my front yard, and we slid off, I felt compelled to offer him a place to rest and recover.

After the dragon took off, saying he'd earned the ribs Val had promised him, I asked, "Do you want to set up your cot here?" I waved toward my house, the lights off, though I sensed Tinja sleeping inside. "I can crash on the couch if you want privacy."

"That is not necessary. I will return to one of my houses to meditate and repair my wounds."

When we'd first met and he'd spoken of multiple homes, I'd thought him a rich bastard with way too much money to throw around. I was sure he *was* wealthy, but now my mind translated *houses* to *bolt-holes*. Places where he could hide from enemies and go when his other homes were destroyed by dragons.

"Okay. Thanks again for helping tonight."

Sarrlevi never said *you're welcome*, but he did incline his head in a small bow. "Do you have another lead that you will pursue next?"

He asked it casually, but his eyes were intent, reminding me that he still wanted to find my mother. After all the injuries he'd received and the time he'd spent on this quest, he had a lot invested in it.

I continued to hope that he'd told me the truth about why, because he thought bringing my mother back to her people would prompt King Ironhelm to forgive him and speak kindly about him to King Eireth, the elf who had the power to let him come visit his mother before she died.

"Maybe," I said. "I'm hoping something will come of old letters that someone is translating for me now."

His eyebrows rose. "Princess Freysha?"

"Yes." I squinted at him. "Don't even think about showing up at her place and questioning her before *I* get the results of the translations. Or at all." The way he'd beaten me to Artie and questioned her with a hand around her throat came to mind.

"Given that *her place* is either the well-protected elven capital or Thorvald's also well-protected home, I'm not tempted to try."

"Good. I think they may be mostly love letters anyway."

"The natural place to search for clues of great importance."

"They probably won't hold anything, but... my only other thought is to try to talk Zavryd into flying us around the state, hoping to chance across magical dwarven enchantments strong enough to sense from miles away."

"Such as those air conveyances."

"Yeah."

"But you believe they are stored within mountains insulated to hide magic, do you not?"

"I'm not sure, but it wouldn't surprise me. That's where the stolen artifacts were hidden."

"Once I've recovered from my injuries," Sarrlevi said, "I may return to this world and speak with magical beings living in this city in an attempt to gather more clues."

I doubted random people around Seattle would have any ideas and squinted at him. "You're not going to visit my mother's two dwarven friends again, are you?"

"Have they returned to their domiciles?"

"Not the last I checked."

"Then I will have to search elsewhere. I lack the contacts on this world that I have on others, but I am not without means." Sarrlevi bowed to me, then lifted a hand. To make a portal?

"Do you want anything to take with you?" I envisioned him returning to a home he hadn't visited in years and that might be devoid of food. "There were some dinner leftovers. Not ham, I admit, but some of the other things."

He lowered his hand and looked at me.

"Or did you hate my dinner? It's okay if you did. You can tell me. I'd rather know so I don't keep inflicting my food on you."

"I didn't care for the dinner *company*," he said.

"They were unplanned. You didn't even like Freysha though? She seemed inoffensive."

"To a goblin, perhaps."

"And a half-dwarf. I like a lady who carries tools around instead of a purse."

Sarrlevi rocked his hand in the air. In agreement? Indifference? "I do not find her personally offensive. It is the family she represents."

"The family that won't let you return home?"

"Yes."

"Maybe if you did a favor for *her*, it would soften their views toward you."

"Unlikely. She is young, and it's doubtful her elders are swayed by her opinions."

"Well, the next time we share a meal, I won't let anyone else crash it. Did you like any of the food? I only ask so I'll know what to get you—or not—in the future. I promise not to be terribly crushed. Besides, *I* know my three-cheese scalloped-potatoes-and-ham recipe is *amazing*."

One of his eyebrows twitched. "Do you find all foods smothered in cheese to be amazing?"

"Uhm..." I debated if I'd ever encountered something I didn't like when it was dominated by cheese. "At the least, everything is much more palatable that way. Even nasty fibrous green vegetables." I smirked at him, certain he hadn't forgotten about what I'd *thought* had been a surreptitious way to dispose of the unpleasantly chewy green stalks he'd given me. "For example, melted cheese has the power to turn broccoli from disgusting little trees into a delicious side dish."

"Even elves do not eat trees. For the most part. Some barks are used in our medicines."

"Broccoli is a vegetable, but it *looks* like little trees." I attempted to share an image of broccoli, bare, steamed, and painfully bland, next to another image of it baked with garlic and cheese. *Much* cheese.

"I see. I would like to try it someday." Sarrlevi looked toward my house. "And I will accept leftovers of the greens if you do not desire them."

"Good. I know there are some of those. You, Freysha, and Zadie were the only ones who took decent portions of them. I noticed even Val seems to share some of her dragon's carnivorous tendencies."

"I'm amazed she's able to acquire meat for herself when he's around," Sarrlevi murmured, following me into the house.

When we reached the kitchen, I turned on a light and headed for the refrigerator but halted abruptly. Three dark-brown bottles with labels in a language I couldn't read sat on the counter.

The writing on the labels was beautiful, loopy and elegant, reminding me of calligraphy. The bottles were less elegant. With homemade wax stoppers, they looked like something crafted in someone's garage. A small envelope lying on the counter next to them hadn't been opened.

"A gift for Tinja from a goblin admirer?" I asked, though I immediately shook my head.

If my roommate had brought them in the house and been the intended recipient, she would have opened the note. And nobody else would have brought them in. The dinner party had broken up before we'd left. Further, it had been late enough that there shouldn't have been any delivery services still out, dropping off parcels.

"A little weird," I murmured, reaching for the note. The envelope didn't have a name on it. "Do you recognize the writing?"

"It's Elven," Sarrlevi said, his voice quiet and without inflection. He was staring at the bottles.

"From Freysha?" I unsealed the envelope. "I don't know that many elves."

Sarrlevi said nothing, only watching me pull out a folded piece of paper. Nerves danced in my belly, and my fingers trembled as I opened the note. Even though I wanted this to be nothing but a thank-you gift from a dinner guest, my instincts—and Sarrlevi's reaction—told me it was something else.

"The berry mentioned on the bottle *is* from the elven home world," he said, "and we do make sodas like this, but..."

"It's suspicious. Yeah."

The writing inside was in English, penned by what looked like a different hand and in a simpler style than the labels.

My mongrel female, please enjoy this gift from my home world. Varlesh.

"I did not send that," Sarrlevi said, reading over my shoulder.

I believed him, both because every other gift he'd given me

had involved cheese and because when he'd had something delivered, the note had used my name instead of calling me a mongrel. But, if he hadn't come in with me, would I have thought anything suspicious of these drinks?

My heart hammered against my ribcage harder than it had when we'd been fleeing the prison.

"Do not drink them." Sarrlevi rested a hand on my shoulder, his face grave. "Do not even open them and risk inhaling the air that comes off the liquid."

"Do you think *she* sent them?" I looked at him, thinking of his words that my mother and the king wore charms to protect themselves against poisoning. *I* did not have a charm with such capabilities. "My aunt?"

"It's possible. It could be someone trying to poison you to more easily get the hammer. Either way, you must destroy the beverages."

"Oh, I will."

"I won't send you anything else via a delivery service so you'll know that anything that comes is a threat."

"Well, anything that comes in a language from another world."

"*Anything*," he said sternly. "For now, do not accept anything from anyone."

"All right." I forced a smile, though I was shaken. "Thank you. Here." I grabbed the containers of Kaleo Twist and Chard Rock out of the fridge, though I hesitated before giving them to him. "You don't think she would have come in here and bothered the leftovers, do you?"

"Probably not. I sense your roommate here and trust from her snores that nobody came by and deeply disturbed her."

I smiled. I *could* hear goblin snores drifting down the hall.

"Though I may run a few tests before consuming them." Sarrlevi accepted the containers, then touched my arm. "I'll return soon. Be careful."

"I will. Thanks."

For a moment, he gazed into my eyes, and if I hadn't been shaken from what I could only assume was an attempt to kill me, I might have leaned in, hoping for a kiss. But he might have been hanging out with my mother's evil sister of late, a thought that helped me refrain. Maybe he remembered that too, for he only patted my arm before walking out the door.

The magic of a portal forming plucked at my senses, and then he and it disappeared.

I should have been relieved, not disappointed, but what was becoming a familiar ache filled my chest, a desire for him to be more than an acquaintance working with me toward a common goal. A desire for him.

"Not going to happen," I told myself, glancing at the note before heading to the garbage can.

When I lifted the lid to toss it in, I found myself staring at a brown bottle identical to the ones on the counter. An *empty* brown bottle.

13

"I FEEL FINE," TINJA SAID FROM THE PASSENGER SEAT OF MY TRUCK. Rain pelted the windshield, and darkness pressed in from all sides. "Truly. I'm a most hale goblin."

She'd declared her haleness three times already, once when I'd roused her from sleep and forced her to dress and twice more since we'd started the drive toward Val's house.

"I'm glad," I said, "but it may be slow-acting."

"It tasted like a fizzy soda. A berry flavor. Nothing odd. It was good."

"Poison delivered in a dreadful-tasting concoction wouldn't be that effective." My phone rang, and I answered.

Val. Thank God.

After realizing Tinja had consumed one of the bottles, I'd called Val, but it had gone to voice mail. I'd left a frantic message, saying I needed to come over and hire her alchemist, and barely explaining before grabbing the keys and hefting Tinja into the truck.

"What exactly happened?" Val asked as soon as I answered.

I did my best to explain, but it was possible I was as frantic as

I'd been when leaving the message. If Tinja ended up dying because someone was out to get *me*, I wouldn't forgive myself. And I damn well wouldn't forgive Barothla. I was *sure* she'd sent those bottles.

"All right," Val said. "Yes, come over. Zoltan is full of himself, but he's also knowledgeable and talented. He can probably figure out what's in there and maybe an antidote. Hopefully, you'll get lucky and it'll just be soda."

"I doubt that, since someone felt compelled to forge a note from Sarrlevi to go with the bottles."

"This is Zoltan's day, so he should be awake, but I'll meet you at his door and go in with you. He tends to charge for his services, an exorbitant amount."

"That's fine."

"It's not really, but I'll help out if need be."

"Thanks. We'll be there soon."

I looked bleakly over at Tinja, whose expression had grown more fearful as I'd explained things to Val. The rest of the way, I drove faster than the speed limit. It was almost four in the morning, so there weren't many cars on the road. I hoped no police were lurking either. *My roommate drank weird elven soda,* didn't sound like a plausible excuse for speeding.

When we reached Val's house, I was relieved that its oddness —or *her* oddness—kept people from parking out front, since the streets in the old residential neighborhood that predated garages were otherwise packed. I pulled up in front of the topiaries, grabbed one of the bottles, and sprinted for the gate in the fence, not waiting for Tinja.

But she hopped down and jogged after me, no doubt wanting answers as badly as I did.

As she'd promised, Val waited at the basement door and held it open for us. She must have warned Zoltan that we were coming, for he stood inside and bowed after we entered his laboratory, infrared lights providing enough illumination for him to work by.

"Here." I thrust the soda bottle at him without preamble. "Can you test it and see if there's a weird dwarven poison in it?"

"*Dwarven* poison?" Zoltan accepted the bottle but frowned at the label. "This is elven writing and an elven soda, is it not?"

"Yeah, but I suspect a dwarven alchemist might have poisoned it. It was meant for me. She, if it was her, wanted to make it look like a gift from Sarrlevi so I wouldn't be suspicious of it."

"Sarrlevi?" Zoltan looked at Val. "Is that not the elven assassin who tried to kill you?"

"Yeah."

"A gift from such a person would make me *more* suspicious, not less."

"That's because he's not into you."

Zoltan's gaze shifted to me, eyebrows raised in inquiry.

"He's not *into* me either. He's just a friend. Check that, please." I waved him toward his microscope, though I had no idea if that was the tool one used to search for poison in a substance.

"But is it not the goblin who drank the beverage?" Fortunately, Zoltan headed for the counter as he asked and started pulling equipment from his shelves.

"Because I thought it was from him too," Tinja said. "All his other gifts were really good. And this was really good too. It didn't taste poisoned."

"All his other gifts?" Val asked.

I shook my head, not wanting to discuss my relationship, such as it was, with Sarrlevi. All I wanted was to make sure Tinja wouldn't die.

"All the delightful cheeses," Tinja explained. "And the pickled root vegetables. These sodas arrived like last time. A goblin messenger rode up on a bicycle with them. The same guy!"

"Root vegetables," Val said. "Romantic."

I glared at her.

She lifted an apologetic hand. "Zoltan will be able to find a solution, if it's necessary."

"Good. Thank you." I pushed a hand through my hair and wondered if it would be possible to find out where that goblin messenger lived so I could question him about who'd paid for the delivery. Not that I had any doubts. As Sarrlevi had pointed out, it was *possible* someone else who wanted me dead had done it, but poison struck me as a likely killing method for an alchemist. The orc mercenaries had merely tried to lop off my head.

Why did Barothla want me dead anyway?

I lowered my hand and attempted to draw a steadying breath, telling myself I didn't yet know the soda had been poisoned. Maybe she'd stuck something in it that delivered bowel-wrenching cramps or something else irritating but not deadly. Maybe she wanted to send a message that I'd made a mistake in refusing to work with her.

"You told her about my rates?" Zoltan asked Val as he made a slide.

"That they're exorbitant bordering on extortion? Yes."

"Extortion? Really, dear robber. I'm not threatening or applying force on anyone. It is she who intruded upon me in the middle of the night."

"Isn't the middle of the night your preferred laboratory hours?"

"I don't have *hours*," Zoltan said. "I'm not a pharmacy. Now, if you'll leave me alone so I can work? Being unfamiliar with the base substance, and trusting there is no record in any *Earth* data-base listing the ingredients, I'll need to run numerous tests and make calculated guesses."

I winced. I'd hoped it would be easy to pick out a menacing substance in what should have been nothing more than sugary soda, but my chemistry knowledge was limited.

Tinja's shoulders slumped. "I have a virtual study group tomorrow, and we're being assigned a new project soon. Also, I must continue work on my side project. I've already purchased a domain name. I have to get my tiny-house plans online and available for sale. I can't be... *sick*."

More worried she would end up dead, I patted Tinja's shoulder and made myself smile. "We'll find a solution. Maybe there's not anything wrong, and I overreacted."

I *hoped* so.

Tinja rubbed her stomach.

"Are you starting to feel... something?" I yawned, the long and fraught night catching up with me. I'd dozed sitting up for a few minutes on Zavryd's back on the return trip, but that had scarcely been refreshing.

"I don't know. Maybe?" One of her pointed ears drooped as she looked bleakly around the laboratory and at chairs in the corner of the basement that held Zoltan's coffin and non–chemistry-related belongings. The black-painted wood-framed chairs with red velvet cushions weren't decorating choices I would have made, but they had enough cushiness to make me think of a nap.

"Should we sit and wait?" Since Zoltan was ignoring us, I looked to Val.

"Yeah, but not down here." Val pointed upward to indicate the rest of the house. "You do not want to fall asleep in a vampire's lab. Trust me." Her pointing finger shifted toward my throat.

"Really, dear robber," Zoltan said without looking back. "I don't drive food out of your refrigerator."

"The carrots and cold cuts are relieved. Come on, you two. We've got guest rooms." Val led the way toward the door.

Wanting to know whether Tinja was poisoned as soon as possible, I was hesitant to leave, but we wouldn't be going far. And alchemists probably didn't work well with cranky half-dwarves breathing down—*up*—their necks.

"You can go home if you want," Tinja told me as Val led us out of the basement, across the patio, and through a back door into the kitchen. "There won't be anything you can do here."

"Except pay the bill?"

"I'm sure the vampire will find a way to get that to you if you don't wait."

"He'll give it to *me* to give to you," Val said dryly, heading for stairs leading to the second floor. "Though he is a modern vampire and accepts payments online."

I could sense Zavryd's aura in the bedroom at the end of the hall, the little tower with numerous windows overlooking the lake, and trusted he'd gone to sleep already. Val turned down the hall in the opposite direction.

"I don't want you to miss your date in the morning because you're here with me," Tinja added in a whisper.

Hell. The date with Tyler. I'd forgotten.

It was only six hours away, and I hadn't gone to bed yet. The urge to cancel came over me, but I would have to wait until daylight, not call him at 4 a.m.

"Date, huh?" Val smiled back at us.

"With one of my brother-in-law's friends." I eyed her, wondering if she would judge me for seeing someone else when we'd had conversations about Sarrlevi. Despite my numerous and vehement denials that I felt anything for him, I didn't think Val believed that. Unwisely, I'd joked about having sex with him.

"A normal guy?" Val didn't appear judgmental, only curious.

"Yeah. I'm apparently capable of attracting a few of them."

She snorted and thumped me on the shoulder. "Of course you are. Here you go." At the end of the hall, she pushed open one door and then another across from it. Both guest rooms looked out over the backyard. "When she's here, Freysha stays in the room we just passed. You guys can share the bathroom across from it. There are some unopened toothbrushes in one of the drawers."

I'd barely noticed Freysha's aura with Zavryd's also on the floor but nodded, glad she was there. Hopefully, I could get the translations of the letters while I was here. Since the dinner party had run late, Freysha might not have looked at them yet, but I would knock on her door in the morning.

"Zav and I have our own bathroom off our bedroom," Val said, "so you *shouldn't* run into him tonight, and I've recently had a talk with him—again—about nudity not being appropriate outside of one's bedroom and bathroom when one has roommates or guests on the premises."

"I didn't realize your dragon has nudist tendencies," I said as Tinja shuffled into a room overlooking a conservatory, the high-growing green plants visible through the glass ceiling.

"Well, you might have noticed that dragons don't wear clothing when they're in their native form. It's not exactly natural for them. I'm not sure he would bother at all, but that elf robe of his is soft and comfortable."

"The Crocs with the meat charms in the holes can't be," I said.

"No, but my ex-husband told him they were lucky, and dragons either have a superstitious streak, or Zav likes whimsy more than he admits."

As I remembered Zondia and her male companion tearing Sarrlevi's house to pieces, it was hard for me to imagine any dragons with a whimsical streak.

Speaking about Zavryd made me wonder if *he* could do anything about Tinja's problem. "In case Zoltan can't figure this out... can dragons heal poisoned people?"

Val hesitated. "I'll ask, but I know Zav's abilities as a healer are generally limited to repairing wounds. Other dragons specialize in more, but getting them to help lesser species is complicated." Something about her grimace suggested she knew that from personal experience. "Exorbitant rates or not, Zoltan is a better bet."

"All right." After another yawn nearly cracked my jaw, I said, "Thanks for letting us stay."

"No problem. Tinja is welcome to stay here tomorrow while you go on your date. With all of Zav's defenses, not to mention a few additions that Freysha has made on her visits, it's probably the safest place in the city. And we know how to deal with goblins around these parts." She smiled.

"Oh? I'm still trying to figure that out. I've heard sound beatings when they disassemble your small appliances are frowned upon."

"*They* certainly frown upon them. I've learned to order boxes of junk and keep them in the closet under the stairs for when Gondo comes over. We're employing the same methodology at the Coffee Dragon. It doesn't keep them from making what they consider *improvements* to the place, but at least they don't disassemble anything important."

"I'll have to visit your shop sometime." I'd always avoided it, since I'd heard the Ruin Bringer was a partial owner. Never would I have imagined going on missions with her and crashing in her guest room.

"I would suggest you bring your date there, but you said he's a normal guy, right?" Val didn't bring up Sarrlevi or appear as judgmental as I'd feared. If anything, she smiled encouragingly. Maybe, like my sister, she thought a normal guy would be a *good idea.*

"An accountant at a tech company."

"That might be a little staid for the Coffee Dragon."

"He seems okay so far," I said, "but I've heard the goblin gamers that hang out there use catapults to launch dice across the room."

"We've shooed the gamers into the upstairs now, but it's still a weird place to people not familiar with magic."

And those who *were* familiar with it, I wagered.

Val bade me goodnight. After telling Tinja to wake me up if she felt worse or needed anything, I got ready for bed.

Despite my weariness, I didn't know how well I would sleep while worried about my roommate and wondering what I would do if the letters didn't reveal any clues. Sarrlevi would be back soon, expecting me to have ideas about where to look next for my mother. And I also had more reasons than ever to want to find her. Her *and* my father. Whatever the reason Mom's captors wanted him, it couldn't be anything good.

But if the bad guys could magically hide their bases, we wouldn't stumble onto them even flying around on a dragon's back. The only encouraging thing was that, since they'd shown up at the Army post on short notice, they couldn't be that far away. Not unless they'd been planning to retrieve my father for a while. But I had a feeling that wasn't it. I suspected that they had somehow figured out *I* was seeking him and had wanted to make sure I didn't get a chance to chat with him.

Who could have told them or how they could have learned that, I didn't know.

14

SINCE I'D GONE TO SLEEP THINKING ABOUT MY ENEMIES AND HOW I could find them, I was surprised and embarrassed to wake up in the throes of an erotic dream with the blankets tangled around my body and the pillows on the floor.

I glanced at the door, relieved to find it shut, not that Val had magical laundry-cleaning devices that came in to swipe one's clothes, nor did she seem the type to intrude upon one's privacy. Even so, I couldn't help but feel embarrassed since I was in someone else's house. I hoped the dreams hadn't been... vocal.

"Going on a date with a new guy," I grumbled, swinging my legs out of bed, "while dreaming about the old guy that I shouldn't trust. I'm sure this will work fine."

With luck, I could avoid mentioning Sarrlevi or anything about how strange my life had gotten lately to Tyler. Or should I cancel?

I glanced at the time, grimaced at the thought of the lecture Penina would give me for bailing, and decided I would let the results of Zoltan's experiments make up my mind. If Tinja was all right, I needed to go back home anyway, and I was supposed to meet Tyler at a coffee shop eight blocks from the house. After being up most of the previous night, the thought of swilling caffeine made that sound appealing.

A soft knock sounded, and I sensed Freysha in the hall.

"One sec," I called, my cheeks warming again as I hurried to straighten the blankets and put the pillows in a more logical place than the floor.

Freysha wouldn't know I'd been having erotic dreams unless she poked into my thoughts while I was thinking about them, but as a full-blooded elf... she *could* do that. I hoped she wouldn't have any reason to. Since her father hated Sarrlevi, I especially didn't want Freysha to know he and I were... anything. And we weren't.

"She'll only want to talk about the letters," I told myself firmly and attempted to plant them at the front of my mind as I opened the door.

"Good morning, Matti." Freysha inclined her head toward me.

"Hi, Freysha." I glanced at the door across the hall, but it was still closed, and I sensed Tinja inside. Sleeping? I couldn't tell.

When I stretched out with my senses, I detected the quarter-dwarf roommate downstairs, a man I'd only met briefly thus far, and Zoltan in the basement. Morning sunlight streamed in the windows, so I didn't know if he was still up and working, but I hoped so. Zavryd must have flown off somewhere, for I didn't sense him. Val was down in the kitchen.

"I've translated your letters." Freysha held them toward me along with pages of notebook paper with English words on them. "One was a little spicy." Her cheeks grew a touch pink.

If a *letter* could embarrass her, I would definitely keep my dreams locked down so she wouldn't glimpse them in my mind.

"I'm hoping there was more to them than that," I said. "While it's nice to know my parents loved each other—and, ah, lusted after each other—I need clues about who might have kidnapped Mom thirty years ago."

And who might still have her today.

Freysha nodded. "Val told me a little about your quest. I hope you are successful in finding her. I am surprised... Well, I would not have expected you to work with the assassin Sarrlevi, given his past involvement—" her voice lowered to a mutter, "—his involvement in *many* things, but I trust you are being wary with him."

"Very wary." I focused on the letters and most certainly did not think about the dream that had clearly been inspired by Sarrlevi's kiss when we'd been riding south. As if Zavryd would have permitted us to engage in what my subconscious mind *thought* we should have engaged in while on dragon-back.

"That is good. And, yes, if you seek information about their past and how they met, some of that is contained within the letters. I do not know if they will guide you in finding her current location, but I hope you find them useful."

"Thank you. Do I owe you anything for your work? Val mentioned I should bring you a fern, but I was distracted last night." I waved toward Tinja's room.

"Oh, no." Freysha lifted her hands. "I am happy to help my sister's friends."

"If you ever need furniture carved out of wood or drywall put up or anything, let me know. I'm handy."

Freysha started to make a polite I-won't-but-thanks-for-offering smile, but she paused. "Are you an enchanter? I understand Princess Rodarska was—*is*—quite a brilliant one."

"No, sorry. I lost her—er, she was taken away—when I was four, so there hasn't been anyone to teach me about dwarven enchanting. Or dwarven anything."

"That's unfortunate for many reasons, but you are young. Perhaps one day, you'll find someone to teach you. I sense from your aura that you have great power for a half-blood. Even for a *full* blood." Freysha smiled at me. "I trust you would be quite the enchanter."

"Good to know." I stepped back, wanting to leap into the letters, not talk about things that didn't matter at the moment, but paused. "Have you heard anything about what Zoltan's researching for me?"

Freysha glanced toward Tinja's room, and I trusted Val had filled her in on the reason for their houseguests. "The last I heard, he's still working."

"Okay, thanks."

She didn't seem offended when I closed the door and hurried to a small desk in the corner. My hands trembled as I leafed through the letters, the words *reward you with more kisses* jumped off one, and I placed it at the back of the pile. I might be *glad* my parents had loved and lusted for each other, but I didn't want to read the details.

The four letters weren't dated, but the others were more formal, and I had a feeling the lusty one had been last, after they'd gotten to know each other better. After identifying what I believed was the first, I propped my elbows on the table to read. All except the last were addressed to *my noble soldier* rather than my dad by name, but they were signed by Mom, first as *Rodarska*, no mention of princess, and *Roxy* for the last one.

I'd read them all, leaning back in the chair to look out the window and consider them, when Tinja knocked and came in. Sweat gleamed on her green brow, and bags lurked under her eyes. I'd seen her tired before but not sweaty—fevered?—and dread curdled in my stomach.

"How are you feeling?" I asked, my mouth dry.

"Like I shouldn't have swilled down elven soda from a stranger."

"I'm sorry."

"Me too. What are those?" Tinja waved at the desk, though I wasn't sure if she meant the letters or a cup holding pens, pencils, scissors, and a ruler, all implements a goblin might find creative uses for.

"Old letters from my mom to my dad from before I was born. Shortly after they met, I guess. Well, not *that* shortly, since Dad must have had time to learn her language before she started writing to him in Dwarven."

Tinja hopped up on my bed and raised her eyebrows. "Anything interesting?"

I might have hesitated to share, since they were so private, but she'd heard most of my rants over the last few weeks and had a lot of the details already. Besides, she looked like she wanted a distraction.

"This one is a love letter. Apparently, my dad was quite the hunky stud."

Tinja wrinkled her nose.

"He was in the Army," I explained. "Women dig a man in a uniform."

"*Goblin* women like males who are handy with their tools."

"I thought you, being a more erudite goblin, might prefer a scholarly mate."

"A scholarly mate who knows his way around a toolbox." Tinja winked at me.

"The other letters..." I skimmed through the translations again while considering them.

Tinja raised her eyebrows as she waited.

"She was thanking him for stopping the questioning in this one." I touched a page. "Maybe the *torture*. There are innuendos and, in some places, it almost seems like she was writing in code, beyond them being in Dwarven. Like she was saying things Dad would understand but maybe his superiors wouldn't? I'm not sure, since the fact that they're in Dwarven alone should have effectively encrypted them—how many people on Earth at the time could read it? Anyway, it's clear she was a prisoner. A prisoner of the military. And Dad was brought in to learn her language so he could get the answers from her that his superiors wanted. This must have been right after she came to Earth."

Right after she'd had to flee her world because her sister had hired an assassin...

"It sounds like," I continued, "my father tried to be a protector for her, that he didn't like what his people were doing. There are no letters from him, so I'm guessing based on her messages and what she's referencing. He didn't have enough rank to stop anyone. One time, he brought her a Snickers bar." I pointed to the single word in English on one of the pages, Snickers having no translation in Dwarven, I imagined. "In this last letter, she says that she appreciates him but that he shouldn't give up his career, give up everything, to help her. He must have been offering to help her escape. That lines up with what my grandfather said."

"Why did the Army capture your mother to start with?" Tinja asked.

"None of the letters say, but I'm guessing it was for the same reason they *re*-captured her." I waved in the direction of the mountains where we'd fought the enchanted helicopters. "Or someone did. They wanted her to make them magical things."

"Like what?"

I hadn't told her much about the reactor, since Artie had said such devices were a dwarven secret. But if it was as epic an energy source as Willard had said, I had no trouble imagining people wanting someone who could make more of them.

"She's supposed to be a powerful and gifted enchanter. She made my hammer, among other things."

"That hammer *is* amazing," Tinja said. "I know enough magic to sense some of the intricacies woven into the enchantments. I hope you learn everything it can do someday. I'm *positive* it's not just for demoing cabinets."

"No, though it does handle that with aplomb." I skimmed

through the letters again. "These aren't dated, but I'm pretty sure they're all from before I was born. From when she was still being held. If Dad helped her break out, and they lived in Seattle for the next five years or so... Well, I wonder how they managed that with the Army after them. My memories are fuzzy about the time we were a family, and I think most of what I remember was from that last year, when I was four, but I don't remember ever living anywhere else except that apartment. Grandpa said I was born in Canada. Why did they come back? You'd expect people on the run and hiding from the authorities to live in a camper and stay off the grid wouldn't you?"

I supposed if my hypothesis that Mom had been able to magically hide them in plain sight was true, then they wouldn't have needed to physically hide. Could they have come back after I'd been born so they'd be close to my grandparents? In case anything happened? Or maybe that had been when Penina's mom had gotten in trouble for drug addiction and lost custody of her. *Dad* wouldn't have gotten custody if he'd been AWOL. Maybe my grandparents had taken her even before Dad had been arrested. But I had memories of Penina being around when I'd been little, and she'd been there that night...

"I would flee to another world if I was running from the authorities," Tinja said, pulling me back from my vain attempt to dredge up what my brain couldn't remember.

I opened my mouth to say that wouldn't have been possible, but was that true? If Barothla could make portals, wasn't it likely that my mother could too?

Maybe the Army had possessed some charm or magical handcuffs that had kept her from doing so while she'd been imprisoned, but what about after she'd escaped? Yes, she still would have been worried about Sarrlevi, but she could have gone to another wild world. Had she fallen for my father by then and not been willing to leave him behind? And had he not been willing to leave

Earth for her?

"I think I have more questions after reading these letters," I said, "not fewer."

"Sorry." Tinja shrugged.

Matti? Val asked telepathically, not from the kitchen but the basement.

Butterflies assaulted my stomach like machine-gun fire as I remembered our reason for being here. *Tinja's reason. Yeah?*

Zoltan did find evidence of what he believes is a slow-acting poison. It's magical, but it has some kind of built-in defense to make it very difficult to detect. He found it through testing, not because it gave off a signature.

I looked gravely at Tinja. *Is there a cure? An antidote?*

That was what one took for poisons, wasn't it?

He's not sure what exactly it does yet. He thinks it was custom made rather than something existing in nature. He wants to take a blood sample from Tinja so he can see what it's doing inside of her, but he says if you could get him more information, that would be ideal.

The person I suspect was responsible lives on Dun Kroth.

When Zav comes back, he might be willing to take us there.

That stirred hope within me. *Would he be willing to mind scour a dwarf princess who happens to be an alchemist?*

Val hesitated. *You think King Ironhelm's daughter is responsible?*

I can't prove it, but yes. I think she tried to do in her sister forty years ago, and now that she's learned Mom's still alive, she might want to finish the job.

But why poison you? I assume this was meant for you and not your roommate.

Yeah. I winced, again regretting that Tinja had been caught up in my problems. She'd lain back on the bed and was looking wearily up at the ceiling, none of her usual spunk present. *And I don't know, except that I refused to work with her to find my mother. I might have irked her by not being suitably obedient. Sarrlevi said she's the cold and calculating type.*

Again, Val hesitated before replying. *Don't take this the wrong way, Matti—I know you have some feelings for him—but is it possible he was the one to deliver the poison? Like... on her behalf?*

No. He was with me when I first saw the package and the note. It was addressed to me from him.

Like the root vegetables?

I blushed, wishing I hadn't mentioned that the night before. Or that *Tinja* hadn't. *No. It called me mongrel female instead of by name, like the gift he sent did, and he said he didn't send it. He warned me not to drink it. Val, if he wanted me dead, or was working for Barothla, who wants me dead, he could have killed me any time. Hell, all he would have had to do was stand back during one of our fights these past couple of months and let me die. If not for him, I wouldn't have survived some of these battles related to my mother.*

Maybe the poison isn't meant to kill you but scare you, make you compliant.

I hope that's all it is. Then Tinja won't die.

She wiped sweat from her brow.

Hopefully not, but she is a lot smaller than you. If she drank a dose meant for someone your size, it might be worse for her than it would have been for you.

I closed my eyes, horrified anew at the thought. I wanted to wring Barothla's neck and wished again that I'd tried to hammer her into the pavement when she'd shown up at my grandparents' house.

When will Zavryd be back? I asked, latching onto the idea that he might be able to take me to Dun Kroth.

Later today, most likely. But... if King Ironhelm's daughter is the one responsible, I'm not sure how much help Zav will be able to offer. The Ironhelms are allied with the Dragon Council, which is headed by Zav's mother. He's most definitely not going to mind scour the princess.

Will he take me to her so I can bash her over the head with my hammer and question her in the human way?

Ah, I'm not sure that's a good idea. She's pretty badass, isn't she?

You've met her?

No, but your aura is impressive, so I'm assuming your mother—and her sister—are pretty powerful.

She's a powerful alchemist, not a mage, I said before remembering Barothla had been armed and armored.

I let out a frustrated huff. She might be a capable warrior, and I didn't know that she couldn't use her magic as a weapon.

We can ask what Zav thinks when he gets back, Val said. *He went to fly up and down the mountains to see if he senses any more of those helicopters. He told me about his encounter with one last night and that your stealth incursion didn't go as planned.*

We *were stealthy. It was the other guys that were the problem.*

So I heard. Brace yourself for a call from Willard. There's no way she won't hear about that incident. Is there any chance you weren't caught on camera?

There's a chance. The memory of the camera leering down at us from the wall by the door popped into my mind. *But I'm not sure. I kept activating my camouflage charm, but I guess if you're involved in a fight or blown across a room by an explosion, the magic can fail.*

Yeah, it takes some complex magic to create the illusion, and it doesn't take much to break it. I'll try to keep Willard off your back.

Thanks.

"We need to take a trip down to the basement, Tinja." I patted her shoulder. "Zoltan wants some of your blood."

Her eyes widened in alarm. "He's going to bite my veins?"

"I assume he'll use a needle."

"That's not as reassuring as you might think."

My phone rang as we headed down to the basement, and I grimaced. My sister.

Once again, the fear that bad people were doing dire things to my friends and family forced me to answer, but I would have preferred to let her talk to my voice mail.

"What's up, Penina?" I asked as we stepped into the vampire's light lock.

"Your date is in an hour," Penina said cheerfully. "Are you ready? Are you wearing something cute?"

"Uh." I looked at the clothes I'd not only broken into a prison in but had slept in and was still wearing. "Not... yet. About that—"

"Bob and Tyler got together for lunch yesterday. He's really looking forward to getting to hang out with you alone."

The inner door opened, with Val waving us in and pointing Tinja toward Zoltan, who waited with a needle, not fangs.

"He asked what your favorite coffee drink is," Penina burbled on, "so he can order it and have it waiting for you. Don't be late, okay? It'll be fun. If things work out, we can double date. Bob and I have been thinking of hiring a sitter so we can go out more often. Like we used to before we had kids. We'd love to see more of you. It'll be so fun. Tyler is a good guy."

"My roommate is actually sick, so I'm thinking of—"

"Don't you dare cancel on him," Penina said, her tone shifting instantly from happy and burbling to stern and lecturing. "You were already hard enough for him to get on the phone. And you set this time and place."

"I know."

Val, whose half-elven hearing probably caught everything, waved a hand. "Go ahead, Matti. I'll keep an eye on your roommate. And give her one of our junk boxes to keep her distracted."

"Junk?" Despite her fever, Tinja's ears perked.

"Besides, you need a shower and a change of clothes." Val waved to my dirty and rumpled attire. "If I didn't know what you'd *really* been up to last night, I would assume you'd pulled some random guy into the bushes in a park to have sex on the ground."

I quashed the memory of Sarrlevi's kiss when it tried to spring to mind, only mumbling that it wouldn't have been a *random guy*.

"What was that, Matti?" Penina asked.

"Nothing. I'll be there."

"Good. I'm glad. Don't forget to wear something cute."

"I'll see what I can find that's clean."

"*All of* your cute clothes are, I'm sure," Penina said tartly, "since you never wear them."

"You're a nag, Penina."

"It's my duty as your older sister. Go get ready, and then have some fun, okay? You've been so busy lately."

I sighed as I hung up. I would go on the date, but mostly so I could take Val's advice to go home and shower and change. Once I had coffee and grabbed a few things, I would return and camp out in Zoltan's lab until he had a solution—or until Zavryd came back and he was willing to take me to find Barothla and wring her neck.

15

EVEN THOUGH MY SISTER WAS ACCURATE IN POINTING OUT THAT I didn't have an opportunity to wear cute things often, I did have some clothes that qualified. I thought so anyway. Penina called my fashion tastes questionable, but since most of her wardrobe consisted of slacks and blouses with only a few mono-colored evening gowns and dresses for her date nights with Bob, I doubted she counted as an expert.

Since the sun was out, I took my Harley to the coffee shop, my hammer within easy reach in the saddlebag. Under my leather riding jacket, I wore pale-blue leggings and a colorful peasant blouse with sequined hems that Penina would have called over-the-top or possibly riotous. I liked it, and the wide neckline showed off some of my cleavage. For work, I stuck to henleys, T-shirts, and jeans, but for a date, a little skin was nice, right?

Though I was worried about Tinja—about *everything*—I resolved to be a decent coffee companion for at least an hour before bailing. My sister was right. Though semi-reluctantly, I *had* set this up.

Tyler was sitting at an outside table with two coffee cups

already resting in front of him, and he grinned and waved at me when I rode up. Clean-shaven with short, tidy brown hair, he was about five-ten—a much more logical height for the boyfriend of someone barely over five feet. Elves towering over six feet tall were problematic. Boy-next-door summed up Tyler, though his glasses gave him a geeky vibe.

He was a far cry from the tattooed, musclebound oafs I usually attracted, and I did wonder if he would scamper away in alarm the first time he saw me swing my hammer at someone. Once, my vigilante side gig had been easy to keep on the down low, but everything had changed since Sarrlevi had shown up.

No, I couldn't blame him for the change. It had started when Tinja had picked out the Bridle Trails house, with its startling link to my mother.

Should I warn Tyler about any of that? Such as that I had a valuable magical hammer that people—magical and sometimes *tusked* people—were trying to collect for a reward? Was Tyler ready to hear about such things?

Nobody had attacked me, trying to steal my hammer, for a couple of weeks, so maybe I would get lucky, and nothing untoward would happen while he was around. At least not in the one hour I intended to spend with him this morning. The discussion of the magical world and my tie to it could wait for the second date.

With that thought in mind, I didn't carry the hammer to the table. I *did* park close to the patio, so I could spring over the railing and grab it if someone suspicious approached.

"Hey." I waved and forced a cheery smile as I passed other tables to sit across from him.

"Hi, Matti." Tyler smiled shyly. "I've never gone out with a girl who rides a motorcycle before."

"I'm kind of rough and tumble."

He looked at the sequins on my peasant blouse.

"But not today." I hoped.

His gaze jerked up to my face, and his cheeks grew pink as he lifted a hand. In an apology? Only then did I realize he'd been checking out my chest, not the sequins, or not *just* the sequins. Well, good. Then the blouse was working as desired.

"I'm glad you made it," he said. "You seem really busy. Because you've got your own business, right?"

"That does keep me busy." Even if it wasn't the reason my life was utter chaos this month.

"Do you have an LLC? An S-Corp?"

I stared at him in surprise—these were not questions any guy had ever asked me—until I remembered he was an accountant. "A Limited Liability Partnership. And a guy who does the books quarterly. I'm not—" I stopped short of saying *mathy*, since that might be a ding in the eyes of an accountant, and I wasn't sure if he considered *rides a motorcycle* intriguingly sexy or a point against me. "Like we were talking about, I'm pretty busy, so it's hard to keep up on the bookkeeping and tax stuff on my own."

"Oh." His face brightened. "I'd be happy to help out. Or answer questions and give advice if you prefer your privacy. Partnerships can be problematic."

"Well, I have a partner."

Tyler waved a dismissive hand. "That doesn't mean you have to use an LLP. With an S-Corp, it's treated as a separate legal entity, so if the company incurs debt or is sued, your personal assets aren't at risk to pay off claims." He started to go into more on the advantages and disadvantages of the entities but must have remembered the coffees, for he pointed to the one on my side of the table. "Sorry, I forgot. Your sister said you like caramel mochas, so I got you one."

"Thanks. They *are* one of my favorites. I—" I halted, sensing and catching sight of someone magical. Sarrlevi.

He wasn't walking up but leaning against the railing near the entrance to the outdoor dining area, as if he'd been there for a while. Like the stalker he was. Hell.

He wore the same black outfit that he'd been dressed in the night before, though *he* didn't appear dirty and rumpled. He never did, even when dragons were breathing fire at him. His short blond hair was clean and his face shaven, but I wondered if the clothes indicated he hadn't been to the house he'd mentioned and had camped somewhere in Seattle.

Tyler, noticing my gaze wasn't on him, stopped talking about corporate entities and turned to look.

"Sorry." I gripped his arm, trying to draw his attention back, though it seemed inevitable that Sarrlevi would come to the table. If he'd intended to do nothing but eavesdrop, he wouldn't have dropped his camouflage.

"Who is *that* guy?" a teenage girl at the table behind us whispered, and I didn't have to look to know she meant Sarrlevi.

The black clothing on a sunny day, not to mention the swords on his back, would have stood out even if his striking features hadn't.

"I don't know," her female friend said, "but I'd *like* to know."

They shared giggles.

The memory of the morning's dream came to mind, but I scowled and shook my head. I was not going to fantasize about Sarrlevi while I was on a date with another man. Even if I couldn't control what my libido stirred up in my sleep, I was awake now.

Tyler frowned and turned back to me. "Looks like a weirdo," was his opinion.

The teenagers giggled again and gazed dreamily at Sarrlevi while sipping their whipped-cream-topped coffee drinks.

"Yeah." I asked if there were any tax advantages to S-Corps, hoping to get Tyler talking again about something he cared about, while silently asking Sarrlevi, *What are you doing here?*

Not wanting him to miss the question, I formed the tunnel in my mind and willed the words to project telepathically.

Surprisingly, he winced. *Your next lesson will have to be how to modulate the effort you put into telepathy so that you can be heard by dragons two miles away but don't shout into the minds of people right next to you.*

Sorry, but why are you here? I'm busy for another hour or so.

Two if I let Tyler continue on about business entities and taxes. No, I wouldn't let this go on that long. I already felt guilty about going on a date when Tinja was ill.

I spent the night questioning locals in the magical community, attempting to find more leads that could point us to your mother. This morning, I stopped by your domicile to make sure you were well—it concerns me how many people are targeting you—and you were not there. Sarrlevi gazed coolly at the back of Tyler's head.

What, did he think Tyler was the reason I hadn't been home? As if, as soon as we'd returned, I'd rushed off in the middle of the night to have sex with someone?

I left to acquire food and attend a meeting with someone, Sarrlevi continued, *and when I returned, you still weren't at your domicile. If not for your hammer, I might not have sensed you here.*

A tragedy that would have been.

Tinja drank one of the bottles, I explained. *I took her to Val's—to the vampire alchemist living in her basement. He confirmed the soda had a sneaky magical poison in it, and he's taken a blood sample to study and hopefully figure out a way to help her.* Zoltan had *better* be able to help Tinja. *She's starting to get sick,* I added.

Ah.

I doubted he'd noticed Tinja hadn't been at the house and had grown concerned about *her.*

Just as I had the thought, Sarrlevi surprised me by saying. *I regret that she was brought into what is likely Barothla's scheme. That any of you have come to her awareness.*

Thanks. I nodded at something Tyler said, making a valiant effort to pay attention to him while talking with Sarrlevi, though I would be in trouble if he quizzed me on business entities later. *I don't suppose you can ask Barothla what she used and if there's an antidote. If she's not pure evil, and I hope she's not, maybe she'll feel bad that she poisoned the wrong person.*

Sarrlevi didn't answer immediately, and I worried that meant Barothla *was* pure evil and gleefully went around poisoning people willy-nilly. *I can attempt to get a message to her. As I've mentioned, I'm not any more welcome—or permitted—in the dwarven court than I am the elven one, so I can't show up at her door.*

You wouldn't have to sleep with anyone to get that message delivered, would you? I sure hoped he was done with the elf ex-princess after she'd brought dragons down on his doorstep.

Would it bother you if I did?

I blinked. Was that a yes? That he *would*?

It would bother me if you were doing it on my behalf and not because you wanted to. Okay, it would bother me if he slept with other women *regardless* of the reason, but I wouldn't admit that. *It would really bother me if you had sex with* her. An image of the smug Princess Barothla came to mind, and I didn't hesitate to share it with him.

His gaze flicked to the back of Tyler's head again, and his eyebrows twitched. *Implying what?*

She's not my type, was all Sarrlevi said.

I didn't think the arrogant elf ladies were either. More because they manipulated him than because they weren't stunningly beautiful.

Not so much anymore.

Tyler glanced over his shoulder, and I realized I hadn't been doing a good job of not looking at Sarrlevi while we spoke telepathically. I'd probably missed a question from Tyler.

"Sorry. I know him. I'm trying to get him to go away, but..." I trailed off, feeling guilty, because I *hadn't* been trying to get him to go away. Maybe I should have been, especially since he'd shown up on my date like a stalker, but if there was any way he could reach Barothla and find out how to cure what she'd done, I had to ask.

Tyler opened his mouth, who knew what reply on his mind, but he didn't utter it, for Sarrlevi walked toward us.

What are you doing? I made a shooing motion with my hand. *I'm on a date.*

His eyebrows rose again, a hint of a knowing smirk curving his lips, as if he was sure I'd rather be with *him*. The dream reared up in my mind again, damn it.

I acquired a lead that might be worth investigating further. Your military employer may have more information on this, but I intend to visit the ship tonight when it arrives.

"Can we help you?" Tyler asked, craning his neck to look up at Sarrlevi, who'd stopped beside him and was gazing at me with his usual intensity. I'd grown accustomed to it, but maybe it was alarming to outsiders. Or maybe *he* was alarming.

What ship? I asked silently, then did introductions, because I felt obligated to with Sarrlevi looming over Tyler. "Tyler, this is Varlesh Sarrlevi. He's from Sweden." Since I'd decided to wait for the second date to mention the magical community and my place in it, Sweden seemed like a reasonable explanation for him. "Visiting the US for a while. Sarrlevi, this is Tyler Rochefort, a friend of my brother-in-law's."

Sarrlevi looked down at Tyler. "Accountant, stock options."

Hell, *that* was what he remembered from the call I'd had with Penina in front of him?

"What?" Tyler turned a flustered look on me.

It was my turn for embarrassment to flush my cheeks pink. "Penina mentioned you work for a tech company and get stock options. It's nothing *I* care about, but I guess she thought it would make you seem more..."

Tyler's eyebrows rose.

"Like a good idea," I finished lamely, certain he wouldn't appreciate that my sister had tried to set this up at least in part because he was financially well-off.

"It wasn't already apparent?" Tyler sounded more amused than annoyed but warier than he had been before the comment.

I sighed. "No, it was."

I frowned at Sarrlevi and made another shooing motion.

He pulled a slip of paper out of a pocket and placed it on the table in front of me. "I'll wait for you to finish."

He headed back to the edge of the outdoor dining area and took up his stance leaning against the railing again. I gave him an exasperated look, but he'd folded his arms over his chest and was watching the pedestrians and street traffic rather than me.

"Please tell me that's not his phone number." Tyler eyed the paper.

I read it. It held the address for the North Lake Marina, not a phone number. "Not unless he's taken up residence on a wharf."

Tyler lifted his gaze to mine. "Your sister said you weren't seeing anyone."

"I'm not," I said, though the memory of Sarrlevi's kiss the night before, and the even steamier one after the battle on the mountainside, rose up in my mind, as if to call me a liar. "He's just..." I groped for an explanation.

"A bad idea?" The corner of Tyler's mouth quirked up.

"For so many reasons, yes."

"Well." He glanced over his shoulder and shook his head when he saw where Sarrlevi had stopped. "All right, then. It was nice seeing you. Call me if you want to go out again. Or if you want tax advice." Something about the way his mouth twisted suggested he might have past girlfriends who called him solely for that reason.

"I will. Thank you for the coffee. I really do appreciate it."

"No problem." After another look at Sarrlevi, Tyler headed off in the other direction.

I groaned and clunked my forehead on the table before grabbing the mocha and walking toward Sarrlevi. A big part of me wanted to tell him off, but it was possible he *had* come by because he'd been worried. He knew someone was trying to poison me, after all. Though I suspected his concern had partially been prompted by his finding a lead and wanting my—or Willard's—help in refining it.

A smug smile flirted with his lips as I approached, as if he'd known I would ditch *accountant, stock options* for him. It made me want to flatten his nose with my fist.

"What happens at the marina?" I asked, waving the paper instead.

"A troll-owned barge docks there and is coming in tonight. It reputedly makes trips from Russia to Seattle and back, carrying commodities and ingredients for witches, herbalists, alchemists, and others in the magical community. They sometimes help orcs, ogres, and trolls who wish to relocate to this country do so. I have learned that such beings are not welcome on your commercial aircraft."

"It's tough to get tusks past TSA." I set the mocha cup on the railing so I could push my hands through my hair. "What does a troll barge have to do with my parents?"

"Last month, someone going to pick up some ingredients from them late at night saw humans in camouflage uniforms operating a *forklift*—" Sarrlevi said the word carefully, probably not familiar with the machine, "—that removed a crate from their cargo hold. They loaded it onto a helicopter, then boarded and flew away. The person—a half-dwarf enchanter—said the crate was filled with magical items and that the large helicopter was also magical. He could tell it had been enchanted by a dwarf."

"A half-dwarf enchanter? I didn't know you knew of such people here on Earth."

"I did not, but I went to Thorvald's coffee shop and asked around to see if anyone knew of enchanters. I'd heard a half-troll enchanter works there and thought of her for you, but she was surly, already had an apprentice, and was not using the same type of magic that dwarves would use."

"Most of my teachers have been surly. That's not a deal-breaker for me."

"Are they surly before or after you interrupt them while they're explaining something?"

"Ha ha." I swatted him.

"When the troll mongrel mentioned a half-dwarf enchanter in the city, I thought that might be better. It was luck that he knew of this barge and had seen that cargo being off-loaded. It's not what I went there to ask him about."

"What did you go to ask him about?"

He'd said *for you*. I touched my chest and raised my brows.

Sarrlevi gave me that intense stare again. "As we discussed, you need an instructor to teach you how to use your magic and better defend yourself. Eventually, perhaps one of your own people—a full-blooded dwarf from Dun Kroth—will deign to help you, but it would behoove you to begin learning as soon as possible. With the knowledge and capabilities of an enchanter, you could put excellent protections around your house and also create trinkets such as Thorvald has, trinkets that could assist you against enemies and their harmful magics. And substances."

"I..." I stared at him, not knowing what to say. Had he truly been out hunting around for an instructor for me?

Sarrlevi withdrew a business card from a pocket and gave it to me. "I've arranged payment, and, should you two find each other agreeable, the half-dwarf will instruct you a couple of days a week." He smirked. "Perhaps because of his gender, he finds coin acceptable and doesn't insist that I pay him in sexual favors."

"That's a first. Does your allure not work on men?"

"Rarely. Like your accountant, they're more predisposed to want to punch me. The presence of my swords usually convinces them not to try."

The swords, the muscles, and the aura of badassness that radiated from him—I didn't think someone had to have magical senses to detect it.

I said none of that out loud, not wanting to stroke his ego. "I appreciate you finding me a teacher."

I vowed to pay for this enchanter's services on my own, but I was touched that Sarrlevi had made the effort. I looked into his eyes, expecting to find some calculation there, or maybe accustomed to brushing off his acts of kindness with the certainty that he had an ulterior motive, such as wanting to keep me alive so he could continue using me to find my mother. It was possible that was at the heart of this, but it was getting harder to file everything he did away as that. Especially when I remembered his tender kiss from the night before.

"It's because you need me to survive long enough to help you find my mother, right?" I asked.

When Sarrlevi opened his mouth, it looked like he might object, but he smiled faintly and said, "Of course," instead.

I snorted and leaned against him. He wrapped his arms around me and rested his chin on my head.

"You're definitely a bad idea," I murmured, certain he'd heard every word of my conversation with Tyler.

"Yes," he said agreeably. "You'll come with me to the troll barge tonight to question them?"

"Yeah."

"Maybe there will be another cargo that your mother's captors intend to pick up."

"I would like to capture one of those camoed guys alive to question."

"To *mind scour*," Sarrlevi said coolly.

Though I wouldn't usually wish that on anyone, I wouldn't stop him if he wanted to rip information out of the mind of one of the people behind my parents' kidnappings.

My phone rang, and I groaned when I saw the caller, reminded of Val's warning.

"It's Willard," I said, stepping back.

"She may have more information on the troll barge," Sarrlevi said.

"If some footage of our prison incursion leaked out, she may want to have us both arrested."

Though Sarrlevi didn't reply, he did lift his chin, and his eyes said he doubted anyone on Earth could successfully *arrest* him. Unfortunately, I didn't have that confidence when it came to me. Besides, I couldn't leave the planet whenever I wished. This was my home.

"Yes, Colonel?" I answered warily.

"Come to my office. Is Sarrlevi with you?"

"Uh." I looked at him to see if he cared if I admitted that, but his haughty expression did not change to give me a clue. "Yes."

"Imagine my surprise," Willard growled. "Bring him too."

His eyes narrowed.

"I'll try." I didn't presume I could force him to do anything he didn't wish. "Uhm, now?"

"Yes, now." She hung up.

Willard was usually brusque, except when she was sarcastically busting Val's chops, but that had been terse, even for her.

I sighed. "Will you come?"

"You will agree to meet the half-dwarf instructor later? And will still accompany me to the troll vessel?"

"Yes." I would have done those things regardless of whether he came with me to Willard's office but didn't say so.

Sarrlevi nodded. "I will come. The military colonel will *not* arrest me."

"Not unless she has a dragon for backup, I'm sure."

He scoffed, though it was more likely because he didn't think a dragon would assist a mundane human than because he didn't fear their kind. At the least, he knew to be wary around dragons.

Hopefully, he wouldn't have to worry about that.

16

WHEN I'D CHOSEN TO RIDE MY MOTORCYCLE TO THE COFFEE SHOP, I hadn't intended to pick up a passenger there. Especially not one I was attracted to. With the Harley seat forcing us into even more of an intimate position than riding on Zavryd's back had, I struggled to keep memories of the previous night's dreams—of *many* previous nights' dreams—out of my mind.

Fortunately, Sarrlevi merely rode behind me, his hands resting lightly on my hips. The roar of the Harley combined with the noise from the freeway traffic didn't offer the romantic ambiance of a nocturnal dragon ride. I also had to worry about the police seeing us and pulling me over since my passenger didn't have a helmet.

This seat is less uncomfortable than the one in your larger conveyance, he said as I took the freeway exit toward Willard's office.

The truck is for hauling things around for work. Remembering his critique of my telepathy, I attempted to project my words with only minimal mental thrust. *This is what I ride if I'm going greater distances or just for enjoyment.*

It is like a noisy, vibrating evinya.

Those are the big birds your people ride, right? I remembered him mentioning them once when I'd told him to *hold his horses.*

Yes.

I would love to see one. Perhaps not ride one unless they're a lot more sedate than dragons.

They are domesticated and easier to handle than dragons. If you ever visit the elven world, you will likely see them. My people make their homes in the trees and must fly or levitate to the platforms. He shared an image of a city of wooden homes built into branches—maybe magically sculpted from the living wood itself?—and connected by platforms and rope bridges. No, *vine* bridges.

That doesn't look like the kind of place a dwarf would be comfortable.

When dwarves visit, they tend to stay far from the edges and look nervously at the branches when stiff winds come up.

How do elves feel about visiting dwarves in their tunnels?

We look nervously at the ceilings of their underground cities and have nightmares about cave-ins.

Dwarves are good engineers, right? I would hope cave-ins are rare.

They are, and they use their magic to enchant everything to add further support. His telepathic tone turned dry. *That doesn't keep elves from being uneasy in their cities and vice versa.*

I guess dwarves and elves don't hook up often.

It is an atypical pairing. When it does happen, they often compromise by living on the ground.

Oh, like normal *people?* We were stopped at a light, so I could smirk back at him.

The people of this world are anything but normal. Sarrlevi gave me a pointed look. *They don't even like exquisite elven vegetables.*

Ha ha.

As I navigated onto the street with Willard's building, I decided the ride had been nice. Having a light conversation with him that wasn't about my mother or his quest—or the crazy dangerous and manipulative people in his life—had some appeal. He hadn't even teased me.

I do not sense any dragons, Sarrlevi said as I parked.

I guess you're not going to be arrested then.

He rested a hand on my shoulder before sliding off. *I will not allow you to be arrested either.*

Thanks. I decided not to go into how resisting arrest was also a crime here.

The crater that had been the result of Sarrlevi and Zavryd's duel a few weeks earlier had been filled in and was roped off with tape and signs that warned us to stay off the freshly seeded grass. Since Willard's office wasn't supposed to draw attention to itself, as evinced by the IRS plaque and utter lack of anything mentioning the US Army, I stopped and stared at a surprising sign hanging from the tape. It featured a hand-painted cartoon dragon inside a red circle with a slash over it. Not able to imagine Willard painting such a thing, I decided Gondo had been responsible.

"Well," I said, "we know what's keeping the dragons away."

"Yes, I'm certain Zavryd'nokquetal is sharply deterred by such signage."

The door to Willard's outer office stood open, and Gondo was inside, speaking on the phone. Though he sat on the desk instead of in the chair, I almost praised him for engaging in the work Willard had doubtless hired him for, but he was describing the goblin seating capacity and refreshments available at the Coffee Dragon to someone, so it was possible he was doing something for himself instead of his Army secretarial duties.

He waved at me, though his hand froze in the air when Sarrlevi followed me in. Gondo had to have expected Sarrlevi this time, but he still wilted and glanced downward, as if he was thinking of hiding under the desk.

You don't threaten him when you walk by, do you? I knocked on

Willard's door, her muffled voice audible inside. It sounded like she was on the phone with someone too. Not ordering party favors for the Coffee Dragon, I assumed.

I only look balefully at him, as I do all goblins.

Why?

"One minute," Willard called through the door.

To ensure they don't bother any of my belongings if they ever chance by my camp when I'm not in it.

Does that work?

It does.

Maybe you could teach me the baleful look so I can use it on Tinja while standing in front of my kitchen appliances. I started to smile until I remembered where Tinja was and that her life was in danger. After this meeting, I would call Val to check on my roommate.

You can't be effectively baleful when you're cute, Sarrlevi said.

I blinked and looked at him, certain he'd never called me cute, or said anything to indicate he found me appealing in any way. Too bad *cute* didn't mean beautiful, striking, or sexy. He probably thought Tinja was cute too.

Instead of asking for clarification, I said, *What about if you're menacingly swinging a big hammer?*

That might assist in emanating bale.

"Uhm, Lady Puletasi?" Gondo asked.

That had me blinking again, and I mouthed, "*Lady?*"

"I'm not sure of your correct title," Gondo said. "You're not a boss, so you're not a work leader, and you're the daughter of a princess, but you're not a full-blood or an heir. Among equals, goblins don't use honorifics, but you're..." He eyed my weapon. "You have a big hammer. I am not certain if we are equal."

"She likes it when you call her *plumber,*" Sarrlevi said, a glint in his eyes. "Plumber Puletasi."

Thanks so much, I told him silently, *for managing to go a whole hour without teasing me.*

That was far too long. I feared you felt distressingly bereft. He tousled my hair and smirked.

I should have been indignant, but my body always wanted to lean into his touch, no matter what stupid smirk accompanied it, and I hoped his hand lingered.

"Oh, plumber." Gondo brightened. "Such a noble trade. All building trades are noble. I heard you have a lovely enchanted table that you built. We could use enchanted tables at the Coffee Dragon. The current ones are somewhat susceptible to rowdy patrons. Dimitri and Inga have done some improvements, but they are merely tables at their core, not great slabs of wood with heft that are capable of deterring drunken ogres that pound hard when they lose at games."

"I've heard the caffeinated goblins are more of a problem at that establishment," Sarrlevi said dryly, turning his tousling into combing his fingers through my hair to straighten it—or possibly to make me wish we were somewhere private so I could ask exactly what he'd meant by *cute.*

"If you are seeking table-building-and-enchanting work, perhaps I could speak with the owners," Gondo said. "They adore me."

"I'd better get some lessons from a real enchanter before I put that on my business card." Besides, beyond crafting things for my own home, I was more interested in building houses than tables. I wished all this madness could end, that I could find my mother, and, after a nice visit with her, I could start on the project Abbas and I had been discussing. We needed to put in an offer on that lot soon if we were going to.

"I heard your goblin roommate is ill," Gondo said. "Do you think she would like a gift?"

"Val gave her a box of scrap parts to play with," I said.

"That *is* a perfect goblin gift. Does she like coffee? Perhaps I should bring her some. Her family does not live in the city, correct? She may long for the company of another cultured and urbane goblin such as myself."

"I don't know if she's up for company, but she does drink coffee."

"Excellent, Plumber Puletasi."

I sighed at Sarrlevi.

He smirked again. *It has to be better than being called Ruin Bringer.*

I don't know about that. With a title like that, Val probably manages to be effectively baleful.

The door opened, and I jumped, more because Sarrlevi's hand was resting on the back of my head than because I hadn't expected Willard. She'd hung up her phone and come to open the door personally. The more effective to scowl at me, I was sure. She also scowled at Sarrlevi and his hand.

He brushed his fingers through my hair once more before lowering it, his humor fading and his usual cool and aloof expression returning as he looked at Willard.

"How much trouble am I in?" I asked, though Willard was scowling more ferociously at Sarrlevi than me as she waved us inside and shut the door firmly.

"*You* weren't the one caught on camera down there." She rotated an open laptop on the desk so we could see the screen.

"I wasn't?" I asked in surprise.

Willard brought up camera footage from the prison, not the interior camera beside the back door that I'd noticed and worried about but an exterior camera focused on the courtyard. And a battle going on out front.

Smoke obscured the combatants, but the angle gave a clear view of a tall blond elf in black cutting down enemies with the power of a tornado. The angle did *not* give clear views of his enemies' faces. The men and orcs that had come down from the helicopters wore helmets or hats and camouflage, and could have been, as far as the footage showed, soldiers.

"The Army *and* the police have seen this and have an arrest warrant out for an unknown person fitting your description," Willard told Sarrlevi.

"But not for me?" I touched my chest.

"No. I assume *you* weren't foolish enough to leap into a fray on the doorstep of the building."

Indignation flashed in Sarrlevi's eyes.

I lifted a hand. "He was buying me time to find my father. And it would have worked, but those guys—" I pointed to the men Sarrlevi had been fighting, "—blew a hole in the side of the building before I reached his cell. I got to hear his voice once as he called my name—" I had to pause for a breath as the angst and frustration of the night returned, "—but that's it. I didn't even get to see him."

"*Those* are the criminals that killed your soldiers." Sarrlevi also pointed to the figures in camouflage. "They are who your police should be chasing."

"*They're* all dead," Willard told him. "Along with eight soldiers who were stationed in the facility."

"I killed only the infiltrators who attacked us. Others got away."

"Leaving no wounded behind." Willard shook her head in disgust. "Since you left only bodies, the MPs who showed up didn't find anyone left to question."

"Two helicopters like we fought on the mountain arrived to take their survivors and my father away," I said, distressed that it sounded like Sarrlevi might get blamed for all the deaths. It wasn't as if he had a record here on Earth or the authorities would be able to identify him, but if he was waylaid by the police every time he showed up at a coffee shop or anywhere else, that would be inconvenient.

"Yes, I've already questioned Val about what her dragon was up to last night." Judging by Willard's continuing disgust, she wouldn't have authorized Zavryd's assistance if she'd known about it in advance. "He said he took down a helicopter. We have only his word because by the time soldiers went out there to look for the wreck, they found evidence of a crash but not the actual craft that went down. I don't know how someone got that huge helicopter out of there, especially if it was as utterly destroyed as Zav said."

"Magic." Sarrlevi shrugged, as if moving a helicopter would be a simple matter.

"You—" Willard pointed at Sarrlevi, "—had better go back to your world. It's a miracle Puletasi wasn't caught on footage in any of that, but if she's seen *with* someone who's wanted by the authorities, it won't go well for her."

"I am capable of camouflaging myself from your law enforcers."

"If you're so great at camouflaging yourself, how come you were caught on camera?" Willard asked.

"Engaging in battle breaks the illusion, that which perpetrates the camouflage."

"Aren't you *always* in battle?"

"Only when he's helping me," I said. "Which is unfortunately more often than I'd like. But that's not his fault. The world—at least *my* world—has gotten crazy lately. And he's been amazing about helping me these past weeks. He shouldn't be punished or *glared* at for that." I flung a hand toward the laptop, though the footage had stopped playing.

Willard shook her head again as she looked at me, her expression more pitying than angry now. Why, because she thought Sarrlevi was playing me?

I glowered, imagining her and Val talking about how I was falling for Sarrlevi and not being rational when it came to him. But that wasn't true. I knew I couldn't trust him 100 percent. That didn't mean it wasn't worth keeping him around. And being decent to him. He *deserved* decency.

Sarrlevi stepped closer to me, his chest brushing the back of my shoulder as he stared at Willard. "I will remain on this world and continue my quest. Mataalii will continue to assist me."

Willard's pity turned to exasperation.

I spread my hands. "We're all looking for the same person. It makes sense for us to keep working together."

"I just want to find her reactor," Willard muttered. "And to figure out who's stealing artifacts and hoarding them and why."

"I hope you'll forgive me if I care more about finding my mother. And we have a new lead. *Sarrlevi* found a lead." I willed her to realize how helpful he'd been and told her about the troll barge.

She didn't appear impressed, nor did she beam warmth at Sarrlevi. I hoped she didn't think he had killed any of the soldiers in the prison fiasco. That had *not* been complete footage of everything that had happened.

"That sounds like last month's lead," Willard said, "but you can check it out. You and *Thorvald* can go check it out. You don't need him."

"*I* will also go," Sarrlevi stated.

"Why do *you* have to be involved in this?" Willard asked him.

"It was my quest before Mataalii even believed her mother still alive. I will complete it."

Willard opened her mouth, but Sarrlevi cut her off.

"And *I* do not care about the dwarven energy source. We are not at cross-purposes, human."

Willard squinted at him. "You sure you're not at cross-purposes with Puletasi?"

Sarrlevi hesitated. It was a very short hesitation before he said, "We seek the same person," but I caught it.

And once more, I felt uneasy about the assignment he'd once been given. And that my aunt still wanted him to complete?

"Uh huh." Willard gave me a significant look, and I nodded to let her know I wasn't unaware of the danger Sarrlevi represented, even if I liked him touching my hair and using my birth name. "There will be security cameras at that marina," she said, pinning Sarrlevi with her gaze again.

"We'll be careful to avoid them," I told her. "As we were in the prison, until those other guys showed up."

"Puletasi…" Willard rubbed her face.

My phone rang, Val's number popping up. "Hold on. This may be about my roommate." I didn't know if Val had told her boss about the poisoning, but I could explain later. "Yes?" I answered.

"Zoltan has an update for you," Val said. "He thinks he has a formula he can make that will cure Tinja, but there are a couple of ingredients he doesn't have."

"Are they something I can get? I'm happy to stop at any market in the greater Seattle area."

"They're not going to be found at any market in the greater *Earth* area."

17

RAIN FELL AS I NAVIGATED TRAFFIC AND TOOK THE BACKSTREETS toward Val's house in Green Lake. Once again, Sarrlevi rode behind me. I was relieved he'd been too obstinate to consider leaving when Willard told him to. I needed him. I hadn't even glared at him when Gondo had said, "Goodbye, Plumber Puletasi," as we'd left the office.

Val had said Zoltan would write down the special ingredients his formula required and that Tinja wanted to see me. Fortunately, if the troll barge didn't arrive until nightfall, we had plenty of time. Of course, I would drop that lead if necessary to focus solely on collecting whatever Zoltan needed to help Tinja.

After parking in front of Val's house, I grabbed my hammer, hopped off the motorcycle, and took several steps up the walkway before remembering the home's defenses. Among other things, the topiary dragons, with their glowing crimson eyes and smoldering nostrils, would attack Sarrlevi if he stepped foot on the property.

"I'll ask Val to lower the defenses so you can come in," I said.

"She will not do that." From the sidewalk, Sarrlevi clasped his hands behind his back and nodded that he would wait. "Bring me the list of ingredients that can't be acquired on Earth, and I will attempt to find them."

"I..." The offer didn't surprise me, but, for once, I couldn't brush it off as something he would do only because it furthered his goal of keeping me alive and finding my mother. My roommate's life meant a lot to me but had nothing to do with his mission. With emotion swelling in my throat, I ran back and hugged him. "Thank you."

"Your gratitude might be premature," Sarrlevi said, patting me on the back. "Depending on the list, the items may be difficult for even a well-traveled and capable assassin to acquire."

"I hope they aren't, but I appreciate you being willing to help regardless." I rose on tiptoes to kiss him on the cheek. Technically, more the jaw since even tiptoes couldn't give me the height to reach his cheek, but he did bend to make the gap less substantial and touched the back of my head.

I would have run around the house to the basement, but Val opened the front door and waved for me to join her inside.

"Zoltan is sleeping," she said, nodding toward the daylight sky, "but he said to wake him up if you're able to get everything."

"How's Tinja doing?"

"She's stopped tinkering with the junk-box items and is in bed."

"Stopped tinkering?" Fresh unease crept into my gut. "She must feel lousy."

"I think so."

Val closed the door once we were inside, and I sensed her roommate Dimitri in the dining room. Neither Zavryd nor Freysha was in the house, but I also sensed Tinja upstairs in the room she'd been given.

In a quieter voice, Val said, "Zoltan believes she has a couple of days but not much longer."

I rocked back, bumping my hammer against a shelf full of magical knickknacks. They rattled, and one flashed at me in protest, but I barely noticed. I'd been afraid the poison would be deadly, but I'd *hoped* it wouldn't be.

"You haven't seen the person who delivered the poisoned sodas, have you?" Val asked.

"The person responsible for the delivery? No. Not since I refused to help her find my mother. That was before the poisoning."

"You're sure it's her? Your mom's sister, you said, right?" Val fished something out of her pocket. A list with two items circled.

I would give that to Sarrlevi. "I'm not sure, no, but she's an alchemist, and she paid me a visit the same day the sodas arrived."

Val nodded. "Zoltan did think it was the work of another alchemist. He also said that the dosage he believes was in the soda might not have been deadly to someone larger. She might not have meant to kill you."

"Just make me cripplingly sick?"

"Something like that. You said you refused to work with her?"

"Yeah."

"It might have been meant more as a message than a murder."

"If it kills Tinja, I'll give *her* the message of knocking her conniving head off." I hefted my hammer, wishing there were something around for me to smash. I longed to take out my aggressions.

Val steered me away from her shelves of knickknacks and held out the list. Most of the items had checkmarks by them. "Zoltan has an extensive collection in his lab and has these items. The circled two are all that he needs."

"The venomous tail of a manticore and... two drops of blood from the person who crafted the poison?" I grimaced.

"Yeah. You better make sure your auntie really did make it before you stab her."

My auntie. Right.

"I admit, I have no idea where to find a manticore, even though I've used substances made from their venom before. When Zav gets back, maybe he'll know." Val dug an empty vial and syringe out of her pocket and also a large plastic zip baggie reinforced with magic. "Make sure not to touch the tail. Dwarf blood ought to be safe to touch, other than the fact that the owner may kick your ass when you attempt to take it."

"I have no doubt." I wasn't even sure how I would find her. *Sarrlevi?*

Yes? he answered promptly.

Val waved for me to follow her upstairs to see Tinja.

Do you know where manticores live? I need one of their tails.

They're rare creatures and not simple to find or kill, but I do know which worlds and which forests they're native to.

Good. I can come with you to help battle one as soon as I see Tinja. But, uhm, there's one other ingredient I'll need assistance getting. The blood of the alchemist who made the potion. Two drops.

Sarrlevi was silent for a long time, and I worried he would say that would be impossible to get. If Barothla was back in the protected dwarven city, and he couldn't get in, there might be no hope. Or if Sarrlevi was, as I still feared, an ally of hers, he might not be willing to attack her and subdue her long enough for a blood draw. It also sounded like she was powerful enough that he might struggle to get through her defenses even if he *were* willing to attack her.

Even worse, if Sarrlevi attacked King Ironhelm's daughter, would the dragons get involved again? I had no idea how the Dragon Council felt about her. Zondia had mentioned that my mother would be a preferable heir, but that didn't mean the dragons would be blasé about an assassin they were already irked with attacking the back-up heir from their chosen line of rulers.

As the silence went on, I worried. We'd reached Tinja's door, and Val knocked lightly.

Let me retrieve the manticore tail, Sarrlevi finally said, *and I'll consider how I might acquire her blood.*

Don't you want me to come along to help? You said manticores are dangerous, right? I know you're a badass, but I can help. I squeezed the haft of my hammer. *You know I can.*

I do know that, but it could take some time to hunt one down. I would prefer you meet the troll barge when it arrives and continue our quest.

Okay.

It seemed a fair tradeoff. *More* than a fair tradeoff, as the trolls wouldn't try to sting me with a venomous tail.

"One sec, Val." I held up a finger, then ran back down the stairs.

As I opened the front door, I sensed a portal already forming. *I have something for you,* I told Sarrlevi.

He'd moved into the intersection, the glowing silver disc hovering in the air before him, but he paused to look at me. *Another kiss?*

A baggie for the tail and a syringe for the blood. Kisses aren't appropriate, right?

He smiled sadly. *They are not.*

If he hadn't said that, I might have kissed him on the jaw again, to say thanks and for luck, but his face had grown grave. Something told me that my musings had been on point and that he would get in trouble—maybe a *lot* of trouble—if he tried to steal some of Barothla's blood.

"Be careful, please," I said as he accepted the items. "And thank you for doing this."

Sarrlevi bowed to me, then sprang through the portal. It and he disappeared.

Not wanting to keep Tinja waiting, I hurried back inside.

Val was speaking with her, explaining that something called the *Goblin Fuel* blend might not be appropriate for a sick person, but she stepped out when I arrived and waved me in.

"Hey." I navigated past clutter on the floor, half-assembled projects next to an empty box labeled *junk*, and sat on the edge of the bed.

Sweat dampened Tinja's usually fluffy white hair, and her pointed ears had an uncharacteristic droop. Her green fingers gripped blankets pulled close to her chin, as if she were cold. Green goblin skin didn't seem to get pale, like human flesh, but she didn't look good.

A lump in my throat made it hard to say more. "I heard you wanted to see me," I managed.

"I need something, Matti." Tinja put a can of ginger ale, a bendy straw thrusting from the hole, on the nightstand and clasped my wrist.

"Some homework picked up? Books? Tools? A smoothie?" I glanced at what looked like the goblin version of a gift basket on the nightstand: an apple crate filled with springs, broken strips of metal, empty soda cans, and two frisbees, the sides chewed by dogs. Several Kit Kats, one bar already devoured, and two bags of roasted Goblin Fuel coffee were the only items I might deem normal.

"My homework is all online, and Val picked up my laptop for me."

I couldn't keep from wincing, feeling I should have been there to pick it up, instead of having coffee with Tyler. That had been an admittedly short date, but I could have called to ask Tinja if she needed anything while I was at the house.

"I'm glad," I made myself say, and I was. It still boggled my mind that the *Ruin Bringer*, someone I'd spent a long time avoiding because the magical community swore she was cruel and evil, was a decent person. Even her haughty dragon mate was kind of okay.

"I need something much more important from you, Matti."
Tinja gazed solemnly into my eyes. "I may die."

"You're not going to die. Zoltan found a formula that can fix
you up. Didn't they tell you? We're gathering the ingredients now."

"Difficult-to-acquire ingredients, yes?"

I hesitated. "There are a couple that are challenging, but
Sarrlevi is helping." With one, anyway. I worried about getting
Barothla's blood.

"The assassin? I'm doomed." Without letting go of my wrist,
Tinja flung her free arm over her eyes and dropped her head back
on the pillow.

"You're *not* doomed."

"Because I may be doomed, I must make a request from you."

I had to fight the urge to keep telling her she would be fine. If
she had a serious request, I had to listen and grant it. If I could.
"Go ahead."

"While I've been lying here wasting away, I've realized that the
best way to sell my tiny-home plans would be to have a demo
model of an actual tiny home."

"Oh?" I watched her warily, hoping her dying wish wasn't
going to be for me to build one, though I supposed I would.

"Yes. And then I could record videos and put them on YouTube
and establish a vast following and have *free advertising* for my tiny-
home-plan empire."

"Have you been talking to Zoltan?"

"Obviously." Tinja lowered her arm and winked. "I'm his
patient."

"I'm not sure *patient* is the correct term when an alchemist is
taking your blood and experimenting on you."

"But my plan is good, isn't it? You told me I must learn to
market on a *shoestring budget*. Zoltan doesn't spend any money,
and he has legions of followers who buy what he creates."

I hadn't seen his channel and didn't want to, but I suspected his legions of followers had arrived because he was handsome, if in a pasty kind of way, and had an exotic accent. Even so, I nodded encouragement to Tinja. "It does sound like a good idea."

"Yes. So you will help me build a tiny home in your backyard?" She beamed a smile at me.

"You're milking this illness, Tinja."

"I could *die*." She flung her arm over her face again.

I wished she were being melodramatic and her life weren't truly in danger. "When you're better, I'll help you build a demo tiny home, but maybe not in the backyard. If Abbas and I are able to snag that five-acre property, that would be the place for it."

"That would be acceptable." Tinja squeezed my wrist. "You are a good roommate, Matti. I will let you hang out at the urban goblin sanctuary that I will have constructed for my city-loving people once I'm wealthy."

"Hang out at it or build it?"

"Would you *like* to help me build it? I could hire you. I will have vast human monies when my business becomes successful."

"Let's just do the tiny home first, okay?"

"Yes. This is a good idea." Her smile faltered, and concern crept back into her eyes. "I want to live, Matti, but what ingredients is Sarrlevi getting? I am afraid to owe a favor to an assassin."

"I think *I'll* owe him the favor." I doubted someone who'd dismissed Tinja as a servant the night before would have gone out of his way to collect ingredients for a formula for her.

"I do not think it is good for you to owe an assassin a favor either."

"Probably not." I patted her shoulder. "Do you need anything else? Do you want me to stay for a while?" I kept from glancing at the clock on my phone. It was still daylight, and I had time to hang out with her.

I did need to ponder how I could get Barothla's blood if Sarrlevi wasn't willing to help with that. Zavryd was my only other option, but he'd already balked once when I'd requested he take me to the dwarven court. I suspected he would *really* balk if he saw in my thoughts that I wanted to attack a princess there—or at least subdue her sufficiently enough to draw her blood.

"Come back later," Tinja said. "I am tired now. And I must think about my tiny-home empire."

"All right. Maybe we can have some of the special coffee there when you're better."

"Gondo brought it for me." Tinja smiled shyly at me.

"Is that a good thing?"

"I haven't decided yet."

I patted her shoulder again and stepped outside. Sensing Val in the kitchen, I went down to thank her for watching over Tinja and to see if she wanted to visit the troll barge with me. Willard had told me to take her—and *not* take Sarrlevi.

But when I stepped into the kitchen, Val was on the phone.

"How many hydras are we talking about?" she asked. "And are they *in* the water or accessible from shore? Zav isn't here right now, so I'll have to drive, and I don't have a boat."

I paused in the doorway, not wanting to intrude. Was that an assignment coming in from Willard? Or someone else needing the Ruin Bringer's assistance?

"How did the hydras get here? I've only fought one once before. They're not the typical magical beings that flee to Earth to hide out." Val noticed me and lifted a finger as she listened to the reply. "Ugh, did anyone *see* fae? You know they're not my favorite people to deal with. My chocolate stash is low too." After a pause, Val glanced at her phone. "If traffic isn't horrible, I'll be there in two hours."

"Was that Willard?" I asked when she hung up.

"Yeah. I've got a new assignment. I've got to head up to Deception Pass and lop off some hydra heads. Dimitri should be around to keep an eye on Tinja if you need to leave. He's working on projects at the house today."

"That's good. Thanks."

"How's she doing?" Val pointed toward the guest room.

"I'm a little heartened that she's well enough to scheme."

Val raised her eyebrows.

"Due to her impending death, she got me to promise to turn one of her tiny-home plans into an actual tiny home."

"For someone with a huge hammer and a short temper, you're a softy."

"Yeah." I shrugged and decided not to bring up the troll barge. It sounded like Val would be gone, risking her life for the rest of the day.

"Do you think you can get those ingredients?"

"Sarrlevi said he would hunt down a manticore for me, but I may be on my own when it comes to collecting Barothla's blood."

I was about to ask if Val could talk Zavryd into making a portal for me, but she frowned, lifted her eyebrows, and asked, "Sarrlevi volunteered to get you a manticore tail?"

"He's doing it as we speak."

"I don't think manticores are easy to find. And they're deadly." Val scratched her jaw.

"You don't think he can handle it?" Maybe I should have tried harder to invite myself along.

"He probably can, but..." She frowned thoughtfully at me. "I thought Willard was going to try to get him to leave Earth."

"He didn't want to go."

"Matti..."

"I know I shouldn't trust him, and I don't fully. Nothing has changed, okay? But if he's willing to help out with Tinja's problem, I'm going to let him. I can't even reach Barothla without his help, not unless Zavryd is around and might take me?"

"He had to leave Earth. There's a meeting of the Dragon Council."

Hopefully not one that had anything to do with an elf assassin.

"I'll have to get Sarrlevi to take me to her then," I said. "One way or another."

"I'm not sure if I should hope he keeps helping you or not." Val headed out of the kitchen and toward the front door, gesturing for me to follow. "I want your roommate to make it, but I'm worried about you, Matti." Val grabbed her keys off a hook. "I'd hate to see you wrecked because you found your mother after thirty years only to watch an assassin stick a dagger in her chest and kill her."

I closed my eyes, the graphic image disturbing. "I don't think that's what Sarrlevi plans to do. I mean, I don't *know*, but if all he wanted was for me to lead him to her, he wouldn't have to keep saving my ass."

"If you died, that would make it harder for him to find her."

"I know, but why would he be helping *Tinja* if he meant to screw me over in the end?"

"It could be," Val said slowly, holding open the door for me as we stepped out onto the porch, "that he's helping your friend *because* he means to screw you over."

"I don't follow."

Val shrugged. "Maybe he feels guilty about what he's got planned."

"I highly doubt career assassins are plagued by guilt."

I was tempted to share some of the story that Sarrlevi had told me, about how he wanted to reunite my grandfather and my mother so King Ironhelm would speak fondly of him to the elven king, who might then permit him to visit his mother. But Val would accuse me of being naive if I believed all that. And maybe she wouldn't be wrong.

She shrugged again. "All I'm saying is that he might originally have planned to use you but decided along the way that you're

okay, and now he feels a little bad about what he intends to do."
She hesitated. "Willard said he uses your name now, not *mongrel*."

"So clearly, he's deeply in love with me."

"Clearly," she said dryly.

"Look, I'm not saying there aren't some questions I would ask
him if I knew for certain that he would answer truthfully, just that
I'm aware that he's potentially a threat. I'm not lowering my guard
around him." Never mind that I melted with pleasure when he
rubbed my hair and kissed me. I could melt and keep my guard up
at the same time. Really.

"Good." Val thumped me on the shoulder. "Willard hates to
lose operatives, especially those who call her *ma'am* and don't put
their boots on her desk."

"You'd think a lot of people would be like that with a colonel."

"Oh? Huh."

As Val drove off, I tried not to think about what I would do if
her version of finding my mother came to pass. For the moment, I
needed to worry about curing Tinja, but if one of these leads
panned out, and Sarrlevi and I actually got close to my mother...
Well, I would have to plan for that. I would have to come up with a
way to keep anyone from hurting her once I found her.

I slid my hand into my pocket for the card of the half-dwarven
enchanter. Since Sarrlevi had said the lessons were already paid
for, I would call to set up the first one. I had few delusions about
magic being easy to master, but maybe I could learn enough to
make items that could stave off enemies.

I closed my eyes, not wanting Sarrlevi to be an enemy.

18

If someone had asked me which docks in the greater Seattle area would be most likely to attract troll smugglers, the North Lake Marina in Kenmore wouldn't have been the place. Poised along Lake Washington, not Puget Sound, it attracted private sailboats and yachts. A bicycle trail passed behind it, a nearby park was full of kids and dogs playing on the grass, and well-maintained condos looked out over the marina.

I gripped my chin as I studied the handful of docks, not seeing anything that could be considered a barge, nor sensing any magic. But Sarrlevi had said the trolls were due in that night. Maybe the place got rougher after the sun went down.

Sensing the approach of someone with magical blood, someone with *half-dwarven* magic blood, I turned and waved my hammer.

"Ah, Ms. Puletasi?" The fiftyish man had a tidy gray goatee, mustache, thinning hair, and wore a black polo shirt with the same landscaping logo that was on his business card.

That card had surprised me when I'd looked at it, and I'd

thought Sarrlevi might have grabbed the wrong one, but I supposed one couldn't blatantly announce one's enchanting side hustle. My new mentor carried a similarly logoed canvas tool tote, and I envisioned him teaching me how to enchant hedge clippers so we could have an *Edward Scissorhands* moment.

"Hi. You can call me Matti. And you're Santiago Ortega?" I waved the card, assuming he was the one I'd texted about the appointment. "Sarrlevi didn't actually mention your name."

"He called me mongrel."

"Sorry. He's only recently stopped calling me that too."

"Oh." Santiago tilted his head. "How did you get him to stop?"

"I..." The memory of our first kiss leaped to mind. "I went into battle with him a few times and didn't embarrass myself overmuch."

"I'm not much of a fighter."

"Not even against Himalayan blackberry brambles?" I pointed at the logo on his shirt.

"Not anymore. I have a son and a crew to handle the grunt work. These days, I kick back, answer the phones, and enchant their tools."

Hm. Maybe there *would* be an *Edward Scissorhands* moment. I'd been hoping more for something that could help me travel to other worlds and defeat enemies, but I supposed I could get drops of my aunt's blood by running her over with a magical riding lawnmower.

"I'm not a customer-service type," I said. "I would rather wrestle weeds than answer phones."

"So I gathered when you waved your hammer at me for a greeting." He smiled and offered me his hand. "Yes. I'm Santiago. It's a beautiful hammer. Not from anyone on this world, I gather?"

"My mother made it. I'm not sure when and where but probably not in the apartment my family lived in when I was little."

Santiago blinked, then smiled. "Probably not. There are usually magical forges involved in dwarven weapon-smithing."

As handy as I was, *smithing* wasn't anything I'd ever tried. "Does one need a forge to make useful magical charms?"

"You'll need an enchanted toolset and to learn the basics before you can make much of anything, but I'm highly motivated to help you learn to craft whatever you wish, whatever is in my power to teach anyway."

"Highly motivated? Sarrlevi didn't threaten you, did he?" I frowned. He'd said he'd *paid* the man, but he'd been known to get his way by wrapping his hand around people's throats. "I was surprised when you said you'd come to me for the lessons, starting immediately. I didn't realize... I don't want to inconvenience you, sir."

"He did not threaten me, though I did gather from his weapons, menacing aura, and unsettling stare that such would have been in his repertoire."

"It is." I almost mentioned that Sarrlevi was an assassin, but Santiago already looked a little disturbed. If he was like me, he'd spent his whole life on Earth and didn't know much about the Cosmic Realms or the infamous assassins who worked in them.

"He paid me well. *Very* well. He either likes you a lot, or you rob banks together."

"Uh, no. I flip homes. The only bank involvement is the gouging they do to me on the loan rates."

"I did notice his gold coins weren't stamped by any of the known mints. Known *Earth* mints." Santiago raised his eyebrows.

"Yeah. He's not from around here. I would guess the gold is real though. He's well-off enough to have multiple houses and access to the rarest cheeses in the Cosmic Realms."

That earned me a few slow blinks.

"It's a long story." I smiled, but the talk of gold coins rattled me. How *much* had Sarrlevi paid this guy? I'd assumed I could take over paying the instructor myself—I didn't feel bad about lightening Sarrlevi's pockets of cheese, especially since it was part of our original deal, but I was no gold digger, damn it. But what if Santiago asked for hundreds of dollars—or the precious-metals equivalent—per lesson? "I'm really glad you came, and I'm eager to get started. I would, however, like to handle payment myself going forward. I can give you my phone number or email for invoices, if that works."

"Ah, Ms. Puletasi, the lessons are already paid for. For as long as you want them."

"I can't accept— I mean, he shouldn't have done that."

Why had he done that? Val's warning ran through my mind.

"You will have to discuss that with him, but perhaps we should begin our instruction, and you can decide if we are compatible? I told him I would not cash in any of the coins until we determined that." Santiago smiled. "It was an easy promise to make, because I'll have to do some research about how to cash a large quantity of gold coins from another planet without bringing suspicious authorities to my door."

I rubbed the back of my neck. A large quantity. Hell.

"It's had me flashing back to my youth when I wasn't in this country entirely legally, but I am a citizen now and have built my business and pay my taxes and want no trouble. Maybe I will simply lock them in a box and leave them to my children."

"So *they* can get in trouble?"

"Well, they're kind of pains in the ass." He winked and waved at the grass. "Let us sit, yes? I have brought something for you to practice on."

"Sure." I sat on the grass next to him though I kept an eye toward the marina in case any troll-laden barges that emanated magic docked early.

Santiago opened his tool tote and plucked out a pipe wrench. "I understand you are a plumber?"

I issued something between a snort and a groan as I flopped back on the grass.

"That is not correct?" Santiago asked.

"No, it's fine. I suppose if I could enchant a garbage disposal to never back up or break, my homes would be in high demand. I admit, I'm hoping to learn something that could best a powerful enemy who's got it out for me. Or to heal a sick friend, in case... well, she was poisoned. By an alchemist."

"You sound like you lead an interesting life."

"Tell me about it."

"I'm afraid to say that, as with many things, we must start with the basics before you can enchant useful items. We are also limited by our blood. I have books I've acquired written by dwarves, and I was trained as a boy by my father before he returned with the others to his world, but I could never be as powerful as he was, because I'm only *half* dwarven."

"I don't care about being powerful. I'm just hoping to be able to make useful stuff."

"That can thwart powerful enemies and heal the dying?" Santiago raised his eyebrows.

"Yeah. Is that too much to ask? I wouldn't mind a magical wrench, but..." I spread a hand, needing more. If Sarrlevi couldn't —or wouldn't—get blood from my aunt, I would have to find a way on my own. And I didn't have much time.

Maybe this had been a silly thing to start today. What had I truly expected to learn in the single lesson we had time for?

"I believe you will have the potential to make very good artifacts and tools, should you put in the time to learn, for you have a strong aura for a half-blood. At the least, you can in a few lessons learn to better use the tools you already have." He extended his hand toward my hammer.

That made me sit up with interest. I only knew a few of what could be many power words. What if I could learn the rest of them? And what if something already keyed into the hammer would help me against Barothla?

"I'm very open to that," I said.

"Good. What is the hammer's name?"

"I don't know. My mother didn't wield it a lot when I was in the crib."

His eyebrows rose.

"She's been gone since I was four." I paused. "I *was* out of the crib by then, but not far out. And until the soldiers came to get her... I didn't see her go into battle often."

"Interesting. May I?" Santiago had eyed the hammer a number of times but hadn't presumed to touch it.

I hesitated, always protective about it, especially now, with people gunning for me.

"To look at the runes. They're not all familiar to me, but I can read the ones that are typical in the day-to-day Dwarven language. Some are from ancient texts."

"Yeah. Sorry. People have been trying to steal it from me lately to turn in for a reward." I extended the head, the part engraved with runes, toward him but couldn't bring myself to let go of the haft. "A hundred thousand dollars and an enchanted trinket can entice a lot of thugs."

Santiago merely smiled. "I haven't weighed the gold your friend gave me yet, but I believe I may have already received that reward."

I gaped at him, but he was too busy running his fingers along the runes and scrutinizing the hammer to notice. Sarrlevi had *that* much gold to throw around? Shit, no wonder he'd scoffed at *stock options*. How much did his clients pay him to assassinate people? Or was there some Cosmic Realms stock market where he'd had his money compounding for three hundred years?

Santiago murmured a few words in Spanish before saying,

"She is magnificent," and giving the hammer a pat before handing it back to me.

"It has a sex?"

He chuckled. "I'm not sure, but it may. There is a sentience enchantment underlying many other powerful spells."

"What does that mean? It's—uh, *she's* alive in some way?"

"She has an awareness and intelligence, yes. Should you learn her name, she may even be able to speak with you."

"I..." I didn't know what to say to that, but I remembered the night I'd held one of Sarrlevi's swords. It had shared what I believed had been the memory of one of their battles. "Is that common in magical weapons?"

"Not in the least. Very few enchanters, and only dwarven enchanters as far as I know, have been born over the generations who are capable of crafting such tools. They tend to be treasured and even revered by their people. You say your mother made the hammer?"

"That's what I was told by my grandfather—her father. I guess he would know."

"Indeed. I encourage you to learn the name as soon as possible. If you use it, and the hammer accepts you as her wielder, *she* will be able to tell you all the power words and what she is capable of doing."

"What if she doesn't accept me?" Disappointment thundered in my mind as that seemed not only possible but probable. "I'm only a mongrel, after all."

His eyebrows rose. "Your benefactor believes in your worth. Surely, he would not have invested so much in your education if he did not."

My benefactor? Sarrlevi?

"I'm not sure his *investment* is indicative of anything except..." Val's words rang in my mind again. Guilt. "Well, we have a complicated relationship. And it might not be that much money to him."

"Relationships with deadly men with two swords *do* seem like they would be complicated," Santiago said dryly, "but do not sell yourself short. As I said before, I believe that even as a half-blood, you will have strong potential if you work hard."

"I'm willing to do that."

"Good." Santiago lifted the wrench. "Shall we begin?"

19

Santiago departed at sunset, leaving a rudimentary understanding of how enchanting worked and what it could do in my mind. Also swimming around in there was the information he'd given me on my hammer. Now that I knew it—she—had intelligence, I ached to learn her name. Would my dwarven grandfather know?

A honk came from the marina. Feeling guilty, I checked it again for trolls or other magical beings.

During the lesson, I hadn't paid much attention to the marina, but since Sarrlevi had asked me to watch for the barge—and he was risking his life hunting for a manticore in return—I didn't want to screw up and miss it.

I grimaced as a new feeling toward him blossomed within me, the desire not to disappoint him. It bothered me that he'd given all that gold to Santiago on my behalf, but it also made me not want to waste his money, to genuinely become someone who could craft things that were worth that and more. Maybe I could one day make something for him that would be an equal trade. Were there enchantments I could learn to make his next house dragon-proof?

That seemed unlikely. Besides, if Sarrlevi was gunning for my mother, all I ought to be focused on was making sure he didn't succeed. Based on what Santiago had said, my mother not only meant a lot to me, but she might be a treasure to the entire dwarven kingdom.

I flopped onto my back in the grass, more emotions than I could name tangling in my gut and making me feel a little sick.

A familiar figure stepped into my view, startling me since I hadn't sensed his approach. Only when he stood above me, looking down with a blond eyebrow cocked, did I grow aware of his aura.

Still wearing the black outfit, Sarrlevi was as neat and tidy as always, with no dirt or dust in sight. He wouldn't have appeared like he'd been in a battle, but a fresh gouge on the back of his hand ran up under his sleeve, and the skin was puckered and inflamed along the wound. That hand also gripped the baggie that I'd given him, with what looked like a hacked-up giant scorpion tail inside. Droplets of a viscous liquid dotted the interior of the bag. Venom?

"Your enchanting lesson was tiring?" Sarrlevi looked toward the marina, but only for a moment before returning his gaze to me. He'd probably already checked for trolls and magic.

"Mentally draining, yeah." I rolled to my feet to face him. "Look, Sarrlevi. I really appreciate you helping out and also lining up an instructor for me, but you shouldn't have paid him all that gold. I... I'm an independent kind of person, and I don't like asking people for favors."

"You did not ask."

"I know, but I don't like accepting handouts either. I like to make my own way in the world and not be a burden on anyone. Also, that was a *lot* of money. I can't ever repay it. I mean, maybe I can someday after more years working on my business, but... "

"I am not a bank," he said dryly, "and I was not making a loan."

"I know, and I get it, but..." I gazed into his eyes, so tempted to ask him if he was doing this because he was after my mother and wanted to make amends for that in advance. Make amends to *me*. "You can't kill her, Sarrlevi," I whispered. "Not just because she's my mother, but because... I'm only now realizing how important she is to others. To her people."

His expression didn't change, but he held my gaze instead of looking away. No, he did more than that. The faint itching sensation under my skull told me he was trying to read my mind.

I scowled and was about to tell him off when my phone rang. Normally, during a serious discussion with someone, I would have let it go to voice mail, but I tugged it out, stepped away, and answered before looking at the caller.

Hopefully, Sarrlevi's mind reading would fail if I was distracted by something else. I didn't care if he knew about my ongoing suspicions about him, but I didn't want to throw Val under the bus. He didn't trade insults and glares with her the way he did Zavryd, but if she vexed him, maybe he would leap to take the assignment the next time someone came to him, wanting her assassinated.

"Hello?" I answered while watching Sarrlevi.

He clasped his hands behind his back, the manticore-tail bag still dangling from his grip.

"Matti," Penina said.

I winced, certain Tyler had reported my less-than-attentive presence on our date. If not directly to her then to her husband. "That's me. What's up?"

"I just wanted to know how your date went. Are you going to see him again?"

"Uh." Maybe Tyler *hadn't* reported anything. "I'm not sure yet. He bought me a mocha. That was nice."

I watched Sarrlevi, who'd bought me a lifetime's worth of enchanting lessons, expecting his eyebrows to twitch, but he'd shifted his gaze to the marina. With the sun setting, a fog was creeping in from the lake. That wasn't typical weather for this time of year, and I wondered if he, with his keener senses, detected anything magical. Were there artifacts that could alter the weather? I didn't know.

"He's a good guy, isn't he?" Penina asked. "I know it's too early for you to make plans or think about anything serious, but I hope you'll keep an open mind. You're thirty-four now, you know."

"I do know that. I math good." I couldn't keep from rolling my eyes. Well, I'd wanted my mind distracted…

"I'm just saying that the options get slimmer as you get older. You can't be too picky, not if you want to get married and have kids. You *do* want that, don't you? It would be good for you. I'm sure you'd settle down if you had to take care of others."

I thought of Tinja, who needed someone to take care of *her*, and glanced at the manticore tail. Instead of arguing with my sister, I ought to rush that bag to Zoltan while trying to talk Sarrlevi into taking me to see—and possibly pummel—Barothla. My concerns about my mother and Sarrlevi's intentions toward her could wait until Tinja was better.

"I'm building my business, not thinking about having kids, not right now." With my temper, I wasn't sure I'd *ever* be a good mother, but I hadn't ruled out the possibility.

"I want you to have what I have. I think you'd be happier."

"I'm *not unhappy*. I like my work." I wasn't that tickled that magical bad guys were taking shots at me left and right now, but hopefully that would be temporary.

"Work isn't life, Matti. You don't want to wait until you're old to figure that out."

"I know. I get it. Thanks."

"Will you come to brunch next weekend? You can bring Tyler."

"Will he be there whether I *bring* him or not?"

"Maybe." Penina sounded like she was smirking.

I rolled my eyes again. "Okay."

By then, Tinja would be better. Or she'd be... No. I shook the half-finished thought away. She *would* be better. There was no other option.

"Great," Penina said. "Bye."

"Your older sister watches out for you?" Sarrlevi asked as I stuck my phone back into my pocket.

"I guess. I know she cares, but she doesn't understand that I don't want what she wants, and I don't need her setting me up with men."

"Better misguided caring than indifference."

I wasn't sure what to say to that.

"Thorvald doesn't know me well. As you're aware, we began our acquaintance as predator and prey." Was that Sarrlevi's way of saying Val's hunch was wrong? Had he seen her words in my mind?

I was sure Val would have objected, had she heard Sarrlevi refer to her as *prey*, but if he were hunting me, I would feel that term was appropriate. Thus far, I'd been attacked by orcs, trolls, and werewolves, but no deadly assassins had tried to take me out. It was bad enough that Sarrlevi veered into chilling and unsettling when he appeared behind me without warning or admitted he'd been keeping an eye on me. That stuff had stopped bothering me as much, but maybe it shouldn't have.

Sarrlevi removed his scabbards and extended a hand toward the grass. "Sit with me for a moment."

"Does that make it easier for you to read my mind?" I remained standing as he sat on the slope, but the sight of the manticore bag reminded me that he was helping me, and I shouldn't give him a hard time right now.

"Touching your head makes that easier. Sitting is irrelevant."

I grunted and sat beside him, facing the marina. Fog now

wreathed the docks, the masts of sailboats rising up from it. The sun had set, and it was growing darker.

For a long moment, we sat in silence, Sarrlevi with his arms draped over his knees, his swords on the ground beside him.

"My father was known by all for his temper," he said, "but he was, as I told you, a powerful warrior and mage. He helped defend Veleshna Var, the elven home world, during the Troubled Century, when a couple of the other races banded together and tried to take control of our land. Of *us*. Because of that, my father was respected by his colleagues and honored as a hero." Sarrlevi's mouth twisted, showing what he thought of that. "He had a brother, who also lived in the city and who came by now and then. He knew my father well and knew about his temper and what an ass he was to my mother and to us children. He knew what my father hid from the rest of the world and that my mother was always too afraid to speak to others about it."

Sarrlevi kept looking toward the water as he spoke, but I found myself watching him, his profile. Why he was telling me this, I didn't know, but I listened intently, longing to know more about him, about what motivated him. Wanting to know if I could trust him.

"After my father and I fought, after I killed him, there was an inquiry. I stood before the king—this was before Eireth's time—and his noble advisors. I gave my version of the story, and the king asked if anyone would speak on my behalf. Nobody came forward to do so." Sarrlevi continued gazing toward the water as he spoke, but his blue eyes had grown unfocused, the eyes of someone lost in the past. "My mother was so distraught that she didn't come to the inquiry. I did not blame her. I had, however, thought that my uncle, who'd been present before when my father struck her, might speak the truth. He never had in the past, but I'd believed it was because he feared repercussions from my father, who was the stronger mage of the two. But my father was gone. There would have been no repercussions."

Sarrlevi paused, his jaw tightening. Seconds passed before he continued, and I caught myself lifting a hand toward his arm, but I pulled it back. Still not sure.

"Instead of speaking on my behalf or admitting to them what a monster my father was to his family, he told them I'd always been a brooding sullen boy overly obsessed with weapons training. He said that my outburst had been inevitable. *Outburst.* That was what he called what my father and I both knew was a fair duel. One that had been years in the making. It was what motivated all my training." He paused and took a breath, letting it out slowly. "After the king and the nobles conferred, they agreed I was too dangerous to remain on the elven world, and they cast me out. They said it was only for my mother's sake that they didn't have me executed, that she'd already lost too much."

"I'm sorry," I said quietly. This time when I lifted my hand, I let it rest on his arm.

"I do not seek your pity. I tell you this so you will know that I never had anyone to stand up for me when I was young." He looked at my hand on his arm and then to my face. "And rarely after that."

Significance emanated from his gaze, but it took me a moment to realize he was pointing out that I'd done that. And it had meant something to him.

Sarrlevi smiled faintly as my understanding came. "I've certainly never had anyone stand up for me against *dragons.*"

"Well, I'm not that wise."

"Fortunately for me." He wrapped an arm around my shoulders. "I understand wanting to excel without assistance from others, wanting to *prove* something, if not to those around you, then to yourself. I do not seek to take that from you. But it is not a failing, and it does not lessen your accomplishments, to let someone help you now and then, especially someone whom you've already helped." His voice grew softer. "And who appreciates that."

I leaned against his side. Was that what was motivating him to help me? Not guilt but... gratitude? "I thought you were ambivalent about the punishment and rehabilitation, that you believed having your mind wiped and starting over might not have been the worst thing."

He snorted softly. "That was a momentary musing once the danger was past. Besides, there are two years of excruciating torture before they steal your memories and imprint a new persona on you. Nobody could want that."

"I wouldn't think so, but assassins are odd."

"Very odd, yes."

With his arm still around my shoulders, he bent his head down to rest it atop mine. I swallowed and blinked unexpected moisture from my eyes as I let myself lean against him, enjoying the closeness.

"I assume this oddness," he said, his tone lighter now, "is why your sister has not invited *me* to your family brunches."

"It's because the only time she met you, you were bleeding all over the floor. She assumed you'd gotten in a fight and were trouble."

"A bad idea," he said.

"*Clearly.*"

"I apologize if I overstepped my bounds in paying the enchanter, but I wanted to make sure you would be set, even after I'm gone."

"Thank you," I said, my throat tight.

I supposed I'd always known that he would leave eventually, once his mission was complete, and return to his life in the Cosmic Realms, but the thought saddened me. Still, he was here now, and I let myself lean more fully against him. I closed my eyes as we sat together, trusting he would keep an eye on the marina—and on me—and let myself bask in the warmth of his body—of *him*—as the fog and the night deepened.

Before I went on the manticore hunt, he said, switching to telepathy, *I sent a message to Barothla. After we investigate the barge, I'll return to see if she's agreed to meet with me. I'm still debating how I can get a blood sample from her without starting a war with the dwarves* and *the dragons invested in their rulers. Right now, whether she's an appealing candidate or not, she is your father's heir.*

She said he'd changed that, that she wasn't.

If that's true, I've not heard about it. It's possible he has, but it's possible she was lying to you.

Yeah.

I sense the troll ship approaching. Sarrlevi didn't release me, so maybe we had a few more minutes. *Did you learn anything from the enchanter?*

Some foundational basics. And that I should do my best to learn the name of my hammer.

He chuckled. *Yes.*

Do your swords have a sentience? He said the hammer does, and she might be woken with her name. He also said it's a very powerful enchantment and few can make such tools.

That's right. There may be fewer than a hundred such weapons in all of the Cosmic Realms, as it has been—had been—a few generations since an enchanter capable of crafting them existed. If your mother can make such weapons... Well, it was unwise of me to accept that mission forty years ago. I'm surprised the dwarves didn't hunt me down and implore dragons to destroy my home sooner.

All your homes.

Indeed. One of my swords is sentient—sapient—yes. The one I lent you.

The one that belonged to your father?

Yes. The story I heard was that he received it as a gift for helping the dwarves in a war they were fighting at the time—centuries ago. Traditionally, such weapons are handed down from father to son or mother to daughter, and the name is shared with the new owner then. My father refused to tell me the name of the sword as he was dying. Not surprising. I'd just delivered a mortal blow to him, after all. I supposed a part of me hoped he might accept that I'd defeated him honorably—and that he deserved to be killed for what he'd done, but he was bitter and spat at me with his dying breath. Sarrlevi shrugged. *However, after several decades, the sword roused and told me his name. I think it took him that long to decide I was worthy to know it.*

I frowned, assuming that meant the hammer *didn't* think I was worthy. Though if it typically took such weapons decades to assess those wielding them, maybe that wasn't surprising.

Abruptly, I felt chagrined that I'd used the hammer so often to demo cabinets. It was by far the best tool I had, but if I'd known she was intelligent... Hell, I'd probably deeply offended her. Even if I somehow learned her name, she might not consider me worthy, and she might ignore me.

That sucked. She had, however, responded to the power words when I'd learned and used them. Maybe there was hope. But just in case, I vowed to get a sledgehammer for demoing purposes and enchant it as soon as I knew how. I'd reserve the hammer for more noble pursuits, such as bashing in the head of a conniving dwarf princess.

Sarrlevi squeezed my shoulders, then released me. He stood and pointed toward the foggy blanket that had descended fully over the lake. Now, none of the ships at the marina were in view, but I sensed something magical out in the water.

"Time to investigate our lead," Sarrlevi said.

"I'm ready." The sooner we questioned the trolls, the sooner Sarrlevi could check on Barothla and find the final ingredient for Zoltan's potion.

20

As Sarrlevi and I activated our camouflage, me using the charm Artie had given me, and him using his own magic, we headed toward the fog-shrouded marina. A few lights were on now, attempting to pierce the misty air, but they did little to illuminate the docks or the ships berthed there.

Before, I hadn't sensed any magical beings in the area. Now, as we stepped onto the pavement, I detected someone. A troll?

He was coming down from the bicycle trail and angling toward the marina.

Company? I silently asked Sarrlevi. *Someone here to pick up a cargo? Or greet refugees brought across the Pacific?*

Maybe he'd sensed the visitor earlier and that was why he'd switched to telepathy.

Possibly, but it's a young troll. I doubt he has much responsibility. There could be others with camouflaging abilities.

Do you think he sensed us?

He may have when we sat in the grass. He shouldn't be able to now. As to the cargo and possible passengers, I... do not sense many living beings on the ship. There are a few, but I think they are yaku, not trolls.

Yaku?

Something akin to your dogs. They're native to the troll home world and trained to guard their masters and their belongings. The image of a brawny four-legged creature that Sarrlevi put into my mind had the height and mass of a great slavering grizzly bear. It did not make me think of dogs, not in the least. Instead of fur, it bristled something like porcupine quills, and I was positive I didn't want to receive a swipe from its long claws. *The crew may be camouflaged,* he added.

They must be. I assume the dogs *aren't steering the ship.*

Likely not. I do sense magic within the barge. I can't tell if the craft itself is magical or if it carries artifacts.

Artifacts that someone might show up to collect? I glanced in the direction that I sensed the young troll, but he had stopped at the far end of the marina, the fog shrouding his body from view.

Perhaps, but I don't sense any of those magical aircraft in the area. Just because those who have your mother picked up cargo from this ship in the past doesn't mean they will tonight. I merely hope to learn more about them by questioning the crew.

Okay. I admitted hoping for more. I was tired of those guys eluding me and regretted that Val and I had inadvertently kept Sarrlevi from being taken to their base where he might have learned all about them. Though... as I'd been thinking earlier, I wanted to be with Sarrlevi when we found my mother. Just in case.

There were several docks, but Sarrlevi chose a particular one and headed down it. A guess? Or did he know?

I trailed behind without questioning him. When I'd seen the marina before the fog came in, there'd been a number of berths available but not that many that would accommodate larger vessels. This one did have a large open slot at the end. If Sarrlevi was wrong, he could levitate himself to another.

When we reached the end, he drew one of his swords and

stood ready, his head cocked. Listening as well as sensing the barge's approach?

It had no sails, nor was there any breeze, but I didn't hear the rumble of a motor. Maybe one of the artifacts we sensed was a magical propeller.

The dark boxy shape of the vessel loomed out of the fog. Though full night had come, not a single lamp lit its deck. It wasn't as large as I'd expected when Sarrlevi had called it a barge, but it was bigger than the surrounding sailboats and yachts. Something told me its crew didn't pay for a regular berth.

Its crew that I still couldn't sense. I *could* sense four living beings. The *yaku*. They prowled the deck, and I feared they were as large as Sarrlevi's image had suggested.

If they're guarding the crew, he told me, *we may have to fight them.*

I flexed my hands on the haft of my hammer. *I'm ready.*

Back to back. Their fangs are more dangerous than their claws.

I nodded, though I remembered him fighting werewolves back-to-back with Val once and thinking that his style—*their* styles—had been too quick and dance-like to complement mine. Though my training had made me reasonably agile, dwarves were more like tanks than dancers. Hopefully, I wouldn't clunk him in the back as I swung my hammer.

Growls came from the deck of the barge, and I crouched, not sure if the creatures would spring onto the dock with us, or if Sarrlevi wanted to leap onto the vessel to fight them.

Claws clattered on the deck as all four creatures ran toward us, dark shapes indistinct in the fog. Magic emanated from Sarrlevi, and power blasted toward them. It slammed into the side of the barge, shattering wood and bending the railing inward, but it didn't affect the *yaku*.

They're wearing collars that protect them from magical attacks. With luck, our weapons will be powerful enough to work on them.

Follow me. Sarrlevi sprang over the railing and onto the deck, landing to face two of his bristled opponents.

The walkway was narrow enough that the back two couldn't reach him, not from that direction. They were smart enough to figure that out and run around the cabin to come at him from the other direction.

I wouldn't allow that.

As much as I wanted to leap right after Sarrlevi, I couldn't clear the railing in a single jump and had to climb over. I stepped on something, startling me. The limb of... a dead *yaku*? What the hell?

I didn't have time to contemplate it. Two *living yaku* had rounded the cabin, and they pounded toward me. Sarrlevi and I would have had to fight back-to-back whether we'd planned to or not.

Trusting nothing would get by him, I lifted my hammer and braced myself, assuming my two opponents would attack together. Even on four legs, they were both taller than I, and they would bring a lot of mass to the battle.

"*Hyrek,*" I whispered, willing the power of lightning to infuse my weapon and hoping it was stronger than the magic Sarrlevi had tried on the *yaku*. I also added, "*Eravekt,*" to make them easier to see in the dark.

The hammer glowed and hummed in my hand as I swung to stop the creatures' charge. They must have sensed that my weapon was dangerous, for they stopped outside of my range. With it raised, I was tempted to creep closer and lunge, but if one got by me, it might reach Sarrlevi's back.

Though he could probably handle all four by himself, I didn't want to fail in my duty to guard his back. Just as he was guarding mine.

Snarling, the creatures overcame their hesitation. They

crouched and sprang as one, both angling their jaws toward my throat.

I whipped the hammer toward the fanged maw of the one closest to the wall of the cabin and shifted away from the other as much as I could without giving ground, without opening the way to Sarrlevi. My target jerked its head to the side, avoiding my hammer. The second *yaku* snapped toward me as it landed. Accustomed to using my legs in battle, I kicked at a joint in one of its legs as I swung again at my other foe.

This time, my hammer clipped it, branches of lightning crackling around the hulking body. My kick landed, making the other one pause, but I lurched off balance when something stabbed through my shoe and into my foot. Only as pain blasted up my leg did I remember that the creatures had quills instead of fur. Quills like *daggers*.

Enraged, I stomped my foot down and smashed my hammer into the shoulder of the offending *yaku*. While the other reared back, lightning singeing its fur—its *body*—I swung as fast as I could, my kick having done little to deter its buddy.

With a snarl, I crushed it in the snout, then altered my grip to pound my hammer down on the top of its head. Its skull crunched, but that didn't halt its attack. Teeth gnashed for me, snapping in the air in front of my face.

My hammer gave me longer reach, and I evaded the fangs as I struck the creature again. Once more, lightning flared from the head of my weapon, and the *yaku's* back went rigid before it toppled to the deck.

Fortunately, the other one, shaking its head and panting heavily as the lightning that had struck it faded, hadn't recovered enough to take advantage of my singular focus. Now, it crouched and growled at me, but I leaped in, delivering a crushing blow to its snout and ending the snapping of its jaws. Teeth broke and clinked to the deck. It yowled, but as I stepped in to finish it off, a hint of orange light—flames?—arcing above us made me pause.

Something shattered against the side of the cabin not three feet from me. Distracted, I almost missed the *yaku* lunging toward me. Instincts kicked in, and I reacted in time, hitting it again in its mangled snout. Its head struck the side of the cabin with a thud.

Behind me, magic flared. Sarrlevi sending an attack not toward anyone on the barge but toward the docks. Someone cried out—the troll boy?—then splashed into the water.

In an overhand strike, I brought my hammer down on the top of my remaining foe's head. The *yaku's* legs flew out from underneath it, and it slammed to the deck. Not sure if it was dead, I hit it again before backing away, my weapon still raised. But neither of the beasts I'd faced were moving, and I sensed their auras fading.

My heel clunked against the dead one behind me—the one that had been dead before we'd boarded the ship. I had questions about that, but flames were spreading fast along the side of the barge. The scent of kerosene filled the air. What had that troll thrown? A Molotov cocktail?

As I stepped farther from the flames, my heel crunched on glass. I snarled in pain, though it wasn't the broken glass but the puncture from the quill that stung. It must have driven through the sole of my shoe.

Are you all right? Sarrlevi stepped around the body between us and rested a hand on my shoulder as he summoned magic to squelch the flames. Not surprisingly, he'd vanquished his *yaku* without trouble, probably before I'd finished off mine.

Yeah. I just did something stupid. I'm used to being able to kick my enemies.

You'll have to wear armored boots if you want to employ such maneuvers against all foes.

I'll put them on my Christmas list. Remembering the suit of armor in Hennehok's cabin, I wondered if he had returned home yet. If he hadn't, would he mind me borrowing his armor? Though I would feel silly wandering the 'burbs of Seattle in such a getup.

With the yaku *dead, I don't sense anyone else alive on this ship.* A trickle of magic flowed from Sarrlevi's hand, running through my body and to my foot. *I don't know who killed the first* yaku, *but magical bullets are embedded in its skull.*

His magic tingled as it cooled and numbed my foot, and I was tempted to slump against him, but we weren't out of danger. Just because we didn't sense the crew didn't mean nobody was on board.

I'll look at it more closely later. Sarrlevi's magic faded. *Can you walk?*

Yes, I said before I put weight on my foot to test it. I would walk whether it hurt or not. I refused to be a liability. *Thank you.*

Reactivate your camouflage.

I did so, not pointing out that one was supposed to say *you're welcome* after receiving thanks. He might have detected the next threat.

Sarrlevi looked toward the sounds of splashing—the troll swimming toward the shore—and summoned more magic. To attack him?

He's just a kid. I rested a hand on Sarrlevi's arm.

A kid who was spying on us.

You spy on me all the time.

It's acceptable when I do it.

Is that so? I gave him the wry look the comment deserved.

Sarrlevi grunted, but the magic he'd been gathering dissipated. Good. Molotov cocktail or not, I doubted the kid was much of a threat, and I didn't want Sarrlevi beating up on teenagers.

He stepped over the bodies of the *yaku* and led the way toward the front of the barge.

The cabin lacked windows, so we couldn't see inside until we reached a door. It was open, swaying and creaking on its hinges even though there wasn't a breeze. The movement of the barge in the water was responsible, I told myself, though waves were few on the lake.

I smell blood, Sarrlevi said.

Yaku *blood?*

No. He pointed through the doorway, then at the deck in front of it. *Wait here.*

What happened to back to back?

That's a hard way to go through a doorway, and I have more armor and defenses than you.

Though my curiosity made me want to go in on his heels, I nodded, reluctantly agreeing that he was right. Someday, I vowed with determination, I would be able to enchant armor and defenses to protect myself.

Sarrlevi eased through the doorway and down the steps. A faint *click* came from within. Certain he hadn't made the noise, I crept closer, but I stayed to the side of the door, not wanting to outline myself as a target, in case someone inside could see through my camouflage.

Gunshots fired, making me jump. *Numerous* gunshots. It sounded like an automatic weapon.

I raised my hammer and almost charged inside, but I didn't know how to deflect bullets. Sarrlevi did, though I didn't know if even his armor and magical enhancements could handle such a rapid-fire attack.

A smashing and wrenching came from inside, and the gunshots stopped.

You okay? I asked telepathically.

Yes. One moment.

Another wrenching noise came from a different part of the cabin. Some of the magic emanating from the interior faded. A crack followed, like a sword hitting wood. More magic disappeared. All that remained came from the back of the cabin and the rear of the ship, where the magical propeller I'd hypothesized existed would be.

The crew is all dead, Sarrlevi said. *You can come in.*

Wasn't the goal to be able to question someone? I stepped through the doorway, willing the hammer to glow brighter to illuminate the way.

Sarrlevi sighed into my mind. *It was, but the crew was already dead when I walked in—when the ship arrived. The gun was rigged in such a way to act as a booby trap. And I found a few other traps.*

Can you tell how long the crew has been dead?

Not long.

Are the bodies still warm? A dead green-blue-skinned troll male lay at the bottom of the steps, and I stepped gingerly over the corpse.

They are, yes. Also, the yaku would have grown hungry if nobody had been feeding them on the way across the ocean, and they would have eaten their masters.

Grisly.

Not venturing much farther inside, I lifted my hammer to shine its light around the interior. The open cabin wasn't compartmentalized, save for the cargo being netted off in the back, while hammocks, a refrigerator, a sink, and a microwave occupied the front.

Sarrlevi stood in front of the cargo, his weapons drawn but lowered. Two more dead trolls lay on the deck near him. There was also a machine gun that had been knocked from an apparatus that had held it aloft and pointed at the door. He'd sliced through the weapon to ensure it wouldn't be used again.

A fourth troll was dead in one of the hammocks, one leg hanging out, as if he'd been trying to get up when he'd been killed. His eyes were frozen open, a bloody bullet hole in his forehead.

Was that... from the booby trap? I asked.

I don't think so. They were all killed by bullets.

And recently, you said. I trusted his assessment and didn't touch any of the bodies to check for body heat. I wasn't blasé enough about death not to find corpses upsetting.

Yes. Within the hour, I believe.

Did one of the crew go crazy? Or... maybe some enemy jumped on board when the barge went through the Ballard Locks.

Or they could have ridden a magical helicopter in and boarded it from above.

You think it's the same people that have my mother? And now my father? Why would they have killed trolls who brought them a cargo last month?

I do not know that it was they. I only mention it as a possibility, since we know they have magical firearms. Sarrlevi looked at the crates behind him. *Also, whoever killed them didn't take the cargo.*

That's weird. Especially if they're collecting magical artifacts.

I sense few items of significant power in the cargo, Sarrlevi said.

I joined him to look at the crates. They weren't labeled and hadn't been opened, but a couple of packs of cigarettes and a bottle of vodka open on a table might have hinted at the majority of the contents.

Someone might have learned that we sought to question the crew and wanted to keep us from doing so. Sarrlevi held up a finger. *The boy has returned with more trolls.*

He strode toward the cabin door, springing over the steps instead of using them, and landed outside on the deck.

I looked around, aching for more clues. If Sarrlevi's hunch was right, how could my mother's captors have possibly known we were coming to intercept this ship tonight? Assuming Sarrlevi was telling the truth, he'd learned about this from Santiago, someone neither of us had known or had any dealings with even a day ago.

After the incident at the prison, I was beginning to think the helicopter owners had a way to spy on us—on *me*—from a distance. Who knew what magical artifacts my mother had enchanted for them over the years? Been *forced* to enchant for them, I assumed. I refused to believe she'd voluntarily abandoned me to do such work. As it was, it was surprising someone everyone kept saying was very powerful hadn't been able to find a way to escape in all this time. But Artie had said my mother wasn't a warrior.

What do you want to do about this? Sarrlevi asked telepathically from the deck.

I hurried out to see what he was looking at. The fog was as thick as ever, but I sensed a group of five or six trolls, including the boy. They were in the marina but not on the docks, and I couldn't tell if they were looking in our direction, but they probably were.

An uneasy feeling came over me as I remembered the gunshots. The crew had already been dead when the booby trap went off, but someone listening from a distance wouldn't know that. What if these trolls suspected us of killing the crew? Whether they were friends of the dead crew, or had been waiting for their cargo, they wouldn't have kind things to say about us when the authorities—or more likely Willard's people—were sent to investigate.

I was on the verge of trying to speak telepathically to them to explain the situation when a swell of magic pinged at my senses. It came from the dock between us and the trolls.

Portal. Sarrlevi raised his weapons and stepped close to me, though he gave me an odd look as the silver disc appeared, floating in the air. *A dwarf-made portal.*

"Uh." What dwarves would be coming to see us? And how would they have known we were here? "If it's Barothla, I'm going to knock her on her ass and try to get some of her blood."

"That should prove interesting," Sarrlevi said mildly.

Though he didn't say it, I was sure he believed she could knock *me* on my ass, if not all the way into the next zip code.

"We'll see," I said grimly, lifting my hammer.

21

THE DWARVES WHO LEAPED OUT OF THE PORTAL WERE FAMILIAR, BUT all the faces were male. Barothla wasn't among them. I recognized the general, the priest, and several warriors who'd accompanied my grandfather when he'd arrived on the plateau by Sarrlevi's house. His *former* house.

Likely recognizing the dwarves as well, Sarrlevi didn't lower his swords. Instead, he glared balefully at them, as if certain they were bringing trouble.

My own expression was more hopeful as I watched the portal, wanting my grandfather to come through. If he did, I would tell him about his daughter's evilness and also ask if he knew the name of the hammer.

The silver disc of the portal faded, leaving the marina shrouded in fog and darkness, the dwarves' faces in shadow. I sagged in disappointment, though I couldn't be surprised that the king hadn't shown up on a random dock in Kenmore. The real question was why these guys had.

How did they find us? I silently asked Sarrlevi.

I do not know.

The priest muttered something, and a globe of golden light appeared, floating in the air ahead of their group. The dwarves were all looking at us. The trolls had backed away and faded from my awareness. Deciding a portal popping up nearby could only mean trouble?

I thought people could only make portals to places they're familiar with. It's hard for me to imagine these guys hitting up Log Boom Park regularly to inline skate. I waved in the direction of the grassy recreation area, though night and the fog hid it from view.

I am certain they do not.

The priest and the general strode toward us, and I lowered my hammer. Though I understood why Sarrlevi would be tense around the dwarves, I didn't want to threaten them in any way. Without a doubt, they would report this meeting to my grandfather. Maybe he was the one who'd sent them.

I don't have Val's translation charm with me anymore. I grimaced, about to ask Sarrlevi if *he* could translate if needed but remembered that he didn't understand much more Dwarven than I did.

I have one, but if you speak telepathically with them, you should be able to understand each other. He nodded toward me without taking his gaze from them. *You've improved at that quickly.*

The priest and general stopped at the end of the dock with four sturdy armed and armored dwarves spread out behind them. A few glanced at me, but they were too busy glaring at Sarrlevi to give me more attention than that. Had they come to see him?

Sarrlevi said nothing, merely glaring back.

Hi. I smiled and waved cheerfully, keeping the hammer at my side. *Can I help you guys?*

We have come for an update on your quest, the general spoke into my mind.

My quest to find my mother? I'm still working on it. I pointed at the barge, though they couldn't have known the dead trolls had anything to do with my mother. Even *we* didn't know that for certain. We had only guesses. Unfortunately.

The general and priest looked at the lifeless barge.

Is that so? the general asked.

We followed a lead to this place, Sarrlevi told them.

They scowled, looked at him, and then looked at me.

Why is that one here? the general asked. *He cannot be trusted.*

He's handy in a fight, I replied.

Oh, we know. Still scowling, the priest pointed at Sarrlevi and addressed him. *You will leave the mongrel alone. You will not follow her to Princess Rodarska so you can finish your vile work.*

I'm here to protect Mataalii. Sarrlevi shifted closer to me, his shoulder brushing mine, his swords still out. *She has a name. Since she's the granddaughter of your king, perhaps you should learn it.*

Perhaps you should stay out of dwarven affairs, assassin.

I lifted a finger. *How did you guys find me? And do you want to stay here on Earth and lend me some assistance in seeking my mother?*

We found you through the hammer. The priest pointed to it.

Uh, how? I looked at Sarrlevi.

He spoke softly into my mind, the words only for me: *It has a powerful aura, as you know, but it emits no beacon that I can detect.*

The priest must have guessed at my confusion. *I am familiar with your mother and her work, and I have something she once crafted.* He touched a charm infused in the chest plate of his armor. *Using my magic and the guidance of the gods, I was able to track the hammer. I once thought I might be able to track* her, *and maybe I could, if I were on the right world and she weren't hidden behind protective magic...* He shook his head. *All I can track here right now is the hammer.*

Good to know. I didn't want to be tracked, but at least the dwarves were better than murderous orc mercenaries.

We bring you a warning, but we will not speak it in front of that enemy of the princess. The priest's eyes closed to slits as he pointed again at Sarrlevi. *Of Princess Rodarska.*

Did the emphasis on her name mean he didn't believe Sarrlevi was an enemy of Princess *Barothla*?

You will go, assassin, the priest said.

I will stay and protect Mataalii. Give her your warning, and leave if you will not use your magic to help her find her mother.

We have looked for her before. I will hope for the king's sake that the mongrel does find her, but I doubt she will. When she fails, we will come and take the hammer back to Dun Kroth, to our people, where it belongs.

It belongs with its original owner's descendants, Sarrlevi said. *Is that not your way?*

Not with half-bloods, the priest said. *Not typically. If the mongrel is to prove she is worthy of wielding that hammer, she should do it without your dubious* help.

The general lifted his own weapons. *Step away from her, assassin. You are skilled, but you would not be able to best all of us. And we would relish the chance to end your life. Unlike the dragons, we do not rehabilitate those who try to kill our royals.*

Sarrlevi clenched his jaw, looking more irritated than afraid of the dwarves. But there were six of them, and they had powerful auras, especially the priest and the general. If they all attacked at once...

I turned toward Sarrlevi and rested a hand on his chest. *Will you go for a while? I want to hear their warning, and I don't want you to get in a fight when there's nothing to gain. I don't want you to be hurt again either.* I glanced toward the gash on the back of his hand, though I was thinking of the rockfall that had collapsed on him, the wounds he'd received in the prison, and all the other times he'd been hurt since we met. Since he'd started helping me. *Not because of me,* I added.

His eyelids drooped, and I sensed that he wanted to object. I wasn't sure he was that thrilled about my hand on his chest either. Well, too bad. This wasn't a battle he needed to spring into.

Please, Sarrlevi.

Varlesh, he replied softly.

What? I asked, even though I knew it was his first name. *You want me to...*

Use it. If you wish. Not taking his gaze from the dwarves, he slung his magical backpack off and pulled out the bag with the manticore tail pieces inside. He handed it to me. *If I'm able to arrange a meeting with Barothla, I will come later and let you know.*

I accepted the bag. *Thank you, Varlesh.*

Be wary of these dwarves. They may be your grandfather's allies, but I doubt they consider themselves yours.

Yeah, I gathered.

He inclined his head toward me, backed a few steps away, then conjured a portal on the deck of the ship. Not until it was ready did he turn his back on the dwarves and leap through it.

Once the silver disc disappeared, I eyed the dwarves uncertainly, hoping I hadn't made a mistake in sending Sarrlevi away.

They relaxed visibly and lowered their weapons. One even cracked what sounded like a joke in Dwarven. I didn't understand it, but the others chuckled, and longing swept through me. A longing to understand and to belong.

The general exhaled slowly. *Girl, you cannot trust that one. We believe he still seeks to slay Princess Rodarska.*

I don't think he does, but I'm aware of his past, and I don't trust him.

He shook his head. Maybe I shouldn't have put my hand on Sarrlevi's chest if I'd wanted them to believe that. I almost told them I was using him, but I couldn't bring myself to voice that.

We came to warn you, the priest said, *that Princess Barothla has learned of your existence and may be a threat to you.*

Tell me about it. They'd traveled all this way to deliver *that* warning?

The priest and the general glanced at each other in confusion.

I sighed. *I already knew. Barothla not only visited me, but she poisoned my friend. She was trying to poison* me, *but the wrong person drank the soda.*

Several of the dwarves swore.

I told you, the general said, pointing at the priest.

They started arguing aloud in Dwarven. I rubbed my head.

"Hey, guys?" Silently, I continued: *What I really need now is a cure for that poison.* I met the priest's eyes. *Is there any chance your magic could help? My friend is innocent. She didn't deserve this.* I didn't think *I* would have deserved it either.

The priest shuffled his feet and looked at the dock. *If a lesser alchemist had been responsible, my healing magic might have been enough to reverse the effects of a poison, but Princess Barothla is powerful. Even if I could thwart one of her potions, I...* He glanced around at his buddies. *I think we would all hesitate to cross her.*

I scowled and wanted to call them cowards. But Sarrlevi was hesitant to cross her too. Though that might have more to do with bringing the wrath of dragons down on his head—again—than him fearing her power. Since he was already on the dragons' radar, he had to step lightly around them—and their chosen rulers.

Elves are more experienced and more typical practitioners of alchemy, the general told me. *They would be the ones to ask for help.*

You chased away my only elf ally.

That one is not *an ally.* The general flung an arm toward where Sarrlevi's portal had been. *If he's standing at your side, it's because he wants something. Watch your back.*

I am.

If you want to keep your hammer—

Yeah, yeah, I'm working on it.

The general looked at the priest. *I would not have expected Rodarska's daughter to be so... impudent.*

It must be the tainted human blood, the priest said.

I rolled my eyes and barely kept from pointing out that my

dwarven blood might have a few issues too if it had created my aunt.

Now that our warning has been delivered, the general told me, *we will depart. It is unwise to vex Princess Barothla, but we knew the king would want you safe.*

I'm glad someone does. I started to wave, but blurted, *Wait!*

The dwarves looked curiously at me.

You're going back to the dwarven court where Barothla lives, right? Will you tell her that she got the wrong person? I didn't drink her poisoned soda, but my roommate did, a little goblin without a lot of body weight. She's going to die if a cure isn't found. I still didn't know whether Barothla had intended for *me* to die or not. Since there had been multiple sodas, it was plausible that I could have swilled two of them and been in the same position that the smaller Tinja was in. Or worse. *Tell her if she doesn't want to be a complete bitch and super villain, she should come heal my friend.*

The priest's and general's faces were grave when they regarded each other, but they didn't appear surprised by any of this. Wonderful. Princess Barothla was a known evildoer. Why hadn't the king ostracized her from his court and his life instead of simply removing her as his heir? Had he even done that? Sarrlevi hadn't thought so. I had only Barothla's word on that.

Several of the dwarves murmured to each other in their language while shaking their heads. What, nobody was willing to risk Barothla's ire by delivering the message?

The general turned from the others and lifted his chin. *If we encounter her, I will give her this information.*

Thank you.

I doubted anything would come of it, but I would hope for the best. If nothing else, Barothla might show up on Earth to try again when she realized she'd missed her target. If she did, I would have a chance to get that blood sample.

My phone rang. A local number that I didn't recognize.

"Hello?" I answered.

"This is Zoltan."

Fresh concern for Tinja flooded into me. What if she'd gotten worse? What if she didn't have as much time as Zoltan had originally thought?

"I've got the manticore tail," I blurted.

"Goodness, what a breathy announcement. Do you always proclaim your ingredient status when you greet callers?"

"Always. Is Tinja okay? Where's Val? You didn't gnaw her veins and render her unable to use the phone, did you?" As soon as the words came out, I remembered she'd left on a mission up north.

"*Gnaw?* I am a vampire, not some carnivorous dragon. Should you ever allow the touch of my fangs at your throat, you would feel how gentle I am."

I shuddered at the thought, watching as the dwarves formed a portal and disappeared. Why it had taken a pack of them to come deliver that message, I couldn't guess. Maybe they thought Earth was a bad neighborhood.

"Bring me the tail as soon as possible, dwarf mongrel," Zoltan continued when I didn't respond. "I've gathered the rest of the ingredients and made preparations, but all of the components must be heated and mixed at once. Have you acquired the blood of the alchemist who concocted the poison?"

"Not yet, but I will. A... friend is trying to reach her now."

"Ah, yes. I spoke to Thorvald about that *friend*. She does not believe he will be willing to perform a forced blood draw on someone who hired him."

"If he doesn't, I'll find a way to do it myself." With the dwarves gone, I clambered back onto the dock and headed toward my motorcycle. "I don't suppose Zavryd has returned?"

"He has not."

"I need an artifact that can make portals so I don't have to rely on others for rides," I muttered, wondering if enchanters were capable of making such things.

"Crafting such is not within my repertoire as an alchemist," Zoltan said. "I need the blood within twenty-four hours, if my formula is to be delivered in time to save your friend."

I closed my eyes. "I understand."

22

In the guest room at Val's house, I sat on the floor, chewing my fingernails, with Tinja's bed at my back. She was sleeping, but her breathing had grown raspy. Courtesy of Zoltan, a humidifier rested on the nightstand, wafting vapors into the air. Smelling of eucalyptus and tree bark, the concoction was supposed to make it easier for asthmatics to breathe. It was the only help Zoltan could offer until he had the last ingredient.

Which I had no way to get. All I could do was wait for Sarrlevi to return, hopefully with news that he *could* get it.

My helplessness was making me want to smash things, which I couldn't do in Val's house. Unfortunately.

Instead, I pulled my hammer into my lap. To pass the time, I was trying to practice the exercises Santiago had given me.

He'd said that detecting the enchantments that others had laid on artifacts, and analyzing what they did, was part of learning. Mom's weapon, with its layers of enchantments, was good to practice on. But with poor Tinja ill behind me, I struggled to focus.

As I gazed at the hammer, I considered the people who'd been able to track me through it, first Barothla at my grandparents' house, and then the dwarf priest at the marina. Going forward, I would have to keep in mind the possibility of others doing the same.

The dwarf priest had also said he might have been able to use his familiarity with my mother's work to track *her* down. *If* she were out in the open, not somewhere insulated from beings with magical senses. It didn't surprise me that she likely was. Whoever these people were had been holed up in a protected mountain before and had probably moved to another remote base.

I slid a hand along the haft and thought, *If there's any way you can lead me to my mother—to your maker—I would be grateful.*

A hint of sadness seemed to emanate from the hammer. A figment of my imagination? Or me superimposing my own emotions on it?

I wasn't sure, but Sarrlevi's weapon had shared feelings and a vision with me. And it sounded like the hammer was its equal.

"I wish I knew your name," I whispered, "and could unlock your powers. And that they would help me find her. I'd happily give you back to her if we did. She made you, and she's the rightful wielder. I would miss you though." Feeling sheepish at speaking aloud, I glanced at Tinja, half expecting a snarky comment, but her eyes remained closed.

I wished she *were* awake and well enough to deliver snark.

My senses pinged with awareness as a magical being came within my range. Not Val or Zavryd or any of the people who lived in or visited the house. It was someone only vaguely familiar. It was...

I surged to my feet. "It's *her.*"

Fingers tight around the hammer, I peered out the window, but the guest room faced the wrong direction. My senses told me Barothla was coming from the street.

Zoltan? I attempted to project my thoughts telepathically toward the basement as I ran down the stairs to the front door.

I can hear you. You needn't yell.

Yelling is appropriate right now. Trust me. Not certain how the senses of vampires compared to full-blooded magical beings from other worlds—or half-bloods such as myself—I asked, *Can you sense the dwarf outside? Princess Barothla.*

I pushed aside the living room curtains to peer out.

I do sense her, yes. Is she bringing you a sample of her blood?

I highly doubt that's the reason for her visit.

There she was. Wearing the same armor and even more weapons than before. Had she come for a battle? If she had, I would give it to her, whether that was wise or not. I couldn't hide inside the wards while the blood that Tinja needed was scant yards away.

Would you like to join me for a battle? I wasn't above gathering allies.

Goodness, no. And certainly not one that takes me outside of the house where miscreants with blazing automobile headlights drive past, their invasive beams blinding my sensitive eyes.

What if I could lure her into the basement?

Barothla stepped onto the sidewalk and gazed at the house, the dragon topiaries, and toward other defenses that could only be detected with magical senses. Was she powerful enough, or did she have charms strong enough, to get past them?

I would be more prepared to fight a battle here in my stronghold, but Lord Zavryd's wards should keep all but the most powerful beings from reaching my front door.

From what I've been told, Princess Barothla is a most powerful being.

That is possibly true. Her aura is significant. The assassin Sarrlevi once got past the defenses, though I believe Lord Zavryd has since strengthened them.

After studying the defenses—she hadn't tried to destroy any of them yet—Barothla turned her gaze toward the front of the house. No, toward *me*. She looked through the window where I stood.

I'm going out to talk to her. Or pound her. One of the two. *Wish me luck.*

Should you nobly die in battle with her, do try to fling some of her blood toward my basement door before you perish.

I'll do my best. Wishing I had armor and maybe a magical firearm like Val's, I opened the door and stepped onto the porch. *But you might have to come around to the front yard to get it.*

A car drove past at that moment, the headlights on.

Dreadful, Zoltan said, as if he'd seen it.

"Any chance you're here to cure my friend?" I called to Barothla, who hadn't reacted to the car. Her gaze was locked on me.

She tilted her head, and I repeated the question telepathically, though she'd shown last time that she had a translation charm.

It was not my intention that she drink the elven beverage.

I tried to tell if her words sounded remorseful. Not really. It was more like she'd indifferently stated a fact.

The special brew was for me, huh?

Barothla smiled. *To demonstrate to you that it's wise to work with me. And unwise to work against me.*

Nothing like fever, labored breathing, and impending death to convey wisdom.

I've found that to be true.

If I bring her out here, will you heal her? Still on the porch, I tilted my thumb over my shoulder toward the house.

I did not bring with me the alchemical equipment necessary to craft an antidote.

Then why did you come? I prowled down the steps and toward the sidewalk. If she wouldn't cure Tinja, I would have to get her blood. I'd given the syringe to Sarrlevi—maybe I should have run down to get another one from Zoltan—but something told me that if we ended up fighting, blood would spill aplenty. A hammer strike to her nose ought to make it gush...

To give you another chance to join me in finding my sister. Should you agree to do so, I'm willing to return and create an antidote for you to give to the goblin. She smiled again, though her eyes were narrowed now.

The now-familiar itching sensation under my skull came over me as she tried to read my mind. Her touch wasn't as painful as Zondia's had been, but it was a lot more uncomfortable and intrusive than Sarrlevi's.

But I see you believe some pedestrian vampire alchemist from this benighted world could thwart my work. Barothla laughed shortly. *That's amusing.*

I stopped five feet away from her, at the edge of the boundary of protection. It hadn't occurred to me that Zoltan's concoction might not work. *He* hadn't suggested it was doubtful, but I hadn't thus far noticed humility or uncertainty from him in regard to his talents. Or anything. Was that confidence warranted?

And you want my blood. How crude. Barothla chuckled. *But this world is crude, with less native magic than a wilted* dakyor *flower. I shouldn't be surprised.*

You still want to kill my mother—your sister—don't you?

Who told you such a thing?

I almost said Sarrlevi's name, but something told me not to. *Someone said not to trust you. Your own people are afraid of you.*

Nonsense. It is as I told you. In order for me to regain my father's favor, I must bring my sister home. Alive.

I think you want to kill your sister and *your father. And that they've known for a long time to be wary of you. That's why they wear charms to protect against poisoning, isn't it?*

Her smile disappeared as her eyes narrowed further. *Who have you been speaking with?*

Some of your people warned me about you. I shared an image of the priest and the general and the dwarves who'd come with them, caring less about throwing them under the bus than Sarrlevi. If they'd wanted my loyalty, they could have been more helpful.

And you believed them? When they call you a mongrel and have made it clear you're not worthy of that hammer?

It's easy to believe the truth.

Step out here if you wish to do battle with me and attempt to steal some of my blood. Barothla pulled the twin hammers off her weapons belt. *I see the longing to smash my nose in your thoughts. You truly are a heathen. It's ludicrous that my sister lowered herself to rut with some human to produce a savage like you.*

My jaw clenched, and I almost sprang, but the smug certainty in her eyes made me worry that she would get the best of me. That feeling grew stronger when she summoned her power, and it wrapped protectively around her. As if her armor hadn't been enough, my hammer would have to get through a magical barrier as well.

Maybe it would be smarter to play along and try to jab a needle in her when she wasn't on the defensive. But how did one *play along* with a foe who could read minds?

It does make it challenging, Barothla whispered into my thoughts. *Tell me which of the dwarves spoke ill of me. I will make certain he is removed from my father's court. Such disloyalty must not be permitted.*

The itching under my skull intensified, making me want to claw at my head. Aware of her digging deeper, I tried to blank my mind. Even if I didn't like any of my grandfather's advisors, I didn't want one of them to end up dead from poison. Especially when Sarrlevi had been the one to tell me everything.

My attempt to blank my thoughts didn't work. Unbidden—or perhaps dredged up by her power—the memory arose of Sarrlevi and me flying on dragon-back, with his arm around me as he warned me how cold and manipulative Barothla was.

Her eyes widened. *Sarrlevi! He spoke against me?*

I clenched my jaw again, furious that she'd plucked that information out. I squeezed the hammer haft and willed the weapon to use its power to help me guard my thoughts and protect myself.

Don't tell me you've seduced him. Barothla sneered and looked me up and down. *Does he like that height your human blood gives you?*

Oh, yeah. He can't keep his hands off me.

She seemed to think I was serious, for fury ignited in her gray eyes, and the power radiating from her intensified.

If I could goad her into springing forward, would the topiaries roast her? Even if their fire wasn't enough to kill her, it might distract her, giving me a chance to jump in and swing.

He's an amazing kisser, I said. *Too bad he didn't find you appealing. I guess full-blooded dwarves don't have the beauty to appeal to elves.*

Instead of losing her temper, Barothla snorted. *Now I know you're lying. Assassins aren't into intimacy, just sating their needs. He doesn't kiss anyone, even the pretty elf sluts.*

The comment caught me off guard, and I was slow to react when she blasted magic toward the property's defenses. It struck like a thousand hammer blows, bashing alarms and booby traps all around the house and yard. The glowing eyes of the topiaries went dark, their magic fading, and Barothla strode toward me with her hammers swinging for my head.

Though startled, my instincts kicked in. I whipped my weapon up, striking her left hammer, then her right, and keeping her from reaching me.

I launched a straight kick toward her groin, knowing it wouldn't hurt her through her armor and magical defenses, but hoping to knock her back. I might as well have kicked a steel lamppost. The ball of my foot struck an unyielding invisible wall two inches in front of her armor.

She swept one of her hammers in to knock my leg aside, but I retracted it before it struck me. My ability to defend against her opening blows didn't keep her from charging at me, both weapons swinging.

Barothla lacked the speed and agility of an elf, but she launched a steady combination of feints and legitimate attacks, enough to keep me busy dodging and parrying. Clangs rang out as I deflected blow after blow. As I backed around the yard, careful not to end up trapped against a wall or tree, I assessed her.

Not as ambidextrous as Sarrlevi, Barothla favored her right hand, the swipes from the hammer in her left less refined. When I started parrying and launching attacks of my own, I focused on that side. With growing confidence, I decided I could defend adequately against her and grew more brazen, shifting to offense whenever I got a chance. The trouble was that even when my hammer slipped past hers, I struck that impenetrable barrier around her.

Don't you know any of the power words for your mother's hammer? Barothla sounded dry, not concerned in the least that I might be the faster fighter.

When she had magic to call upon as well, why would she be?

"*Hyrek!*" I snarled and lunged for her, knocking her left hammer high, then sweeping the head of my larger weapon under her arm.

My target was a seam in her armor, and my weapon *should* have pounded into her hard enough to send her flying, but the magic of her defensive barrier held. Lightning sprang from my hammer, arcing all around her, but the crackling electricity never touched her.

Barothla smiled, unconcerned. *Did you think I wouldn't know how to defend myself against the weapon I watched my sister forge and enchant? I do wonder if I might use it to find her. I have other charms she crafted in her earlier days of enchanting, but they are not as power-ful. Perhaps her hammer is exactly what I need.*

Frustrated, I swung again and again. Barothla lowered her arms, not bothering to defend, only funneling her power into increasing the strength of her barrier.

So much lightning crackled in the air around us that she should have exploded. Even as the wielder, I felt the hair on my arms rise, and the scent of burning ozone filled the yard.

You're a fool to strike against me, mongrel girl. Barothla pointed one of her hammers at me, and a battering ram of power struck me in the chest.

Pain blasted me as my shoes left the ground and I flew across the walkway. Before I could twist to get my feet under me, I landed hard against the steps. Wood cracked underneath me. I was lucky my *bones* didn't crack. The blow stole my air, but I hurried to rise, raw fear flooding into me for the first time.

Barothla hadn't moved, but she attacked again with magic. Great power pummeled me from above, as if she were pounding me with her weapons. The power was so tangible that I heard the thuds as it struck me, each blow sending agony through my body.

Hefting the hammer, I tried to parry the attacks, but I couldn't see them. I couldn't *block* them.

A smash to my face made me bite my tongue. Another to the top of my skull hammered me so hard that my knees buckled. I crumpled to the cement walkway, falling back against the broken steps again. The relentless blows kept coming.

As much as I wanted to keep fighting, to find a way to hurt her, all I could think of in that moment was defense. But neither my martial-arts blocks nor hammer parries were sufficient. I couldn't stop invisible magical attacks. Blood ran warm from my nose and ear as I curled on the ground, covering my head.

Are you sure *you don't want to help me find her?* Barothla asked, standing right beside me now. Preparing to deliver a killing blow? *As I said, it's unwise to work against me. If you change your mind about that, I'll let you live. I'll cure your friend. And maybe I'll even let you keep this.* She bent and grabbed the hammer, trying to pull it from my grip.

"*No!*" With a surge of fury, I thrust the head upward toward her chin while willing the weapon to help me, to drive through her defenses and find its target.

After she'd defeated my every attack, I didn't expect it to work. But the hammer punctured a hole in her barrier and clipped her chin. The blow was hard enough to send her reeling back in surprise, and, for a blessed moment, the attacks pummeling me halted.

So much agony gripped my body that I couldn't rise, however, and I soon sensed her gathering herself and reapplying her magical barrier.

If that is your answer, then I shall kill you and take that hammer back home. It does not belong with you. It— Barothla cut off her words, switching to Dwarven and yelling something aloud. "What are you doing?"

I recognized and could translate the simple words, but they confused me until I realized she wasn't talking to me. Zoltan had come outside, goggles covering his eyes, and was using an atomizer to spritz a liquid at the topiaries. Whatever it was, it caused them to flare back to life. Red beams shot out of their eyes, almost clipping Zoltan's shoulder.

"Beastly things," he cried. "Find the intruder!"

But they *were* targeting Barothla. He'd merely been in the way. When he darted to the side, they cut cleanly through the air toward her.

As they did, Zoltan ran around the yard, spraying other things —other defenses around the property.

With my breathing ragged and my whole body in pain, I could barely track him. As I'd hoped earlier, Barothla was distracted by the beams. This was my chance to slip past her defenses again and get some of her blood, but, when I tried to push myself up, such pain came from my joints that I couldn't put weight on them. She might have broken my bones, *many* bones.

"Away, dwarven invader," Zoltan cried, waving his atomizer. "You are not welcome here."

Barothla, whose defenses were proving sufficient to repel the beams from the topiaries, snarled and stalked toward him. Zoltan skittered back, already looking like he regretted intervening.

Reminded of the command the king had given me to call back the hammer after throwing it, I drew myself into a sitting position and hurled the hammer at her while once again willing it to crush through her defenses.

And it *did* puncture her barrier and get through, but my throw had been weak, my injuries hampering me too much. The head only clanged off her armor and bounced to the ground.

But she'd stepped into the fairy ring of mushrooms on one side of the yard, and, with Zoltan spritzing them, they stirred to life and spat something green at her. Whatever it was didn't get through her defenses, but she scowled at them instead of rushing over to attack me again.

"*Vishgronik,*" I called to the hammer.

As it lifted from the ground and flew across the yard and into my hand, magic swelled above the roof of the house. A portal appeared in the air, its silver glow flooding the yard.

"Lord Zavryd returns!" Zoltan called. "He will vanquish the intruder."

Barothla swore and looked toward the rooftop, then backed toward the street.

"I need her blood," I blurted.

Willing my limbs to find more strength, despite my pain, I hurled the hammer at Barothla again, aiming for her unarmored face.

It spun head over butt toward her with easy accuracy, but she was prepared this time and used her magic to thicken the barrier in front of her. The hammer struck it, lightning flaring around her, but it fell to the ground without getting through her defenses.

She paused, glancing at the portal, and reached for it.

"*Vishgronik!*" I cried again, terrified that she would grab it before the magic pulled it back to me.

Zavryd, in his natural dragon form, flew out of the portal.

Cursing again, Barothla left the hammer to levitate back to me and spun, erecting a portal over the sidewalk.

What intruder dares step foot upon the premises of a dragon? Zavryd cried telepathically as he flapped his wings and circled the yard.

He summoned power, and I hoped he would flambé Barothla, but maybe he recognized King Ironhelm's daughter, for he didn't strike.

I'll return for that hammer and for you, Barothla spoke into my mind, scowling over her shoulder at me before she sprang through the portal she'd made and disappeared.

My mind wanted me to charge across the yard and spring through after her, but my body was too battered to obey. Instead, hammer back in hand, I slumped to the walkway, half propped against the partially destroyed wooden steps. Her portal disappeared.

I hadn't gotten her blood.

23

ZOLTAN APPROACHED, PEERING DOWN AT ME THROUGH HIS GOGGLES.
"You said you would fling some of her blood in my direction, but I
believe that's your blood." He flicked a finger at the steps. "Also
that." He pointed at the walkway under me. "And that." He waved
toward a splotch halfway to the sidewalk. "Really, my mongrel visitor. You're a mess. And you accuse *me* of gnawing veins. That
dwarf pulped you."

"I know."

Zavryd shifted into his human form and strode toward me.
This is unacceptable.

"Sorry." I glanced at the broken steps. "I didn't do it. I mean, I
did, but only because she threw me into them. I can fix them."
Even speaking hurt, and I slumped as bleakness overtook me.
How would I get Barothla's blood in time to help Tinja now?

*Even a princess should not presume to step foot on a dragon's
premises. And what did she do to my wards?*

"Stunned them," Zoltan said. "I do not think she had the
power to thwart them fully, but I had to revive them. It is fortunate
for our visitor that I had some Ode to Life in my laboratory. Have

you the power to heal her? If not, I believe the proper course is to call an ambulance."

Even though I hurt everywhere, a night in the ER with IVs stuck in my veins and monitors beeping did not sound appealing. I thought longingly of Sarrlevi's magical touch. On numerous occasions, he'd said he wasn't a healer and could only repair basic combat injuries, but he'd taken away my pain several times and left me in close to full health.

"That is not necessary." Zavryd crouched and rested a hand on my shoulder. "My mate would wish me to heal this one. But where *is* my mate? She did not inform me that she had trips planned."

"Deception Pass," I said. "Willard sent her off to fight hydras."

"*Hydras?* Those are dangerous and not native to this world. She is a capable warrior, but I will fly up to assist her after I repair the broken bones of this one."

"Matti. Or Puletasi, remember? And thank you."

Magic trickled from Zavryd's fingers, his touch more brusque than Sarrlevi's, but warm and healing nonetheless. I closed my eyes, relieved that Val liked me enough that her mate felt obligated to spend time fixing me.

While lying there, I let myself muse over Barothla's comment about Sarrlevi not kissing anyone. He'd kissed *me*, so that clearly wasn't true. If he didn't deign to trade tongue touches while gazing intimately into the eyes of the elven females who manipulated him, that might not be that surprising.

I shook away the musing. It wasn't important.

"Is there any chance you know where Barothla went and would make a portal so I can chase her down?" I asked Zavryd.

It was a foolish request, given that Barothla had handily kicked my ass. But I couldn't give up on Tinja, especially when Sarrlevi was probably looking for Barothla on the dwarven home world while *she* was lurking here on Earth. It was possible she'd gone back to Dun Kroth, but her parting words rang in my mind. She might not have gone far. She might continue to track me through my mother's hammer and pounce as soon as Zavryd was gone.

"As a relative who has been slighted, you are perhaps the only one who could navigate political entanglements and get away with attacking her," Zavryd said, his magic continuing to flow into me as he spoke, "but it appears that your methods for battling her were inadequate."

"I guess Sarrlevi shouldn't have been so quick to say I didn't need fighting lessons from Val."

I wished *he* were here to help me. Whether he would be willing to raise a hand against my aunt, I didn't know, but I had a feeling he would support me and help me reach her if I asked it. But I'd foolishly obeyed those dwarves and sent him away. And they'd offered nothing useful.

"I will point out," I added to Zavryd, "that I was holding my own—*more* than holding my own—against her when we started and she was only using weapons. Her magic is what thumped me into the pavement. Er, your porch steps."

"The Ironhelm line is known for its powerful mages. It is one of the reasons they hold rule so easily. The blessing they received from the Dragon Council centuries ago was perhaps not needed."

A car drove around the corner, its headlights sweeping across the yard, and Zoltan hissed and raised his atomizer, as if he would run out and squirt the windshield. The driver didn't so much as slow down. If he was a neighbor, he was probably used to weird things happening on the lawn in front of this house.

"I will return to the lightless interior and check on the goblin," Zoltan said.

"Thank you for your timely help," I called as he headed for the backyard.

"You are welcome, mongrel." Zoltan paused at the gate. "Perhaps you will remember my chivalrous assistance and feel obliged to offer me a taste from your veins when you are less mangled.

This talk of the power of your family makes me curious to learn how delicious and invigorating your blood might be."

"Gross, dude," I said.

"I think it will not be, actually." Zoltan winked and bowed before leaving.

"I don't suppose there's any chance you can get two drops of blood from Barothla?" I asked Zavryd, already feeling stronger, though several of my injuries were itching like mad. The sensation came from deep within my limbs, so I couldn't have scratched to relieve the itch even if I'd wanted to. I imagined bones knitting themselves together at top speed.

"To take the blood of a royal would be considered a heinous act."

Still hoping for his help, I didn't point out that forcibly taking the blood from *anyone* could be considered a heinous act. "Even if it was only two drops? A tiny prick with a needle from a syringe? And if it was for a potion to cure someone she'd poisoned? Shouldn't there be *political entanglements* for her? She's murdering innocent people."

"Should she report an attack, even a small blood draw, to the Dragon Council, I would have to answer to them and explain myself. It is unlikely that dragons would care about the poisoning of a goblin. They are considered to be among the lowest of the intelligent lesser species. Further, the princess might lie about being responsible for that, and powerful full-blooded dwarves are difficult to effectively mind scour."

"So you're going to let Tinja die in your house?" I sat up, frustrated on her behalf. Even though I appreciated Zavryd healing me, I hated that he was essentially dismissing Tinja as not worthy of getting in trouble over. She was worth it to me, damn it.

"I will seek my mate and discuss this matter with her. Perhaps she will have some ideas, though she is not herself beloved by the Dragon Council." Zavryd knelt back, the magic flowing into me dwindling. "The queen now tolerates her as my mate, due to extenuating circumstances, but in general, none of the lesser species are considered worth breaking laws for."

"Then I'll ask you again: will you please open a portal and send me after Barothla?" I stood up, my muscles weak, my legs shaky. Even though my body didn't hurt as much, twinges remained, and I had no idea how I would win in another fight against her.

Zavryd rose from his crouch, and I made myself meet his gaze, though I had to look up. He was as tall as Sarrlevi.

"I do not think I can, since I believe that portal went to her home in the protected royal quarters of Dun Kroth. There are measures in place to keep even powerful dragons from going straight into that area. Even if she'd gone elsewhere, I would not open a portal. My mate would not wish me to send you to your death. Should you come up with a less suicidal solution, perhaps I can assist you." Zavryd stepped back, then turned into a dragon again. *After I've assisted my mate with her mission, we will return.*

He sprang into the air, his great wings stirring the breeze as he took off.

I slumped, afraid Val's mission might not end until after it was too late. The only thing heartening about the discussion with Zavryd was that he thought I might be able to get away with thumping Barothla without being jumped on by the Dragon Justice Court. Maybe it was assumed that relatives could deal with relatives without outside interference. Or maybe dwarves in general were trusted to handle their own justice when transgressions took place among their people.

With that thought in mind, I walked around the house to the basement door. I had a hunch that Barothla, after being piled on by Zoltan and the house's defenses—and almost a dragon—wouldn't come after me again here. If I went back to my house and was alone, might she be drawn to attack me there?

The booby traps Tinja and I had set hadn't even kept out trolls, so I highly doubted a powerful dwarf alchemist would find them vexing. She would see me alone, think she could get the best of me, and come to finish me off and take the hammer.

And that was exactly what would happen in another confrontation if I didn't come up with a clever way to take her by surprise.

I knocked at Zoltan's door.

Come in, my earnest mongrel.

I have a name, you know. I passed through the light lock and entered his abode, a single infrared light in the laboratory keeping it from full darkness. Why he didn't mind the red lamps when even car headlights were offensive, I didn't know.

Do you? How lovely. Zoltan stepped into view and smiled, his gaze drifting to my neck.

Without Val or anyone else around, it was creepier in the basement with him, but I reminded myself that he'd helped me in the fight, so he probably wasn't that bad of a guy. Just... hungry.

"You've recovered nicely and so quickly. Dragon magic is incredible, is it not?"

"Definitely. Do you have any potions or sprays or, I don't know, *grenades* that I could purchase? I'm trying to lay a trap for the princess. If she shows up on Earth again, I *have* to get her blood."

"Grenades. Really." Zoltan sniffed and looked around his lab. "You should visit the Ruin Bringer's weapons-crafting acquaintance, Nin."

"I wouldn't be opposed to that, but... I think I need something more powerful than she could make." I knew from Val's discussions with Sarrlevi that he didn't have trouble repelling her magical bullets, bullets from the gun Nin had made. And my own senses could tell me that her firearm weapon, though doubtless fine for battling lesser magical beings, didn't have the power of her sword or my hammer.

"Having witnessed the prowess of the dwarven princess," Zoltan said, "I am inclined to agree. I have some acids with the power to eat through magical barriers."

"I'll take acids. Can they eat through armor too?"

"Ah, with enough time, perhaps, but I believe you might need a vat of acid to dip the armor in."

"That might not be practical in the middle of a battle."

"Indeed. Also, I am without vats currently. My lab space is limited."

"It must be tough working within the confines of a residential basement."

"Quite." Zoltan hummed and started poking in cabinets. "You say you're prepared to pay?"

"Yeah. Are acids expensive?"

"Tremendously so."

I snorted. "Of course."

"My formulations are made from the highest quality—and, therefore, priciest—ingredients that must be imported from all over the world. Sometimes from *other* worlds. Although..." Zoltan looked over his shoulder at me. "I do sometimes accept barter."

"I'm not letting you drink my blood. I'm going to need all of it to survive another fight with Barothla."

"Hm, that is likely true. All of it and more." He returned to poking in his cabinets.

I groped for something else an alchemist might have that would be useful. What I really needed was magical armor of my own and the ability to create those protective barriers. If I could fight Barothla on even ground, with our magic canceling each other's magic out, I could best her; I was certain of it. But even Val, who'd been studying magic with her elven half-sister, couldn't, as far as I knew, create magical barriers. Maybe it was beyond the abilities of a half-blood.

"Is there any way to nullify someone's magic?" I asked.

"That which they wear, such as provided by charms or armor or weapons, or that which they cast?"

"Would a mage in battle conjure up a magical barrier to wrap around themselves, or would it be provided by an enchanted item?"

"The former, generally, especially if it's something that extends beyond the armor they wear."

I nodded. "That's exactly what hers did. She had a barrier *and* armor."

"In that case, distracting the mage adequately can cause their concentration to lapse and anything they're actively conjuring to falter." Zoltan walked over with a ceramic pot. "Acid can be suitably distracting. How much do you want?"

"All of it."

"Oh?" His brows rose. "You must want to fill my vault with coinage. I charge by the ounce."

"Coinage? Can't I send you digital money through an app?"

"As long as it's a great deal. This is easily sixteen ounces of acid, and I believe a thousand dollars per ounce is a fair price, given the rarity of the ingredients."

"A thousand dollars an *ounce*? That's more than gold."

"It is in fact less than gold at the current price on the market. And for one who needs an advantage against a superior opponent..."

"Uh, give me two ounces then. And I'll pay five hundred an ounce." Feeling pressed for time, I didn't want to negotiate, but he was gouging me.

"You offer to buy less *and* pay less? Goodness, mongrel visitor, that is not how economics work. It is when you buy in bulk that discounts are available."

"Six hundred an ounce, and I won't tell Zavryd that you called his topiaries beastly."

"You are a tough negotiator who knows how easily dragons are offended."

"That's me."

"I will prepare your ounces and put the liquid into small vials that you might throw at a magically armored foe so that they break. I will also include another syringe so you can more easily draw the princess's blood, should you reach her."

"This time, I will."

When Zoltan returned with the items, he held up the syringe, a cap on the needle. "Remove this and slip it into a vein, if you can. Of course, you can apply it directly to her blood and draw it in like so should she be bleeding copiously."

"Oh, she will be."

24

WHEN I ARRIVED HOME, THE NEIGHBORHOOD WAS QUIET, AND THE fog that had blanketed Lake Washington earlier was covering my street. It was so dense that I could barely see the house from the mailbox.

I paused before going inside, listening and stretching out with my senses, wondering if Barothla would return to Earth soon. It was after midnight here, but that didn't mean it was late on the dwarven home world. She might have rubbed some healing ointment on her chin—I was fairly certain that was the only injury I'd managed to give her—and decided she was ready to return. She also might not decide that for days.

That thought filled me with bleakness. Tinja didn't have days.

She'd still been sleeping when I'd left, and I hadn't tried to rouse her. That she'd remained unconscious while that battle had gone on in the front yard was worrying. What if she'd already reached a point where she *couldn't* be roused?

Tears pricked at my eyes as I imagined succeeding in getting Barothla's blood, only for it to be too late for Zoltan's formula to work. And if Barothla didn't come at all... I would also fail.

I gripped my hammer, willing it to somehow taunt Barothla and invite her to return. With Zoltan's vials of acid in my pocket, it wasn't as if I had a great secret weapon, but maybe they would make a difference. Now that I'd fought her once, I knew what to expect. Maybe I could come out on top.

My phone rang, startling me.

When Abbas's name popped up, I hurried to answer. He never called late at night. What if Barothla had decided to kidnap one of my friends and wanted to blackmail me into giving her the hammer?

"Hi, Abbas. What's up?"

The long pause made me check to make sure I hadn't accidentally hung up on him.

"Hi, Matti," he finally said. "I thought I'd get your voice mail."

Had he *hoped* to get my voice mail? Why? Because he had some awful news that he didn't want to deliver personally?

"Nope. It's me. I'm awake, battling vile aunts and learning how handy it is to have a helpful dragon around to heal one's wounds."

"I'm sure that would be nice. Are you okay?"

"A little tender, but he fixed my broken bones."

"Broken bones? Damn."

"It seems my mother's sister is... formidable."

"If she broke your bones, she must be. I've seen you fall off a three-story roof and walk away."

"I *jumped* off that roof."

"From my point of view, it looked like falling and flailing."

"It's hard to jump gracefully with the shingles sliding off and the plywood caving in."

"Yeah." Abbas hesitated. "How's Tinja?"

"Not any better. I'm back home, hoping Barothla will come try again to kill me when I'm not surrounded by dragon magic and allies."

"That's an odd thing to hope for."

"I'm an odd person."

"True." He sounded like he was smiling when he said that, but his tone turned grim. "I called because..."

I raised my eyebrows.

When the pause went on, I said, "Because you have a holiday coming up tomorrow and can't come to work?"

He sighed. "No. There *is* a big troll ceremony tonight where we burn a bonfire, drink to the moon, and sing the praises of the gods, but I called because... I can't work on the new project with you. Or, uhm, any other projects. Not right now."

I blinked and stared at the phone. Even though the house-building project was the last thing on my mind at the moment, it sounded like he was doing the business-partner equivalent of breaking up with me. "Why not?"

"My father forbade me working with you. The whole clan did because you... Well, I'm sure it's not true, but my father's people believe—the word got out and a *lot* of people believe—that you killed a crew of trolls over in Kenmore earlier tonight."

"Oh." I grimaced, remembering the boy—and the grownups he'd returned with. They'd disappeared after the dwarves had arrived, and I'd forgotten about them, but I'd worried there might be ramifications when those gunshots went off with Sarrlevi and me on the barge.

"You didn't do it, did you?" Abbas asked. "My father said those guys were smugglers, but that's it. They never attacked anyone. They helped get cargoes over that the magical community might not be able to acquire on their own."

"No, I didn't shoot them. Sarrlevi and I were investigating them because we heard the people who have my mother got a cargo from them a while back. We wanted to ask them questions—that's all—but they were already dead when the barge arrived. Everyone aboard was dead except for their dogs. Uhm, *yaku*." We *had* killed those. Would the troll community be mad about that?

"My father said there were gunshots fired after it was in dock."

"Yes, but they were booby traps that someone set, probably whoever killed them. Sarrlevi said their deaths had been recent."

"I don't think you should hang around with him so much, Matti."

I swallowed. What did *that* mean? That he didn't believe me?

"He didn't kill them, Abbas. And neither did I. I get that it sounded bad to the kid on the docks, but I swear the gunshots were from a booby trap. It almost got *us*."

The long silence that followed made emotion well up within me, and tears threatened. I couldn't lose Tinja *and* Abbas.

"I promise, Abbas," I said softly. "I'd tell you if I'd killed anyone. You know I've fought trolls before."

"Criminals, yeah."

I didn't point out that smugglers *were* criminals, especially since it had sounded like those guys had been helping out the magical community. Maybe the troll clans had considered them the blue-skinned equivalents of Robin Hood.

"I do believe you, Matti," Abbas finally said. "But you know I'm tight with my family. I can't go against my father's wishes. *Everyone's* wishes. Not right now, okay?"

"Okay," I made myself say, though it wasn't. I wiped my eyes. My whole world was falling apart.

"I hope you find a solution for Tinja."

"Thanks."

He hung up.

I jammed my phone into my pocket. Frustration and fury and feelings I couldn't name exploded inside me and I slammed my fist into the door.

It was solid oak, but it dented under my strength. My anger didn't keep the blow from hurting. I almost hefted my hammer to beat the crap out of the door, but this was my home, damn it. Instead, I threw back my head and roared.

A couple of houses down, a dog barked, but the world didn't otherwise respond.

Shaking with anger, I went inside, but not before scouring the yard with my eyes and senses, wanting badly for Barothla to appear so I could take out my frustrations on a deserving target.

But she didn't.

25

PASSING THE HALLWAY MIRROR GAVE ME A START. AFTER THE FIGHT, I wasn't surprised that my clothes were rumpled and stained, but shards of wood—from the broken porch steps?—stuck out of my hair, a bruise darkened my jaw, and dirt and a scrape marred my cheek.

Zavryd must have focused on healing the more serious injuries. Understandable. And I was grateful since I doubted I would have walked away from his yard on my own if he hadn't.

I decided to risk taking a shower and maybe let myself cry under the hot water. If Barothla showed up, I would have no problem fighting her naked in the front yard. I would simply keep the vials of acid and my hammer close while I was cleaning up.

"What has my life become?"

Sighing, I pushed my hands through my hair to dislodge the wood, then shucked my shoes and clothes on the floor in my bedroom and grabbed a towel. In the bathroom, I cranked the water to hot and let it steam up everything before stepping in. The hammer leaned against the wall, and the vials rested on a washcloth on the sink in a spot where they couldn't fall. With the way my week was going, I could see accidentally breaking them and horribly maiming myself.

Promising not to linger long, I let the spray pound onto my head and shoulders, glad I'd remodeled the bathroom after buying the house. It had a quality showerhead that was almost sufficient to relax my tense muscles, but I probably needed a deep-tissue massage. And for people not to want to kill me. And for my business partner not to want to leave. And for my roommate not to die.

I bent over, gripping my knees, and was on the verge of giving in to my urge to cry when someone spoke into my mind.

Your abode is not sufficiently protected for you to be here alone. Sarrlevi.

I lurched upright, at first thinking he was in the house, but I sensed him at the front door. A part of me was tempted to tell him to beat it, that I wanted to have my pity party in private, but if Barothla didn't come here, I needed his help to reach her. Besides, I didn't really want to be alone with my dark thoughts.

I know. I need a powerful elf assassin to camp out on his cot in my front yard to keep bad guys away. I turned off the water and grabbed the towel.

It's foggy and damp. Perhaps I could set up my cot in your house.

Uh. I'm naked. I toweled off and glanced behind the bathroom door to make sure my robe hung there, but I wasn't that sure about wearing only that to let Sarrlevi in. Then I snorted at myself. It wasn't as if he was going to be overcome with lust and paw me over. Besides, he'd already seen me naked.

I'm not certain if that's an invitation to enter your abode, he said dryly.

You can come in. I was surprised he hadn't simply shown up in my hallway. He *was* a professional stalker after all. *I never should have sent you away.*

Not at the behest of some useless dwarves, no.

I assume the king finds a use for them, I said, though I'd had similar thoughts.

After slipping into the robe and tying the belt, I grabbed my hammer and padded out to meet him. He stood at the end of the hallway, his arms folded over his chest as he leaned his shoulder against the wall. His eyebrows rose, either at my robe and bare feet or at the hammer clenched in my grip.

"I knew you took it to bed, but you didn't mention bathing with it." His eyes crinkled, though his gaze lingered on my jaw—the bruise, probably. The water had washed away the dirt but couldn't do anything about wounds.

"I'm expecting company." I couldn't manage a smile at his humor. "Maybe I should say I'm *hoping* for company. I don't know if she's coming back."

His expression grew grave, and he lowered his arms. "Barothla came?"

"Yeah. She doesn't care that she poisoned Tinja. I don't think she needs me either, just the hammer. She did her best to maul me and take it. She walked through the protections around Val's house, and we had a little fight. I tried my damnedest to get some of her blood and thought I might have a shot when she was only swinging her hammers around. She's not *that* great of a fighter, but then she got pissed and unleashed her magic, and I broke Val's steps with my back. Zoltan ran out to help, and Zavryd showed up, so she fled, otherwise..." I clenched my fist. "I hate her. And I hate that I need her blood and didn't get it. I thought by being here alone, someplace less protected, she might come again and try to get me. And I'd have another shot at her. I'm sure it's suicidal to want that, but Tinja doesn't have that long. And I—" I stopped, my voice on the verge of cracking. I'd been okay with the thought of crying alone in the shower, but I didn't want to fall apart in front of Sarrlevi. He'd probably *tease* me about it later.

Or maybe he wouldn't. Aside from his plumber jokes, he'd been doing less of that lately. He'd been a friend.

When he walked down the hallway and lifted his arms, I half leaned and half fell against him. Needing support, I was relieved when he wrapped his arms around me. I didn't want to cry all over him, though, and took several shuddering breaths, trying to get myself under control.

"You can relax," he said gently and stroked the back of my head. "I won't leave again while she's a threat."

It was the soft gentleness of his words that made me lose the battle for self-control. Even if I wasn't sure *relax* meant I should weep all over his shirt, I needed to. And he let me, holding me and stroking my hair, enrobing me in his warmth.

He smelled faintly of the forest, of cedar and spruce. I didn't know if that meant he'd napped in a tree earlier, or if elves emanated an aura of nature. Either way, it was comforting. *He* was comforting.

"Had I realized she was *here*," Sarrlevi murmured after a time, "I wouldn't have gone to two worlds looking for her and trying to arrange an appointment."

"All villains come to harass me sooner or later. You can just stand by my side and wait for them." I leaned back and wiped his shirt, glad I'd only cried and not gotten snot on him. That couldn't be an acceptable addition to the assassin wardrobe.

"You do attract trouble."

"I believe it all started when *you* showed up in my backyard. And you are definitely trouble."

"Yes." Sarrlevi smiled and brushed my jaw with his fingers, a slight tingle flowing into the scrape and bruise.

I leaned my head back, basking in his touch, only realizing then how much more intimate it was when he healed me than when someone else did. Because I cared for him? Or because he was different with me? Not brusque, like Zavryd had been, but... caring.

When I opened my eyes, I found him gazing not at my face but... at my chest. Embarrassment flushed my cheeks. The robe wasn't some skimpy and sexy garment, but it also didn't do a lot to hide one's cleavage, especially not from a tall person.

"If I didn't know better, I'd think you were ogling me, Varlesh Sarrlevi."

His smile widened, no embarrassment lacing his expression, but he did lift his gaze back to mine. "I believe you do not mind."

"That's because you're still a cocky bastard. I didn't think you were into dwarves. And *especially* mongrels." I raised my eyebrows.

With everything going on, it was a dumb time to worry about such things, but I wanted... the impossible, I supposed. For him to have changed his mind. He *had* kissed me, whether it had been appropriate or not. And if Barothla's words had been true, maybe that implied I meant something to him.

"You are a more intriguing mongrel than I originally believed."

What did *that* mean? I wanted to be sexy and star in his dreams, not *intriguing*.

His eyes crinkled again, and I had a feeling he was reading my mind, even if the telltale itch didn't tease my skull. Maybe he knew what I was thinking from my face.

"And you did invite me in." He'd finished healing my wounds, but he brushed his fingers through my hair, warm tendrils of magic that had nothing to do with wound repair flowing through me and making my entire body tighten and tingle.

"Not to ogle me," I said, but if some of his magic trickled down and made my robe fall off, would I object?

"No? When *most* naked women invite me into their homes, it is for sex. And they enjoy being ogled."

"I only said you could come in so you wouldn't sleep on my lawn. People would think that's weird."

A hint of his usual cockiness infused his smile. "That is *not* why you invited me in."

"No," I agreed and leaned in and wrapped my arms around him once more, "but it wasn't for sex either. My friend—"

"I know. I understand." He stroked the back of my head again, the magical tingle fading.

My body was disappointed, but my mind appreciated his understanding. Besides, I wasn't sure if he'd been offering sex anyway. Who knew with him?

"I have a plan," Sarrlevi said, "but I think you will not like it."

"Hell. Should I sit down for this?"

"Possibly."

I dropped my arms but, reluctant to release him completely, clasped his hand. Had the living room furniture not been covered in Tinja's blueprints—a painful reminder that she wasn't here to clear them, or promise that she would clear them later—I would have led him out there. The dining room was too formal. Assuming he would be able to refrain from touching me if I took him to my bedroom, I led him in there and sat on the edge of the bed.

"Tell me," I said.

Sarrlevi paused before sitting beside me, though it was probably to frown his disapproval at the clothing I'd left on the floor than because the intimacy of the spot bothered him. "Barothla sent a reply to the message I was able to get through to her and agreed to meet with me in the—it'll be early morning here. How much time does your friend have?"

"That much, I hope. If you can be quick and get back to Zoltan with the blood."

"She'll be suspicious if I'm *too* quick, but I'll do my best."

"Good. Do you still have the syringe? Zoltan gave me another one." I grabbed my jacket off the floor, but it was only as I fished out the syringe that his words sank in. What they meant and why I wouldn't *like* his plan. With the syringe dangling from my fingers, I stared at him. "Please tell me you're not going to have sex with her."

He accepted the syringe. "I can't *attack* her, for the reasons I've already gone over, but sex is something she's expressed an interest in a number of times."

"Oh, I don't doubt it."

His smile was bleak rather than smug. "She strikes me as someone who won't mind roughness, and, even if she does, I'm sure I can keep her distracted enough that she won't notice a scratch." He eyed the needle. "A syringe may be all that's required."

I couldn't stop staring at him, horrified at the thought of him writhing in bed with that vile woman, with my *aunt*, the person who'd hired him to kill my mother. He couldn't have sex with her, damn it.

"Sarrlevi," I groaned, bending forward, dropping my head to my knees, and clasping my hands over my neck. Airplane crash position, wasn't that the name? It felt right.

He rested a hand on my back. "I did not think you would like this plan."

"*No.*"

"I believe it will work and will *not* prompt the dragon horde to descend on me. If I'm successful in keeping her from figuring out what I'm doing, it shouldn't tug any dwarf beards either."

"She's not going to be suspicious that you suddenly want to have sex with her after rejecting her for forty years?" I assumed that was how their previous encounters had gone. But how many propositions had there been? He'd said she'd made the request numerous times. They shouldn't have had to meet more than the one time she hired him. *If* they'd since broken that contract.

But if they hadn't broken it... If, as I'd feared earlier, he still had something going on with her...

I groaned again, straightening to look at him. "Why, Sarrlevi?"

"You need her blood," he said matter-of-factly, "and it's the least antagonistic way to get it."

I shook my head. "But why do you keep sleeping with all these *horrible* women and not—" my throat tightened around the word *me*, and I didn't utter it. "She's not even hot," I grumbled, even though I knew it had nothing to do with desire. I was just stung, which was stupid, because he would be, once again, doing this to help me.

The tears I thought I'd cried out in the hallway threatened to return. I blinked and looked away, having no intention of letting them fall. Before, when my angst had been over losing my friends, it had been acceptable. But this... this was stupid.

"She is not," he agreed dryly and patted my back.

Deciding I didn't want to guide him down the line of thinking that dwarves were homely, because maybe *half*-dwarves fell into that category for him too, I merely shook my head and looked at the floor. "I suppose I should be... glad that your superpowers go beyond bashing people with swords, but this seems so..."

I stopped myself, not wanting to insult him. Who was I to judge? I didn't even know if elves had cultural beliefs similar to those humans had when it came to sex.

"I know." His tone was still dry. At least he didn't sound offended. "I would rather deal with obstacles with swords. Or magic." His fingers drifted from my back to my head, and he rubbed my scalp. Warm tingles of his magic flowed through me, not to heal but to evoke pleasure.

Since he was going off to boink my new nemesis later, I shouldn't have wanted that, but I couldn't find it in myself to be disgruntled with him. If he got that blood, and it saved Tinja's life, I would fling my arms around him and kiss him. Hard.

I let myself slump against him, lowering my chin so he could more easily rub anything he liked. With his delicious magic making my nerves thrum, I was tempted to crawl into his lap and start rubbing parts of *him*. I was about to clear my throat and pull away, lest I do something he didn't want—and that *I* shouldn't want, not then. But another trickle of magic flowed from him. Not into me this time. It wasn't anything threatening, but I lifted my chin, wondering what he was doing.

My shoes lifted from the floor and floated into the hallway. Toward the storage bench by the front door where they usually went? Next, my clothes rose from the floor and toward my closet.

"Are you serious, dude?" I eyed him sidelong and found him watching me back, a smirk on his lips. "Was the entropy of my room disturbing you again?"

"Immensely."

"You're so odd. FYI, dirty clothes go in the hamper, not in the closet."

"They're not dirty any longer."

"Oh? Your magic can get out dirt and bloodstains?"

"Easily." He pushed his fingers through my hair, as if to remind me I should be enjoying his touch and not worrying about his fastidious streak.

It *was* wonderful, even if his attention was divided.

"What are you going to do if you arrive in *her* room, and there are beakers, test tubes, and dirty laundry all over the floor?" I had no idea what the bedrooms of alchemists looked like, but that seemed a reasonable collection of things to expect. "A powerful mage might object to you touching her stuff with your magic."

"I doubt she'll invite me to her bedroom."

"Just some nameless hotel where they rent rooms by the hour?"

"Something like that."

"Romantic."

"Few assassins seek *romance*," he said, dry again.

I didn't point out that I found the head rubbing moderately romantic. I was doing my best not to also find it erotic, but the magic elevated the sensations to another level, and I struggled to keep my voice from growing raspy. "Just killing and sex, huh?"

"Not usually at the same time, but yes."

"Sounds kind of... empty." I winced as soon as the words came out. I didn't want to judge him, but I was doing a crappy job of not coming across as doing exactly that. Besides, it was only because I wanted him to be with me, not any of them, that I objected to his acts.

"It is. When I was younger, I was angry often and not suitable company most of the time. I enjoyed sex—too much, as the reputation I've earned attests—but I did not care about relationships. As an assassin prone toward collecting enemies, not having attachments was safer. I brought this life upon myself." He shrugged, as if to say it was fine, or that it didn't matter. That he still didn't care. But was that true?

"Did you? Or was it that it was all you had the training to do after your people drove you out at such a young age?"

"It's true that it would have been either this or becoming a mercenary. That doesn't pay well, and you have to take orders from others. There was also more political strife than outright war back then." Sarrlevi snorted softly. "This was a growth industry."

"Well, it's important to go into a field with good career prospects."

"Indeed. And it suited me at the time. As I said, I was bitter and angry, and it was an outlet for that. These days, it's mostly a job that doesn't stir much passion in me. My largest source of... emotion has been my frustration with King Eireth and those who refuse to let me see my mother. I don't think she has much time left, and I'd like her to know... just to know that I still care," he finished quietly.

My heart ached for him, and I rested my hand on his thigh, wishing I could help him in some way. But I was still uncertain how he felt about me. Which seemed silly since he'd kissed me, and he was here rubbing my head, but he'd also said the first kiss had been a mistake and that he was on a mission, so such acts were inappropriate. He'd also stiffened the first time I'd hugged him, as if he had to force himself to accept such overtures from me.

"I hope it works out and that you're able to be with her again," I said as I watched his face to see if he minded my touch.

There was a troubled crease to his brow, but he was studying the floor, not me, so I assumed he was thinking of his mother and the elves preventing him from seeing her. I lifted my hand, wishing I could smooth that furrow and bring back the warm humor that had been in his eyes earlier, but I hesitated.

He looked at my hand.

"Do I get to rub *your* head?" I asked.

A smile ghosted across his lips. "If you wish."

I swallowed, feeling a little silly and nervous, but when he bent his head toward me, I pushed my fingers through his short hair. It was cool and soft in contrast to the warmth of his scalp. I brushed across a line of scar tissue. A wound he'd received before he'd been as well-trained at healing injuries? Perhaps in his fight against his father?

I scraped my fingers lightly over his scalp, wishing it was within my power to send the magical zings of pleasure through *him* the way he did to me. But I had no idea how. All I'd ever done was accidentally enchant a few things I'd worked on, and that was all I would learn to do in my lessons, at least in the beginning. I doubted he wanted his scalp *enchanted*. Still, as I shifted my hand to stroke one of his pointed ears, I imagined I *could* send tingles of pleasure through him, both so he would enjoy it and so he would want me, the inappropriate half-dwarf who was, against the wisdom of everyone she knew, falling for him.

As I brushed my thumb along his ear and massaged the side of his head, he lifted his eyes. I paused, worried elf ears were sensitive or sacred or something like that and I'd explored too far.

But his eyes were molten as they met mine, the heated look like none he'd given me before. "Don't stop," he ordered, almost a growl.

"Okay," I whispered, my heart pounding for some reason. Under that intense gaze, I stroked his ear, his head, and willed whatever magic my neophyte body could conjure to make him enjoy the experience. I caught myself leaning closer, wanting...

He pulled me into his lap and kissed me.

It wasn't like the gentle kisses he'd given me before but a hungry kiss full of the passion he'd implied wasn't a part of his life. It was the most thrilling and arousing thing I'd ever experienced.

With my uncertainties and rational thoughts spilling out of my mind, all I could think about was kissing him back and touching him, making him *want* to be touched, making him want *me*. More than those awful women who wanted to use him. I *cared,* damn it. He ought to be with someone who would have his back in a fight, not set him up to be a target for enemies. I wanted to clobber all the people in his life who'd failed to stand up for him, to stand *with* him.

Though that could wait. Right now... I wanted nothing more than to enjoy this, his mouth and his touch bringing far greater pleasure than I'd ever experienced with a man. Hell, with *anything.*

When his hand slipped into my robe to stroke my breast, his magic arousing far more exquisite a sensation than simple touch ever had, I gasped with such enthusiasm that he smirked against my lips. I knew it was that cocky I'm-amazing-and-I-know-it smirk, but I didn't care. He *was* amazing.

I pushed my hand under his shirt to stroke his taut abs, wanting to explore his body even as he explored mine. He growled with approval and leaned me back on the bed, loosening my robe further. Anticipation and desire coursed through me, and I pulled him down with me, wanting nothing more than—

Sarrlevi halted abruptly and pulled his mouth from mine.

"No, no," I rasped, gripping his shoulders to keep him from drawing back. "We're *not* inappropriate. Really. It's okay. *We're* okay." I almost said *please don't stop*, but I found enough of my pride—my *sanity*—to keep from begging. Besides, he was looking toward the door, as if he'd heard something—or *sensed* something —rather than frowning at me as if he'd come to his senses.

Sarrlevi closed his eyes and took a deep breath, then tugged my robe back in place to cover me. "A number of trolls are walking up your street." He dropped his head. "I should have used this time to put wards around your house."

Trolls? What the hell were trolls doing here?

"No, you shouldn't have," I said, hating the thought of him believing we'd been making a mistake. I'd been enjoying this time far too much for it to have been a mistake. "Besides, I came here to my largely undefended house because I wanted her to show up, because there *weren't* wards or any protections she had to worry about." Admittedly, I hadn't known he had plans to see her later.

"I know, but you don't need to invite her—or anyone who threatens you—here. After we deal with the trolls, I will set wards." He started to sit up but paused, his eyes meeting mine.

I struggled to wipe the disappointment off my face. By now, I could also sense the trolls—a *lot* of them—so I knew he wasn't using their appearance as an excuse to ditch me. They were a genuine threat.

He touched my cheek and kissed me. It wasn't the hungry

passionate kiss of a few minutes before, but it seemed to promise...
later. I *hoped* it did, and I tried to make it good for him, to let him
know I would be ready.

I'm going to selfishly hope you aren't going to kiss her, I said telepathically, though I should have been more mature than that and
not brought her up at all.

I won't. He brushed his fingers through my hair one last time,
then strode out to face the trolls.

26

SENSING NO FEWER THAN THIRTY TROLLS OUTSIDE, I DRESSED AS quickly as I could. Instead of striding out the front door, Sarrlevi had slipped out the back and leaped onto the roof before disappearing from my senses. I trusted he was still up there, considering the trolls as they surveyed my house, but didn't want them to know exactly where he was. It was probably only because they'd sensed him here that they'd paused out front.

A single troll might hesitate to get in a fight with me, but *thirty* ought to feel confident that they could handle a half-dwarf. Rightfully so. Unfortunately. Nobody could fight so many at once, not without magic.

I grabbed my hammer, wishing I'd had time to learn more about *its* magic. As I passed the bathroom door, the vials still nestled on the sink, I debated whether to grab them. The trolls might not have the powerful magical defenses of Barothla, but the acid ought to burn their skin and distract them so we could land our blows more easily.

But were these troll bounty hunters from another realm?

Thugs after my hammer? Or were they only here because they believed I'd helped kill the crew of that barge?

My stomach twisted at the thought. I didn't want to kill or even hurt trolls who were after me because of a misunderstanding.

Their eyes are glazed, and they're not responding to my telepathic questions, Sarrlevi said. *Someone is controlling them.*

The people who have my mother? Are there bracelets? I paused at Tinja's room and leaned in and grabbed her Goblinator gun, though I didn't know how to fire it or even if it was loaded. Still, it might be useful to get a few shots in before we ended up in melee range.

Few have any charms or artifacts that I can detect. One has a modest magical axe. Most have tools instead of weapons, and they wear clothing acquired on this world.

Meaning they're not powerful portal-creating mercenaries after my hammer? Fully dressed, with the vials in my pocket, a washcloth wrapped around them for insulation, I eased out the back door. I didn't sense anyone in the backyard, but it was possible some camouflaged threats lurked there, seeking to take advantage while we were distracted by the trolls out front.

I don't think they know what *they're after.*

Could someone manipulate them without trinkets? With straight-up magic of their own conjuring?

Yes, but it would take someone powerful to coerce so many. And the controller would have to be nearby.

How powerful? I decided it made sense to climb to the roof and join him. *Dragon powerful?*

A dragon could do this, yes, and camouflage him or herself from my senses.

Could Barothla do it? When I reached the roof, I didn't see Sarrlevi, but his telepathic words came from the front of the house.

After a pause, he said, *I don't think so. Not with a coercion spell, but it is possible she could have crafted a potion that would make them susceptible to her wishes. I'm aware that alchemists can make inhalants, but I think it would have needed to be delivered in a higher dose than that. More likely, it would be a liquid compound that they would have had to drink.*

Abbas mentioned that there's a troll ceremony tonight. Something about the moon and swigging a beverage.

I squinted at the trolls lined up in the yard and facing the house. Their eyes were as vacant as Sarrlevi had promised. Clad in overalls, hoodies, jeans, and other Earth clothes, with tooth necklaces and bone bracelets the only hint of their troll culture, they looked like they could be Abbas's relatives. I was relieved *he* wasn't there.

Less relieving were the torches that several of the trolls carried. Worse, at least ten of them had pickaxes or sledgehammers. They were tools plucked from a construction site, not weapons for battle, but they could do plenty of damage to a person's skull. Or their house.

A couple of the trolls faced my carport instead of me, and I ground my teeth. I'd just *fixed* that carport.

That would have been an opportunity to slip them something then, Sarrlevi said. *Are you going to Goblinate them?*

I'd rather not, but if they try to light my house on fire, I will.

Despite the vacant gazes, most of the trolls looked toward the roof. Toward *me.*

A brush against my arm told me Sarrlevi was right beside me. Only when he was that close could I make him out, his camouflaging magic better than that of my charm. The charm that I should have rubbed as soon as he'd mentioned trolls, but I had a feeling these guys would already be destroying my house if they thought I'd fled and wasn't here to defend it.

They shouldn't be able to see me, he said. *I can circle around behind and...*

Yes? After finding the trigger, I raised the Goblinator toward the trolls eyeing my carport.

She's here. Barothla.

Of course she was. *Planning to annihilate a pesky relative before joining you at the Crimson Realms Motel 6 later, huh?*

I don't know. I'll go talk to her and try to get her to leave you alone.

Why would you have that ability to sway her?

I don't know that I do, but I'll try to convince her of... Sarrlevi's swords were in his hands, so he couldn't turn a palm upward, but he did a semblance of that gesture with a blade and finished, *Something.*

As he headed off who knew where—I couldn't yet sense Barothla—tires squealed. A truck took the corner too fast, then vroomed down the street in this direction.

I swore. Some of the vacant-eyed trolls were out in the street and appeared oblivious to the threat.

The driver halted, not bothering to pull over to park, and I sensed a familiar aura inside.

"Abbas," I blurted in surprise as he sprang out.

"Stop," he yelled to the trolls, his arms up. "What are you doing? She wasn't responsible. I *told* you." He ran up and gripped a shoulder, but the troll didn't budge. In that crowd, his six-feet-ten-inches wasn't that substantial. "What's wrong with you all?"

"Abbas," I called, thinking he hadn't heard me the first time.

He spun toward the roof, his eyes widening when he saw me with the Goblinator and my hammer. He lifted his hands, as if to placate me.

"Matti, this is my father's clan. You can't—" He flung his hand toward my hammer. "They're not *criminals.*"

"I know, but they're under someone's control, and I think they're here to kill me."

The trolls hadn't yet advanced, but that would change as soon as Barothla got close and uttered a command. Maybe she already *was* close. She could be as camouflaged as Sarrlevi.

But *he'd* sensed her, so maybe not.

"Under control?" Abbas asked. "What do you mean? Like with magic?"

"An alchemist's magical potion, we think." I was surprised he hadn't been affected, but if the clan had been consuming an alcoholic drink for their ceremony, it made sense that he would have abstained.

"We?" Abbas squinted warily around.

I opened my mouth to mention Sarrlevi, but I doubted his presence would reassure Abbas.

"How can we break the control?" He squeezed past two beefy trolls in overalls to grip the shoulder of another, one with kinky white hair and a sledgehammer. "Matti, this is my *father*."

Dread filled me, though I wasn't surprised, since Abbas had said this was his clan.

"You can't hurt them," he added.

"I don't want to, but if they try to kill me or demolish my house..." I shook my head bleakly.

"How do we break control?" Abbas repeated, snapping his fingers in front of his father's broad blue-skinned face.

"Thump the person who made and gave them the potion." I didn't know if that would shake them of their hypnotized state, but it ought to keep them from doing anything—from *destroying* anything. I was surprised they hadn't already started, but maybe Sarrlevi had distracted Barothla.

"Where is he?"

"She, and I don't know. I—" Abruptly, I sensed her. At the nearest intersection.

Abbas must have driven right past her. Maybe she *had* been camouflaged. But if so, how had Sarrlevi known she was there? Had she *spoken* to him?

Reminded that I didn't know exactly what their relationship was these days, I clenched my jaw.

"I'll deal with her," I told Abbas and reached for my camouflaging charm. Before rubbing it, I called, "Here," and tossed the Goblinator toward him. "Keep them from demolishing my house."

He caught the weapon, but I could tell from the horrified expression on his face that, as much as he might want to help me, he wouldn't attack his own people. I couldn't blame him. Besides, if they were under magical control, they wouldn't be able to stop obeying an order even if he *did* attack. My only hope was that I could get to Barothla before she gave the order for them to destroy my property.

After activating the charm, I jumped down from the roof. Though I wanted to sprint toward Barothla with my hammer raised, I made myself walk slowly toward the intersection so I wouldn't make any noise. I doubted a dwarf alchemist had enhanced hearing, but Sarrlevi was another matter, and instincts that made my gut twist with distress told me I didn't want him to hear me coming either.

I would sneak up on both of them, crack her on the head, and keep her from ordering the trolls to attack. Then I could get my blood sample and save my friend.

Something told me it wouldn't be that easy, and, as I crept toward the intersection, she disappeared from my senses again. Damn it, she *did* have the power to camouflage herself. Maybe Sarrlevi's arrival had startled her, and her concentration had lapsed for a moment.

I kept creeping toward the intersection, hoping they were still there, that she and Sarrlevi hadn't sensed me and believed they could talk. Except that I didn't hear any voices. If they were speaking, it had to be telepathically.

I swore silently, wanting badly to eavesdrop, but how? From what I'd experienced, those using telepathy could speak to a group at large, but they could also make conversations private, pinpointing where their words went. I remembered Sarrlevi's instructions for me to form a tunnel and envision the face of the recipient.

Still, if they didn't know I was there, maybe they wouldn't be *that* worried about being overheard. Maybe if I got close enough...

I'd reached the corner and neither saw nor sensed them. What if they'd moved into one of the yards? I stepped out into the street and squeezed the haft of my hammer, willing it to lend me whatever power it could for this.

The weapon warmed slightly in my hand. Whether it actually helped or I'd gotten close enough to their position I didn't know, but the first telepathic words floated to me. Sarrlevi's.

This is ridiculous. There's no reason for you to kill Rodarska's daughter. She doesn't live on Dun Kroth and isn't ever going to be a succession candidate. She's no threat to you.

She has my sister's hammer, which I believe I can use to track her down, and you—for some reason—are refusing to retrieve it for me. Why?

It does not belong to you.

Are you telling me that you murder people for a living, but you object to theft? Oh, that's rich.

I'm not a petty criminal. Are you the one who put the reward out for the hammer?

There's a reward for it? Then I definitely want it before someone else gets it. Someone powerful that I can't easily quash.

She hadn't easily *quashed* me either. Though if she'd started with her magic, she would have. That made me rage inside. I wanted to be the equal of the woman who'd once tried to arrange my mother's death. And was *still* trying to arrange it?

I clenched my jaw so hard I worried they would hear it creak and tried to loosen the joints. Though I still couldn't see or sense them, I doubted I was more than ten feet away. If I wasn't careful,

Sarrlevi, elven tracker—*stalker*—that he was, might smell or hear me using senses that the charms did not nullify.

I flexed my hands on the hammer, debating if I could charge over there and see Barothla quickly enough to smash her before she reacted. If Sarrlevi saw me first, would he help me by distracting her? Or... would he help *her* and keep me from taking a swing?

It also crossed my mind, Barothla continued, *that if her daughter is dead, whatever group is using Rodarska might lose their lever on her. It's hard to believe my sister could be subdued and forced to work against her will on this backward magic-deprived world for decades.*

I rocked back, stunned by the thought, a thought that had never occurred to me. That sensation of dread and almost sickness returned to my gut.

So you'd kill the daughter to what end? Sarrlevi asked. *You don't care about this Earth organization, I'm sure.*

Oh, of course not. But our father won't officially make me his heir as long as there's hope that Rodarska lives. I need her dead. Without a doubt. And if Rodarska attacks her captors in some fit of rage, believing she has nothing left to lose, and gets herself killed... Well, I wouldn't need your services except to retrieve the body then, would I? Barothla's tone grew icy and snide when she added, *I trust you could handle that simple task.*

My body shook with the confirmation that he was still working for her. He had to be. Val was right. He might have put the mission aside for a time, but, for some reason, he was back on it now.

I can handle much, Sarrlevi said. *Order the trolls to depart, and leave the daughter alone, and I'll finish the assignment.*

The daughter. I didn't know if he was distancing himself from me because he didn't want Barothla to know he cared or because he truly *didn't* care. That thought stung like a dagger driven deep. It was hard to believe his touches, his kisses, had all been an act, but who knew what went on inside his head? It wasn't as if I could read *his* mind. I wished I could.

The assignment you haven't been able to finish for forty years. Forgive me, dear assassin, if I don't believe you're fully committed.

Sarrlevi's tone turned bitter. *You've ensured I am, haven't you? You know all about levers and extortion.*

Don't pretend you haven't tried to manipulate me in return. What's this tryst you suggested really about, assassin? As much as I'd enjoy having your cock between my legs, I'm not a fool. You weren't interested forty years ago, and I'm not delusional enough to believe that my beauty has grown to rival an elf's over that time. If I didn't know better, I'd think you wanted me to let my guard down so you could kill me.

I could kill you anytime.

Her snort was audible and helped me further pinpoint her location. *You could try.*

Don't tempt me.

All of my knowledge would die with me.

I'm aware.

A crash came from the house, and I jumped.

"No," Abbas cried. "Stop! All of you!"

It will be simplest if I handle matters myself, Barothla said.

27

DISTRACT HER! I ATTEMPTED TO MAKE IT A PINPOINT communication, only for Sarrlevi, but when I rushed toward Barothla's position with my hammer raised, she sensed me coming.

When she came into view, a scant five feet away, she already faced me with her hammers raised and that damned magical barrier cocooning her. Sarrlevi also came into view, his swords drawn but lowered. He'd been facing her from only a pace away. He didn't appear surprised to see me, but he didn't move either. With his great power, he might have grabbed her and pinned her. He didn't.

I swung for Barothla's head, betrayal and frustration and fury behind the attack. Only at the last instant did I remember to cry, "*Hyrek!*" to bring out the weapon's lightning power.

Barothla raised her one-handed hammers, crossing them over-head to catch my blow. My weapon clanged against hers, and lightning crackled in the air between us, branches spitting in all directions. Sarrlevi, wrapping himself in his own defensive magic, stepped back.

I dared not glance at him for more than an instant, not when Barothla was pulling her hammers down, already preparing a retaliatory strike, but his face gave away nothing. Would he help me? Would he help *her*? Or would he let us settle this between ourselves?

If that was his plan, I was about to get my ass kicked again. I had little doubt. That didn't keep me from roaring in anger and lashing out again, first with a kick designed to distract Barothla, and then with a swipe toward her head.

My foot struck her magical barrier and never reached her. She barely got her hammers up in time to deflect my weapon, but she did, then spat something in Dwarven.

Cracks and crashes came from my house. Even as she battled me, her drugged minions were destroying my home.

In our first match, I'd let her take the offensive so I could gauge her abilities, but I pressed her hard now. I rained blows toward her head and torso too rapidly for her to do anything but defend. Until she summoned magic, her power forming like a vortex in front of me.

As I'd done before, I willed my hammer to pierce her barrier. If I couldn't do something to distract her, she would pummel me again.

The double head glowed brightly, so brightly that Barothla blinked, and her magic faltered. The brilliant silver-blue illumination almost blinded me as well, but I drove my hammer toward her torso. This time, it punctured her barrier and slammed into her armor. The sturdy metal chest plate was as magical as the rest of her items, but my blow dented it and sent her reeling back.

Afraid she would recover and succeed in summoning her magic, I sprang after her. Again, I willed the hammer to puncture her defenses and reach her. I had to keep her from casting her magic. I swung, certain a skull-crushing blow to the head would accomplish that.

Barothla ducked, getting one of her hammers up enough to deflect mine, but the power of my strike knocked it from her hand. She swore as it clattered to the pavement.

Stop her, you bastard! she cried telepathically, glancing toward Sarrlevi, who'd barely moved since we started fighting.

Stop the trolls, he replied calmly, as if to imply he would assist her if she did.

After shooting him a dark look, I swung again. But Barothla had recovered some of her equanimity, and I sensed her not only wrapping her power around herself but summoning a magical attack. Though I blasted the hammer toward her again, trying to keep her too distracted to concentrate, she was too quick.

As it had before, Barothla's power struck me like a jackhammer. Pain blasted my chest as I flew backward and smashed into something that cracked loudly and gave. A mailbox.

You obnoxious bitch, Barothla snarled into my mind and stalked toward me. *You* will *give me that hammer.*

Though the blow had knocked the wind out of me, I pushed myself to my feet. Willing my weapon to help defend me, I held it up like a shield.

Barothla stretched her palm outward, and a tidal wave of power roared toward me. Some of it struck my hammer, the weapon absorbing it, and some whooshed around it and hit me. I sank low and growled, bracing myself against the assault like I would the wind. But the pain that accompanied the magic made it far different from some mere weather phenomenon.

Either through my willpower or because of the hammer's assistance, it didn't knock me back again. That seemed to surprise Barothla for her eyebrows rose and she glanced back again. Toward Sarrlevi. He still hadn't moved, and he didn't come to help her now.

Snarling, Barothla threw even more power at me. I faltered, almost losing my footing, but raised the hammer higher, my arm muscles trembling from the effort. Wading through the pummeling power, I forced my way toward her, determined to reach her again, to get close enough to swing. And to draw the blood that I needed. That *Tinja* needed.

Five steps, and I would reach her. My leg muscles started quivering as much as my arms.

Four steps. Her forehead furrowed, and I sensed her drawing upon even more of her power.

The magical wave turned into a wall, and no matter how hard I tried, I couldn't break through it, couldn't walk that last three steps.

You have acid in your pocket, Sarrlevi spoke into my mind.

Hell, I'd forgotten about that. But if I took my hands from the hammer, her power would succeed in blasting me across the neighborhood. Maybe that would be worth it.

Before I could rethink the wisdom of my choice, I let the hammer slump, as if I had no more energy left to fight her. And, at that lessening of effort, her power did indeed overcome me. Once more, pain blasted me in the chest and knocked me flying.

As I somersaulted, I glimpsed surprise on Sarrlevi's face—surprise and concern?—but I was too busy hurtling through the air and slipping my hand into my pocket to ponder his reaction.

Though my training urged me to land in a roll and spring to my feet, I made myself crash down hard, as if I had no energy left. My shoulder and hip smashed into a cement driveway, making me regret that choice—I'd expected grass.

The force elicited agony that made me cry out, and the vials almost flew out of my hand. Raw stubbornness let me tighten my grip, keeping them and cushioning them the best I could. My hammer clattered as it hit the driveway, the gritty cement scouring my knuckles, but I also kept hold of it. I wanted her to have to come to *me* to get it.

Feigning that I was dazed—I very nearly was—I groaned and attempted to look limp and defenseless.

"Hah!" Barothla cried and strode toward me.

Her defenses remained in place, but the magic that had been assaulting me stopped. She believed she'd won.

Good.

As she drew close, bending to reach for the hammer, I thumbed the vials open and threw them at her torso.

Barothla reeled back, startled, but then she snorted. As with most of my other attacks, they hadn't breached her magical barrier. If Zoltan had told me the truth, the acid didn't need to. It would cling to her barrier and eat through it. But how long would that take?

Barothla started to say something, but she glanced back. For the first time, Sarrlevi had moved. He'd sheathed his swords, but he was right behind her.

What are you doing? Barothla demanded, whirling to face him.

He glanced toward me, that concern still in his eyes, and I realized he hadn't known that I'd let her get the best of me on purpose, that it had been a ruse.

As quietly as I could, I rose to one knee, the hammer back in both hands. I *wanted* to spring to my feet, but a stab of pain in my hip made me fear the landing had broken it.

If you touch me, Barothla started, still facing him, but her telepathic words broke off as she yelped and looked down at her chest. *Something's eating through my armor.* She clawed not at her chest plate but at her neck. Some of it must have spattered her barrier in front of her exposed skin. *A magical acid!*

Barothla spun back toward me, fury blazing in her eyes, but I was ready. With all the energy I had left, I swung the hammer toward her. I *wanted* to smash it into her face, hardly caring if it would be a killing blow, but from one knee in the driveway, I didn't have the right angle. Instead, it crushed into her chest plate, her magical barrier shredded by the acid and the armor itself starting to erode. My blow dented it further—and likely the ribs under it.

Though Barothla cried out in pain, that fury never left her eyes, and she summoned more power while dipping her hand into a pouch at her waist. As her magic knocked me backward, she pulled out a vial of her own.

She threw it at the ground, glass shattering, and I sensed even more magic forming off to the side. A portal.

"No!" I cried, terrified she would get away again and that I would forever lose my chance to get her blood—to save Tinja.

Acrid blue smoke flowed from her shattered vial and stung my eyes. Again, my busted hip thwarted my attempt to stand, but I jammed my hammer down and used it as a crutch. I rose and hobbled toward her, grabbing for her in air that had grown too hazy to see through. The awful smoke flowed into my nose and lungs, making me cough and weep, but I kept staggering forward. My senses told me she'd backed up but hadn't yet fled through the portal.

Only when I came out of the smoke at the end of the driveway did I see why. Sarrlevi had Barothla from behind, his arm around her throat as he further locked her down with his power. She seethed, pure hatred in her eyes, but she couldn't break his holds.

Relief flooded through me. He *was* on my side.

I hobbled toward her, still tempted to bash her in the head with my hammer, but if she was defenseless, I couldn't bring myself to try to kill her with the weapon. I *would* hit her with my fist. Enough to smash her nose and make her bleed. Grimly, I drew back my arm.

"Stop," Sarrlevi said, his power wrapping around me to ensure I obeyed.

It gripped me so effectively that I couldn't move. I could barely breathe, and a chill went through me as my certainty about whose side he was on vanished.

With his arm still wrapped around Barothla's throat, Sarrlevi removed something from his pocket. The syringe. With chilling accuracy, especially given his position behind her, he stuck it in the vein at her neck.

His magic must have had her ratcheted down too tightly for her to scream, but she yelled, *Bastard!* telepathically.

With his dexterous fingers, he held the syringe and pulled the plunger with one hand, filling it with her blood. He capped the needle and tossed the syringe to me.

Call off the trolls, Sarrlevi told Barothla.

A hedge along the driveway blocked the view of my house, but, now that my fight had ended, I grew aware of windows breaking and wood snapping.

Screw you, Sarrlevi, Barothla replied, again attempting to break his grip.

I sensed her calling upon her magic as she tried to physically buck him off, but she couldn't best him either way. He was implacable and only drew upon more of his own power when hers swelled.

Call off the trolls, he repeated.

You won't kill me. I'm your only hope.

You don't have to die for your night to become very unpleasant. His tone was so icy that it chilled even me.

Even though I'd been ready to crush Barothla's skull in during the battle, I shivered at the idea of watching her be tortured. Sarrlevi's words might have been a bluff, but his face was so cold that I doubted it. His body was taut from more than the effort of restraining her, and maybe it was my imagination, but I thought he *wanted* to hurt her.

His words about levers and extortion came to mind. Forty years ago, he might have accepted that assignment for money, but I was positive that wasn't the reason he was working for my aunt now.

A touch of fear replaced some of Barothla's rage and indignation, so she must have also believed he wasn't bluffing. And maybe she also realized her life was in danger.

All right, Sarrlevi, she said, her voice calmer. *All right. Let me go. Call off the trolls.*

It's hard to do that with an arm around your throat.

Telepathy is sufficient.

Barothla sneered, but she projected her thoughts toward the house. *Hold, trolls! Lower your weapons, and step back into the street.*

The sounds of destruction ended, though even after the pounding noises halted, something clinked, then clattered to the ground. One of my drainpipes? I was afraid to creep around the hedges and look at my house.

Now, go. Sarrlevi released Barothla and stepped back. *And leave your niece alone. If you don't want someone to hire an assassin to kill you after you inherit the throne, you had better not be too vile and conniving of a ruler.*

I couldn't tell if that was a hypothetical comment about her inheriting the throne or if he truly believed it would come to pass. If Sarrlevi was after my mother... maybe he did. My heart wrenched.

Barothla glowered at him. *I hope for your sake that's not an assignment you would contemplate.*

There are many assassins in the Realms. Sarrlevi pointed at the portal floating in the air beside the driveway. *Leave.*

She growled at him but didn't offer another retort, not that I could hear. As she strode toward the portal, she glanced at my hammer and sneered at me. Though she said nothing, I had a feeling she would be back, and that I would regret that Sarrlevi had kept me from smashing her head in.

28

AFTER THE PORTAL DISAPPEARED, SARRLEVI STEPPED TOWARD ME. Conflicted all over again about him, I lifted a hand, intending to stop him. The last thing I wanted was for the assassin *currently* after my mother to rub my head.

He didn't back off but he reached for my hip, not my head. Though I wanted to reject any offer he might make, I needed the healing, assuming that was what he meant to give, if I was going to be able to drive over to Val's house with the syringe. And now that I had it, I dared not delay. Whatever was affecting the trolls might take some time to wear off, but hopefully they were done demolishing my house for the night.

"You'll need Zavryd'nokquetal or a more experienced healer to fully take care of this," Sarrlevi said softly, his hand on my hip, "but I'll do what I can."

I stared numbly past his shoulder, not able to look at him.

Not waiting for permission, he sent his magic trickling into me, as he'd done on the mountainside. It couldn't take away all the pain, but it cooled and numbed and invigorated. The relief that seeped into my body almost made me crumple to the ground, but I locked my knees. Tinja still needed me.

"What hold does Barothla have over you?" I asked quietly.

"Deliver the blood to the vampire. I'll watch the trolls and your home and make sure nothing else happens while you're gone."

I struggled to swallow a lump in my throat. The magic faded, and Sarrlevi stepped back. He looked at me, as if to assure himself I wouldn't topple over, then walked into the street and toward my home.

I glanced at the windows of the house behind me, their driveway having provided the battleground for Barothla and me, but the lights were off and the blinds shut. Because the home-owners had slept through it? Or because they'd realized they should stay out of it and pretend they weren't home?

As I walked stiffly back toward my house, a few curtains in the neighborhood stirred, faces peeking out. If I hadn't been considered the owner of the weird house on the block before, I would be now.

The trolls remained on my lawn and sidewalk, but their sledgehammers and pickaxes hung limply at their sides. Their faces were still slack, their eyes glazed. It was almost as it had been when I'd shimmied off the roof and sneaked away except... I grimaced when I saw the damage.

They'd broken most of the windows on the house *and* my truck. Siding had been ripped off, with great holes pounded in the walls. The door I'd punched earlier was completely smashed in. If they'd gone inside and done further destruction in there, I didn't want to know. Later, I would deal with all this. Now, I had to get to Val's house as quickly as possible.

Abbas jogged over as I dug out the key to my Harley—thankfully the motorcycle, tucked under its cover in the back of the carport, had missed the hatefest.

"I'm so sorry, Matti," Abbas said. "I don't understand any of this."

"I know. The person responsible left, and, hopefully, she won't be back. I'm going to deliver the final ingredient for Tinja's potion. Stay and direct your clan back home when they wake up from this, okay?"

"Okay." Abbas glanced toward Sarrlevi, who'd stopped at the sidewalk to survey the damage. Or maybe he'd stopped there because he knew he wouldn't be welcome inside again.

"He shouldn't bother you." Shaking my head, I ran to the Harley, yanked back the cover, and took off.

Since it was very late—or very early—I thought about calling Val as I drove over, but she might not have returned home yet. Besides, Zoltan was who I needed. Hopefully, he would be in his lab and willing to let me in.

Though I believed Val had made it so I could step onto the property anytime, I eyed the topiaries warily after parking. A few of the mushrooms in the fairy ring that had been damaged in the fight wafted a glowing green mist. It granted the place a Halloween vibe. Giving the ring a wide berth, I jogged toward the backyard.

Ah, mongrel dwarf, Zoltan spoke into my mind when I reached the steps. *You have returned.*

Yes, I have.

If you have the final ingredient, I am prepared for it.

I do. I passed through both doors without knocking and found Zoltan at his lab counter, with a small vat—or was that a cauldron?—burbling on a Bunsen burner. The plastic baggie rested next to it, open with most of the hacked-up tail still inside.

"I had faith that you would succeed in acquiring the blood, so I am ready for it."

"Thank you." I thrust the syringe at him, the memory of Sarrlevi stabbing it into Barothla's neck flashing in my mind.

Would there be repercussions for him for that? Despite his warnings that Barothla was powerful and dangerous, I had a feeling he could have bested her at any point. But she had something he wanted, and he presumably couldn't get it through force or by killing her.

He'd mentioned extortion. That was like blackmail, wasn't it? What could she have over him? It was hard to imagine Sarrlevi caring about some dark secret getting out when the world, at least the elven world, already knew that he'd killed his own father.

"I have collected what I needed of the manticore tail." Zoltan pointed at the bag with his elbow as he measured blood from the syringe. "Do tell your comrade with the huge swords that a small sample acquired with a scalpel would have been sufficient."

"I don't think assassins carry scalpels."

"No? One would expect their kind to be surgically precise in their slayings."

"He was surgically precise in getting that blood. How long will it take for you to finish? Should I bring Tinja down here?" I hoped she hadn't gotten any worse. It felt like ages had passed since I'd left her bedroom to battle Barothla not once but twice. My phone's clock told me it had only been a few hours.

"It will not take long. You may bring her."

I hurried through the house, sensing Dimitri sleeping in his room on the first floor. Neither Val nor Zavryd had returned home. Tinja was much as when I'd left, her breathing shallow and raspy, and she didn't stir when I gathered her in my arms. My hip hurt under the load, a reminder that I needed Zavryd's healing later, but I carried her down to the basement.

Fortunately, Zoltan delivered his formula through a vein in her arm and didn't need her to be awake. He pulled out another empty syringe and withdrew a clear liquid from a vial. As with the formula he'd just made, it radiated magic.

"An immune-system enhancement," he explained as he also

injected it. "I gave her a dose before, but it should be more effective now."

"How long do we have to wait to know..." I stopped myself from saying *if she'll make it*. She *had* to make it. "Until she's better?"

"Only time will tell if her body remains healthy enough to recover after my sublime formula has neutralized the vileness of the poison."

If. I grimaced bleakly. The thought of having gone through all that with Barothla only to lose Tinja anyway made my throat tighten up.

"I believe there is a good chance of her recovery," Zoltan said, "but if she does not live, you should know I've done my best to fight a poison made by a very powerful alchemist. I pray you will not sic your assassin on me."

"I won't. And he's not *my* assassin." Another memory came to mind, of sitting in Sarrlevi's lap while kissing him on my bed, but I shook my head to clear it away. "Trust me."

"No? He looms behind your shoulder like an overzealous bodyguard."

"No," I said firmly. "He lies to me and can't be trusted."

Something Sarrlevi had told me himself numerous times. Could I blame him for being deceitful when he'd warned me? I'd been the fool who hadn't listened.

Determined to wait until morning to beat myself up further, I carried Tinja back up to the guest bedroom and brought her a glass of water and a fresh ginger ale with a bendy straw. After that, I lay on the floor beside her bed, doubting I would sleep after the events of the night, but my battered and exhausted body surprised me, and I passed out within seconds.

When I woke, daylight streamed in the window, and I immediately sensed Val and Zavryd in the house. Val was hard to miss, since she stood beside me, her hand gripping her chin as she gazed down at my face.

I lurched into a sitting position and looked at the bed. Tinja was still out, but was her breathing better? It didn't sound as raspy and distressed now.

"Zoltan said he checked her before the sun came up and that she's on the mend." Val arched her eyebrows. "He also told me to let you know that, since you were injured and vulnerable, he left your veins alone when he was up here."

I frowned at the thought of a hungry vampire standing over me while I slept. That was the stuff of horror novels, wasn't it? "Tell him he can have whatever is leftover of Barothla's blood. I'm not taking any extra back to her."

"I believe he prefers it warm and fresh from the vein."

"Gross."

"Yeah. It's hard to find quality roommates." Val smirked and waved at Tinja. "You better keep that one. Better to have one's toasters destroyed than one's veins perforated."

I rubbed my gritty eyes. "We live in an odd world."

"Tell me about it. I should be able to get Zav to heal you—heal you *again*—when you're up for it." Her eyebrows lifted once more. "I take it you battled your aunt again? Zav said he arrived at an opportune time last night to end what I gather was the *first* battle."

"He did. And so did Zoltan. I guess I owe him one." I frowned again. I would rather *not* be indebted to a vampire.

"He only spoke of a thousand dollars you agreed to pay him for two ounces of a magic-destroying acid and told me to tell you that he has more available if you need it."

"I... hope I won't." But maybe I would. Just because Sarrlevi had ordered Barothla to leave me alone didn't mean she would.

More than ever, I wanted to find my mother. I needed another ally to stand with me against all the dreadful people in the world —and in the Cosmic Realms. I just hoped we wouldn't have to also stand against Sarrlevi. The thought of fighting him chilled me, but I also wouldn't stand by while he sliced off my mother's head as I'd seen him do with so many enemies.

"Maybe I'll buy a little more to keep on my nightstand," I added.

"Probably a good idea."

"Does one pay a vampire in cash? Or gold bullion?"

"Didn't I tell you? He takes all forms of online payment. He's quite internet-savvy."

Something about Venmoing a vampire did not seem right.

"How much will I owe him for Tinja's formula?"

"That's taken care of. So is this." Val delved into the pocket of her duster and held up a vial of a murky gray liquid that looked like it had been scooped from a swamp.

I pushed myself to my feet to accept it. "What is it?"

"A truth elixir."

I stared at the vial in my palm for a moment before the pieces clicked together. "Oh."

"He ate your food at dinner, so I'm guessing you can figure out a way to get it into him."

Anxiety stampeded into my gut as I imagined trying to slip the substance to Sarrlevi. I would probably have a panic attack in front of him. "He can read my mind."

"I figured. You'll have to be careful not to think about it. And from what Zoltan said, I gather that Sarrlevi will remember afterward that he felt magically compelled to blab all his secrets to you, but..." Val turned her palm toward the ceiling. "You should know the motivations of the person who's oddly intent on helping you."

"Val..." I didn't know whether to be grateful or horrified. How many times had I longed to get the truth out of Sarrlevi? He would see this as a betrayal—how not?—but hadn't he been betraying me all along? In a manner of speaking? The whole time he'd been helping me, even doing nice things for me, he'd *known* he would, if possible, kill my mother when he found her. "Thanks," I told her and tucked the vial into my pocket.

I could decide later if I would use it. At this point, I wasn't that sure I needed to, as that conversation I'd eavesdropped on had been revealing. But I *would* like to know what leverage Barothla had on Sarrlevi that gave her the power to force him to do something he didn't want to do. Even if he'd lied to me—everything he'd told me about his past probably *was* suspect—I didn't believe he was eager to kill my mother.

"No problem." Val thumped me on the shoulder. "Mongrels gotta look out for each other."

My mate, Zavryd's telepathic boom came from the kitchen. *We have not yet dined this morning.*

Val snorted. "That's code for *come and make me some food.*"

"Are dragons incapable of opening refrigerators and heating up leftovers?"

"Well, he's a *male* dragon." She winked at me.

"You think his sister would be more capable of feeding herself?"

"I'm not sure. Females are the rulers in dragondom and accustomed to males serving them and vying for their attention. She may be even *less* capable of heating up leftovers. I'll brew some of that Goblin Fuel blend and see if it rouses your snoozing roommate." Val lifted a hand in parting and walked out.

I sank down on the edge of Tinja's bed, hoping she would stir soon but also dreading going home to the mess that was my house. Would my insurance cover troll vandalism?

"Matti?" Tinja mumbled sleepily.

I patted her hand. "I'm here."

"I dreamed you were busy building something." Tinja smiled blearily up at me.

"There was an *incident* at the house while you were snoozing. I'm going to be busy replacing windows and doors and siding." I winced at the thought of paying for all the materials. Was my old beater of a truck even worth as much as a full window replacement on it would cost?

"No, that's not what you were building." Her smile broadened. "You were constructing one of the fabulous tiny homes that I've drawn plans for, and human customers were amazed by its brilliance—and thoughtful use of small spaces—and rushing to give me money to fund the construction of my urban goblin sanctuary."

"Your dreams are a lot more entrepreneurial than mine."

"What do you dream about?"

Sarrlevi's face popped into my mind again.

"Debt and taxes and paying for windows," I said firmly, even if it was a lie.

"How dreadful." Tinja's nose crinkled as she sniffed the air. "Is that coffee that I smell?"

"The special Goblin Fuel blend from the Coffee Dragon, I understand. If it's as potent as I've heard, it'll revive you even better than an alchemist's potions."

"I look forward to sampling it."

"I'm sure Gondo will be pleased if you end up enjoying it."

Her nose wrinkled again. "I don't know if I want him to be *pleased*. The gift was nice, but I am not interested in him in *that* way."

"Oh? Was he flirting with you?"

"I believe so."

"That's not good?" I seemed to recall her smiling shyly when she'd spoken of his gift. "He's a city goblin, like you. Not some rural hick eating unsalted roadkill."

"True, but he is... goofy and not at all ambitious."

"Well, you don't have to marry him just because you enjoy his coffee."

"I know this." Tinja gave me a pointed look. "Just as *you* do not have to marry an assassin just because you enjoy his cheese."

The thought of even hanging out with Sarrlevi, now that I knew his end goal, made me shudder. "I'm sure he doesn't want to marry me, but I'll keep that in mind."

Tinja leaned back against the pillows. "Excellent."

EPILOGUE

IT WAS WELL INTO THE AFTERNOON BEFORE I HEADED HOME, WITH Tinja behind me on the motorcycle. Val had invited her to stay longer, but Tinja wanted to rest surrounded by her projects and blueprints. Apparently, she'd had some ideas while she'd been dreaming about me slaving away on her tiny home and wanted to make updates.

I hadn't heard from Abbas and was worried his troll clan would still be standing slack-jawed around the house, waiting for the coercion potion to wear off, but when I pulled into the driveway, I didn't sense them around. I didn't sense Sarrlevi either. What I *did* sense was a lot of magic emanating from the borders of the property, as well as the doors and windows.

Windows that were completely repaired. The ones on the truck were too. Not a hint of shattered glass lay on the walkway or driveway.

My own jaw went slack as I stared. The rest of the house had also been repaired, in a manner of speaking, but it most definitely was not back to normal.

"Why are there leaves and vines growing all over the place?" Tinja slid off the Harley and also stared. Or maybe gaped.

"I *think* they're only growing in the spots where the trolls did damage."

The thick vines and large leaves had filled in or covered all the places where the siding had been bashed by sledgehammers and pickaxes.

Tinja's brow furrowed as she peered at me. "Why did trolls damage the house?"

"It's a long story." Motorcycles weren't conducive to chitchat, so I hadn't yet filled her in on everything that had happened.

"Those vines and leaves are emanating elf magic."

"I assumed."

"They are likely sturdy and will keep the wind and rain out, but Matti." Tinja propped her fists on her hips. "I am now very familiar with the human building codes of this nation. Vines will *not* be considered a sufficient material for walls. Do you know what the R-value of a vine is?"

"No."

"Neither does anyone else. If inspectors come by, they will insist on changes."

"That's fine. I wasn't planning on keeping the house like this." Though the vines and leaves were quite artfully applied. They almost appeared to be an intentional part of the construction of the house rather than patch materials. "For now, they'll keep the rain out."

I walked to the large living room window and touched a spot I was certain had been shattered before. No vines or leaves were intertwined with the glass, but I didn't see any hint of a break. Maybe elven magic was capable of heating glass to the melting point and re-forming it.

"It's too bad he's dead set on his current career—and working against me." I smiled sadly. "I could use someone handy with windows."

"Do you know who did this?" Tinja poked at a broad leaf on a vine twining up a support for the overhang above the front stoop.

"Yeah. And you do too. I wonder where he went." I eyed the property lines, the strong magic emanating from them, before reaching for the doorknob. Not only was the door back on its hinges, but several leaves had grown out of the wood to cover the damage it had received from pickaxes and sledgehammers.

An address plaque that a troll had ripped off and snapped had been replaced by vines spelling out the house numbers. The holder for the hose reel was now made from vines as well.

Before I opened the door, my phone rang, Abbas's name popping up.

A little wary, I answered it.

"Hi, Matti," he said. "How's Tinja?"

"Better. She's standing next to me prodding the magical elven vines and leaves that were used to repair our house."

"Uh, he must have done that after we left."

"Is your clan okay now?"

"Yeah. They came to about an hour before dawn. They were very confused, but they did remember a weird dwarf joining them at their ceremony circle after they drank the *kaja*. She commanded them to come and attack you and your home, and they were all compelled to obey. My father says to apologize to you about that."

"It's not his fault."

"The elf assassin told them about Princess Barothla and how she's angling for you and blaming you for things. He implied *she* was the one who killed the trolls on the barge."

I didn't think Barothla had been responsible for that. I still needed to find the people who'd taken my mother—and now my father. But I didn't correct him. If the trolls wanted to blame

Barothla for the murders of their people, let them. It wasn't as if they could hunt her down and find her anyway.

"They realized they were wrong to blame you," Abbas added.

"Good."

"My father said I could keep working with you."

"That's *very* good. I'm going to need to make some money to pay for unexpected repairs." Unfortunately, there wouldn't be a combat bonus this time. This hadn't been a job for Willard.

"Does that mean we're going to make a bid on the new place? And build some houses from scratch?"

"We should probably go look at the property in person first," I said dryly.

"Oh, I've already been by. It's a mess with blackberry vines all over the back half of the property, the roof on the original farmhouse half-caved in, and mold growing all over the kitchen walls."

"So, it's right up our alley?"

"Exactly. There's room for three new houses and—" now *his* tone grew dry, "—even the tiny house you're apparently building Tinja."

"She already told you about that?"

"When she called to complain about how awful she felt, yes."

"Not so awful that she couldn't scheme." I raised my eyebrows at Tinja, but she was busy examining more vines. I'd missed the ones on the truck. They formed door handles that had been ripped off and even the frame for one of the side mirrors. All the dents the sledgehammers had left in the truck body had been hammered out as well. Or magically popped out.

"Well, she *is* a goblin. See you Monday."

"Okay, bye."

I held the phone to my chest, my emotions a tangle. Sarrlevi was doing his best to fix my problems—and even give me the education in magic that I desperately needed—even though he'd known all along that I would never forgive him if he was successful with his mission. His words, *I wanted to make sure you'd be set, even after I'm gone,* came to mind.

"Matti." Tinja had finished her examination and joined me on the stoop. "I believe it was the *assassin* who did all this."

"Yeah," I whispered.

"Did you see that he also set wards around the property? *Good* ones. I believe trolls with nefarious intent will not be able to get through again, at least not until the magic wears off."

"I think so too."

"Maybe I was wrong. Maybe Sarrlevi is *not* an inappropriate suitor."

I shook my head sadly. "No, you were right before. He isn't... appropriate."

The inside of the house hadn't been disturbed. Maybe Abbas had succeeded in keeping the clan from bashing their way into the living room, or maybe the battle with Barothla had ended before they'd had time to do so.

Either way, I was glad. Both because Tinja pirouetted into the living room, gathering up and hugging her undisturbed blue-prints, and because I wasn't sure I could handle more vines and leaves sprawling over the interior walls. The shelves Sarrlevi had created in my bedroom were enough nature for me.

In the kitchen, I found a folded piece of stationery with my name on it. I approached it warily, the memory of the poisoned sodas and their message coming to mind. But there weren't any beverages—nor any cheese—alongside this.

Wanting to read it in private, I took it back to my room and closed the door and sat on the bed before unfolding the stationery.

Mataalii, it read, *I apologize for not setting wards sooner. It's not a simple matter, but reasonable protection might be created with a couple hours of work. I should have done that instead of letting myself be distracted by other matters. Then the trolls would not have been an issue.*

The memory of rubbing his head and his heated kiss returned, and *I* couldn't regret that he'd spent time with me instead of setting wards. Even if I should have.

As you might guess, they will not be sufficient to keep Barothla out.

No, even Zavryd's dragon defenses hadn't been entirely sufficient for that.

I hope she won't return to bother you, but I can't promise that. She didn't listen to me before when I told her to leave you alone. Perhaps I'm not as fearsome a foe as I would like to believe.

I sighed. "The problem is that you're *not* her foe." Even if I thought he wanted to be.

I am not as skilled a renovator as Thorvald's dragon, but I attempted to make repairs sufficient enough that you will not feel compelled to spend all your time fixing your house. I urge you instead to meet with the enchanter as often as possible and learn as much as you can. You acquitted yourself well enough during your battle with Barothla that I think she will be wary about coming after you openly again, but... she may seek other ways to reach you and get the hammer. Please be careful. Varlesh.

I turned it over, longing for more, at least for a mention of when he might return, but there wasn't anything else.

What if he *wouldn't* return? What if he, realizing I now knew his intentions, would work on his mission independently from me? Would he try to reach my mother and deal with her without me around?

The thought was horrifying. I *had* to find her first. I had to help her escape those who held her captive so she could return to her world and hopefully confront and deal with her sister. I would gladly help her with that. Maybe if I learned enough *quickly enough*, I could be an effective ally for her. And maybe... I could keep Sarrlevi from getting to her.

"I will," I promised myself. "I will."

THE END